Her Scandalous Suitor

by

Rachel Brimble

The Wild Rose Press, Inc.
PO Box 708
Adams Basin, NY 14410-0708
Visit us at www.thewildrosepress.com

Publishing History
First Edition, 2024
Trade Paperback ISBN 978-1-5092-5524-5
Digital ISBN 978-1-5092-5525-2

Previously Published by Kensington Books 2013
Published in the United States of America

Dedication

I want to dedicate the republication of this book (originally The Seduction of Emily) to all the lovely and loyal readers who have read my novels over the last sixteen years and all the readers who are discovering me for the first time.

You are the best!

Rachel x

Chapter One

City of Bath, 1895

Will Samson stood at the back of the auction house, watching and waiting. Over two hundred people stood around him. Rather than part with their hard-earned cash, he suspected they were there hoping to catch a glimpse of one man in particular. The same man he waited for.

Mr. Nicholas Milne. One of Bath's most eligible bachelors. Milne was a celebrity. A man written about and either admired...or feared. Will curled his hands into fists.

He was a rapist. A woman-beater. A dead man walking.

Today, Will was coming for Milne, ready or not. He lifted his hat and pushed the hair back from his face. The tension in his neck and shoulders grew worse as each second passed, and the ache in his temples throbbed mercilessly.

He turned his gaze once again to the open double doors at the back of the room. "Come on, you bastard. Where are you?"

The furor surrounding the sale of the day's most prestigious lot, a diamond, ruby, and pearl necklace known as the Heart of Kingston, had escalated to fever pitch over the last few weeks. The auction house had taken full advantage of the waiting crowd by dragging out the suspense. What better way to heighten the nerves and hunger of bidders than to have them think the real prize—Milne—might not materialize after all?

Replacing his hat, Will slid out of sight behind a marble pillar. Discretion was key. Although confident the people of Bath were unaware of his real occupation, he daren't run the risk of his carefully prepared disguise as a middle-class gentleman being exposed. When was a confidence trickster ever welcome at a high-class auction?

He closed his eyes and leaned back against the wall, planting the sole of his boot against the white alabaster. His mother's beautiful face appeared behind his closed lids. She'd asked him countless times not to avenge the beating Milne had inflicted on her two years before, but the fire inside Will would not be extinguished until Milne was nothing but ashes.

Resentment and hatred swirled in his gut. The same emotions had long ago burned and scarred any love he was once capable of feeling for another. So many months of tracking Milne down, so many weeks of wanting to get his hands around his neck had left Will a shadow of his former self. Maybe once Milne was dead or behind bars, Will could start living again. He opened his eyes. But, in the meantime, he would make the man's life a living hell until he decided how to ruin him completely. The only promise Will would keep to his mother was he wouldn't hang by the neck for his endeavors. When the fever took her into God's arms, Will's heart and soul filled with the heinous intention to wreak vengeance on Milne. God only knew how many more women Milne had hurt in the months it took Will to track him from Bristol to Bath. That knowledge burned like acid in Will's throat.

The raucous chatter and laughter of the room descended into discreet whispering and elbow nudging. Will pushed away from the wall, and rage shot through his chest. The man of the hour had arrived. Blood roared hot and heavy in his ears. Milne strolled in with a smile that spoke of a man who possessed everything. A man completely unaware of how soon his privileged life would change. The urge to sprint forward and clasp his hands around Milne's throat made Will tremble with suppressed anger. He looked to Milne's left and froze as his gaze swept over his companion.

He released his breath on a quiet whistle, attraction twitching his groin. "My God, tell me you're not his."

He languidly appraised her from the tip of the feather in her hat to her thick, glossy black hair curled and twisted beneath it. Her eyes were big and dark, her skin as smooth as glass over sweet apple cheeks. The vivid royal-blue dress she wore pulled in at a waist small enough to fit in his splayed hands, her stature poised and proud. She was exquisite.

Will smiled. Although her ample bosom was decently covered, the soft white netting revealed the faintest hue of her flesh. What he wouldn't give…He forced his gaze upward and stiffened. She stared straight at him—and her mouth twitched with amusement. He pulled back his shoulders and flashed her a smile.

She didn't lower her eyes as he expected. Intrigued, he tipped her a wink.

A moment passed before she surprised him again. She did not turn away in disgust or demand Milne punch him to the ground; instead the minx winked straight back. Desire hit Will hard in the gut as a bubble of laughter tickled the back of his throat. Who was she? He reveled in the tinge of pink staining her cheeks and suspected that inside, she laughed right along with him.

Their secretly shared moment came to an abrupt end when Milne took her hand and placed it possessively in the crook of his arm. He led her in Will's direction, and Will bowed as they passed, the woman staring resolutely ahead. His gaze fell on the elderly gentleman following slowly behind them. The woman's father? If he was, then although intelligent enough to accompany someone as audacious as his stunning daughter on an outing such as this, the man looked as though he needed to be in bed with a tot of brandy in his hand and a warmed bottle at his feet.

As soon as the party's backsides touched their seats, the auctioneer took his place at the podium. Will smiled. His earlier suspicion had been right. The house waited for Milne. He looked at the woman again. If Milne was after the Heart of Kingston, no doubt she was the beauty who would soon be wearing it.

The bang of the gavel was loud in the room, and the audience fell into abrupt silence.

"Ladies and gentlemen, we are now ready for the sale of today's final piece." The auctioneer gestured to a man beside him, who came forward and stepped onto the dais. He held a red velvet box. When he raised the lid, a wave of drawn breath swept around the room.

The auctioneer beamed, his eyes alight with satisfaction above his half-rimmed glasses. "Et voilà, today's most precious lot, the magnificent Heart of Kingston. This exquisite piece has traveled all the way from India. A fantastically cut ruby, surrounded by diamonds and clasped to a string of the finest quality pearls."

Will sniffed and crossed his arms. "Come on then, Milne. Let's see your cash."

The bidding started in earnest, and Will maneuvered his way closer to the front, unable to stem his grin as the competition gathered momentum. With an open view of Milne, Will's satisfaction grew as the man's nonchalant stance floundered. The flush of his cheeks and the set of his jaw showed Milne hadn't anticipated this intense level of interest. Time and again, he glanced at his beautiful companion as the bidding grew more frenzied. The son of a bitch seemed entirely rattled.

Another ten minutes passed, and two bidders dropped out. The fight remained between Milne and one unwavering opponent. Satisfaction soothed Will's tension as Milne perspired under the pressure. His hand trembled when he raised it for another bid. Why was the necklace so important to him? Or was the presence of his companion the reason behind this rare show of unease? Having tailed Milne for the last two weeks, Will possessed a good idea of what he liked and didn't like, where he went and who he saw. When the time was right to strike, Will felt confident he would have all the ammunition he needed to cut his enemy as deeply as possible.

Milne turned to his female companion, and Will studied him. The first hint of Milne having a need for another person shone in his eyes. Her face was turned from Milne's, her chin slightly raised, and her eyes trained solely on the auctioneer. It wasn't beyond possibility she didn't return Milne's affection, but judging by the way his gaze traveled softly over her hair and profile, Milne wanted her. Badly.

Happiness spread like honey through Will's blood. He'd heard rumors of Milne's engagement but dismissed them out of hand. Who'd ever heard of two people in love enough to marry yet never stepping out together? Now it seemed his dismissal was premature. Was this Milne's fiancée? The woman in blue, whose eyes had shot through Will's carefully armored heart like two sharpened daggers.

She had something Will had never seen in another female of her obvious class. The wink she gave him and the way she bit down on her bottom lip made her hugely appealing. Or maybe her attractiveness came from the fact that she was Milne's. Either way, the smooth curve of her neck and the soft curl of the tendrils caressing her creamy white skin had ensured an inspired change to Will's plan. His heart picked up speed, his blood pumping faster as the thought became more of a must. If he seduced Milne's fiancée, it would be the perfect first cut.

The bang of wood against wood resounded around the room once more.

"Lot number 116 is sold at three hundred fifty pounds to Mr. Nicholas Milne." The auctioneer beamed. "May I be the first to congratulate you on the acquisition of such a fine piece, sir?"

Milne dipped his head and slowly closed his eyes in acknowledgment before turning to the new object of Will's mission. Taking the lady's gloved hand in his, he brought her to her feet and pressed a kiss to her fingers. Her mouth momentarily twisted in disgust before evolving into a wide smile when Milne lifted his head.

Will shook his head and grinned. "You, my fair lady, are going to be the best fun I've had in years."

****

Emily Darson walked from the auction room struggling to keep her serene expression in place. What a farce! Having heard nothing from Nicholas in over a week—happiness for her, concern for her father—he deigned to bring her to an auction for the afternoon. Not only did he insist on arriving late to cause a fanfare, he then bid on the most ostentatious piece of jewelry she'd ever seen. She glanced at him from beneath lowered lashes and inwardly grimaced. What sort of man made such an obvious exhibition of his wealth in front of his intended? It made her nauseous.

He turned. "Do change your expression, Emily. You look as though you would rather be anywhere else than here."

She curved her lips into a perfunctory smile. "Not at all. The day has been nothing short of fascinating."

His eyes narrowed. "Do not think for one minute I cannot detect the irony in your tone."

"I am not being ironic. I am merely—"

"You are being ironic. Now, for goodness sake, can we try to maintain some semblance of affection? Surely you are aware people are here to see us rather than the wares on offer."

Emily glanced around her. "What if I don't want to be seen?"

"The choice isn't yours to make. We're engaged. We're talked about in the papers." His eyes flashed with annoyance. "Most women would enjoy the attention."

"Ah, now there's the problem, Nicholas. I'm not most women."

His gaze appraised her from top to toe. "Indeed you are not."

Angry heat pinched her cheeks. "Can we just leave and—"

"So, do you like the necklace, my love?" Nicholas stared across the anteroom.

The abrupt change in his tone caught Emily off guard, and she followed his gaze. Her father watched them from a few feet away whilst talking to an associate. Comprehension struck. Nicholas was merely intent on keeping up appearances for her father. The man was an out and out fraud. Irritation spread across her skin, making it itch, but she planted on a wide smile and nodded at her father. He nodded back. She and Nicholas were actors in someone else's play—nothing more, nothing less.

"I trust you've something suitable to wear to show off the jewelry I've just bought," Nicholas said, his eyes burning with superiority. "Or will I have to buy you a decent dress as well?"

Emily gripped her hands together. "I have some beautiful dresses already. You know I do."

"What I consider beautiful and what you do are two entirely different things. Once we are married—"

"I'll undoubtedly be forced to wear something you approve of whatever the occasion."

Tension crackled, and her blood heated. No matter that her destiny was to become Mrs. Nicholas Milne in a matter of months, Emily refused to become his lapdog.

He cupped his hand to her elbow, his fingers ever

so slightly pressing the flesh as he led her forward. "Why do you insist on making our union so troublesome? We will both reap the benefits of our marriage."

Frustration burned behind her ribcage. "It's a contract. Not a marriage."

"And you will have nothing without it. It would serve you well to remember that…as your father does."

"My father is dying. His fears are amplified by illness. I, on the other hand…"

"Should learn the art of holding your tongue."

Anger burned Emily's throat.

This is necessary. This is necessary. She repeated the words over and over in her head until her cheeks cooled. Exhaling a heavy breath, she willed her temper into submission. Money was everywhere. In the cut of the clothes, the quality of the shoes, and the shine of the jewelry. Although she was better off than many who lived in Bath, the expensive objects mocked her. Displayed what she might never have for her unborn children if she balked at her and Nicholas's arranged marriage.

Love was not an option for her, but that did not prevent her from imagining new rules and new ambitions. She'd heard of changes on the horizon for women and made it her business to educate herself accordingly. But for now, she was trapped in a world she couldn't escape. She only prayed that one day her children would have options, and as money all too often oiled the cogs of choice, Emily would not deprive them the chance of a life where their decisions were their own.

She surreptitiously studied Nicholas's profile and

tried to see what other women saw in him. The announcement of their engagement caused an onslaught of "oohs" and "ahhs" from their circle and the social columns of Bath's newspapers. Nicholas might well stand at over six feet tall with sandy blond hair and eyes greener than emeralds, but for Emily, the combination did not constitute attraction.

His coldness, his ability to reach out and grip her arm like a striking cobra or turn those green eyes into dangerous pieces of flint were enough to illustrate what her future would become when they were married. A fate she worked hard to accept—but her loyalty to her father and her fight to keep what was rightfully hers stole a little more of her soul every day.

She blinked back the burn in her eyes and forced her hand around Nicholas's forearm. He stiffened and looked down at her, surprise etched on his face. Emily smiled demurely, and he relaxed beneath her fingertips, folding his hand over hers.

"We should make haste." He patted her hand. "It is nearing tea time, and I would hate for you to miss out on your daily refreshment."

Ignoring his condescension, Emily lifted her chin as they walked through the marbled corridors of the auction rooms and outside into the bright afternoon sunshine. The late May day was warm, a gentle breeze whispering the first breaths of summer. The tall elegant buildings surrounding them were built from golden Bath stone and shone beautifully beneath the sunlight. The many windows glinted, and the doves in the cornices cooed their contentment. Emily sighed. Bath was her home, and it would be her children's, too.

When her father joined them, he and Nicholas

struck up a discussion concerning the business, omitting her from the conversation. Her resentment simmered. She had a brain. She had focus. A need to work and do something. The desire for her life to amount to more than a dutiful wife and lady burned hotter every day.

A movement barely inches to her side caught Emily's attention, and she turned, abruptly swallowing the gasp that rose sharply in her throat.

It was the man who had winked at her in the auction room.

He strolled toward her, his shining sea-blue eyes locked on hers. Her courage inside the room promptly abandoned her, and Emily's heart turned over. He stood at least a foot taller than she, his wide shoulders absurdly broad, his confidence disturbing. She bit back a nervous laugh as an entirely inappropriate imagining came unbidden into her mind. Oh, to have him fling her over those shoulders and escape with her into the night!

He flashed her a knowing smile—God spare her, she smiled back. Never before had a man's gaze enticed such inexplicable naughtiness in her. Danger screamed its warning. What was she thinking?

Nicholas's gruff cough snapped her to attention.

The handsome stranger twisted his gaze from hers and touched his finger to the brim of his hat. "Good afternoon, sir."

Nicholas nodded. "Can I help you?"

"I wanted to offer my congratulations." The man held out his hand. "A very fine win."

After a moment's hesitation, Nicholas took his offered hand. "Thank you. Now, if you'll excuse—"

"Yes, quite the battle you had in there." Fine lines crinkled the corners of the stranger's phenomenal eyes.

"Nothing beats a fiery one on one."

He turned and looked directly at Emily, his raised eyebrow referring the sentiment to her rather than Nicholas. She should have been outrageously affronted, yet a burst of delicious excitement rushed through her veins and warmed her body.

"I say—" Nicholas began.

The sound of horses' hooves clattering upon the cobblestones halted his protestation.

"Your carriage, sir." The man stepped back and held out his hand, gesturing them forward.

Emily started when Nicholas drew her hand from his arm and nudged her toward the open carriage with his fingers firmly on her spine. The stranger's gaze dropped to Nicholas's hand, and his blue eyes darkened. Emily hurriedly made to climb into the carriage, lest the man protest, but then faltered when Nicholas spoke.

"What is your name, sir?"

With one foot on the carriage step, Emily turned. The stranger's eyes twinkled with amusement as he looked from Nicholas to her and back again. He bent theatrically at the waist and removed his hat in a grand sweep. "Samson, sir. Will Samson."

Nicholas glared at his bent head, but Emily noticed when Mr. Samson straightened and stared intensely into his eyes, Nicholas took an unconscious step back. She didn't blame him. There was something extremely unnerving about Mr. Samson. Devilishly handsome, tall and strong and somehow completely unsuited to his surroundings. Her gaze lingered over the length and breadth of him. His clothes didn't quite fit the occasion; his bare hands and slightly work-worn shoes alerted her to a possible masquerade. She silently admonished herself for being so entirely judgmental.

Nicholas's eyes narrowed. "What business do you have here?"

Mr. Samson replaced his hat. "I'm sorry?"

Nicholas lifted his walking cane and waved it in Mr. Samson's direction. "Well, try as you might to deceive a lesser mortal, sir. You clearly have no money and thus no reason for attending this auction."

Emily stopped breathing. She might well have hazarded the same thing yet gratefully lacked Nicholas's audacity and complete disrespect for others. She tightened her grip on the carriage door. Mr. Samson said nothing, merely continued to smile as though Nicholas was the most amusing creature he'd ever laid eyes upon.

The tension between them crackled.

Emily looked to her father. He was entirely absorbed in the stones at his feet. Frowning, she turned back to Nicholas and Mr. Samson.

"Mr. Samson?" The address leaped from her tongue.

His mouth curved into a wide smile, and his eyes challenged her with their mischief. "Yes?"

"Didn't I see you bid on the Heart of Kingston yourself?"

His eyes narrowed for a moment as though trying to calculate the reason behind her question—a fruitless task because Emily had no idea herself.

"Indeed you did." He sighed. "But alas, as Mr. Milne so rightly observed, my financial status is well below the value of such a jewel."

"Did you not see anything else you might be

tempted to take home with you?"

His gaze bored into hers. "On the contrary. There was one piece in particular I would love to take home and show how much I appreciate its beauty."

A strange vibration erupted in her stomach. Emily looked to his mouth, and heat flooded her body. She quickly lowered her gaze. "Well, good afternoon, Mr. Samson. It was very nice meeting you."

He touched the brim of his hat. "You, too, miss…oh, I apologize. I do not know your name."

Nicholas stepped forward and gripped her elbow. "That, Mr. Samson, is the way it will stay. Good day to you."

Nicholas urged her inside, his hand insistent on her back. Left with little choice, Emily boarded the carriage. She sat down on the velvet seat and exhaled a shaky breath. Her heart beat a wild tattoo, and her hands trembled around the strings of her bag. She turned to the side window to avoid Nicholas's eyes as he climbed in, yet the heat of his gaze burned into her temple. She didn't need to look at him to know anger raged in his emerald eyes, lighting them with a dangerous fire she recognized more and more as their wedding date drew closer.

The grunts and huffs of her father's exertion as he climbed aboard broke through her resolve. Emily stood and hurried to make him comfortable on the seat beside her. Nicholas remained immobile as she heaved her father's weight forward and tucked a blanket around his legs. When the footman slammed the door, she started. The bolt sounded like a clang of impending doom.

Swallowing hard, she tilted her chin and finally faced her fiancé. "Nicholas—"

He raised his hand. "Not now, Emily. For God's sake, not now."

Indignation stung her cheeks and brought a surge of retaliating words to her mouth. She looked at her father, and he shook his head, his eyes warning her to obey. She pulled her lips tightly closed and fought the urge to turn around and look through the back window for a final glimpse of the wonderfully vibrant Mr. Samson.

Chapter Two

Nausea rose bitter in Emily's throat as she stared at the latest letter from a trusted friend. The words blurred. The dear girl's marriage was an unhappy one, an enforced one, and the passion Emily had exerted to help her friend extricate herself from the same fate as Emily's twisted her heart. Ultimately, her passion had resulted in nothing. Dear Hyacinth's marriage had gone ahead, and now she was trapped in the same miserable existence that Emily would be herself in a matter of weeks. Emily pressed her hand to her stomach. She could not go into this marriage submissive and compliant as so many women did—and as Nicholas expected.

They'd known each other since she was eight and he fourteen. He knew her spirit. He knew her need to work at something real. Growing up, they had talked about so many things, but once he took the helm of the tobacco company following the untimely death of his father, the change in Nicholas had been quick and unnerving. She could bear a future married to a man she didn't love but would never bear her spirit being broken. If their marriage was to work, compromises needed to be made. Emily looked toward the window. The trouble being, Nicholas and compromise did not sit well in the same sentence.

She longed to fall in love with a man who

respected her and with whom she could relish their lovemaking, enjoy the feel of his lips against her neck, his hands on her breasts, and feel no shame, only love. To work side by side in both business and family to ensure a comfortable life and happy, independent children. She closed her eyes. How she feared none of that would ever come to fruition with Nicholas, and her daily efforts to banish her trepidation were futile. She wanted children, a family, and who was she to make the decision that they would live in poverty when her father had paved such a careful path of prosperity for them? She must marry Nicholas to maintain her father's half of the business after his death. The prospect of that dreaded day came ever closer as her father's health diminished in front of her eyes.

The sharp rap at her bedroom door shot Emily's heart into her throat. She brushed the letter into her open bureau drawer, heedless of crumples and tears.

"Who is it?"

The door swung open. "It's your father, dear girl."

Emily rushed across the room to assist her father as he ambled into the room, bearing his weight down on his ivory-headed cane.

"Father, what on earth possessed you to come upstairs unaided?" she cried. "Why didn't you ring the bell?"

"Pah, I don't need aid. I need you downstairs." He met her eyes. "Nicholas will be here soon."

"I know and I am ready." She held her dress and mimicked a curtsey. "Do I suit?"

His gaze softened as he smiled. "You look an absolute vision."

Emily grinned. "Why thank you, kind sir."

He pressed a kiss to her cheek. "Nicholas may not be the most amicable of men, but he certainly has an eye for the finest fabrics and richest colors."

Emily smoothed her fingers over the soft velvet of the ruby red dress Nicholas had arranged delivery of the day before. "He does. However, gowns are mere packaging. It's what is inside a person that matters."

"Indeed." His keen gaze wandered over her face. "And what is inside you, my dear?"

Unease rolled through her, and Emily frowned. "Papa?"

"I speak of the auction."

"The auction?"

"I may be dying, but my eyes are still as good as ever. I see the tension between you and Nicholas. It is more potent than I'd like. Have you had a disagreement?"

Emily swallowed. "No, of course not. We…we're both gaining nerves at the impending wedding, I think. We have things to discuss, things to settle."

"Such as?"

She looked into her father's gaze, and her heart grew heavy. Didn't he suspect that it had become her daily duty to find a way to make a marriage she did not want work? Surely he knew she'd do anything to make his passing easier. Anything to ensure when the dreaded day came, he'd close his eyes in peace knowing his only child had ensured his legacy remained secure without selling her soul entirely to the devil…to Nicholas.

She inhaled a shaky breath and turned to the bureau. "I want our marriage to be a good one, but Nicholas refuses to accept that I am not his to do with as he will once we are man and wife. I want him to respect me as he did before our engagement. He's changed, and I can't say I like it."

Silence.

Emily locked the bureau drawer and slipped the key into her velvet evening bag.

Her father coughed. "Has he hurt you?"

Emily swiftly turned. "Hurt me?"

He came toward her and took her hand. "Has he raised his hand to you?"

"No. Why would you think such a thing?' She huffed a laugh in an effort to dampen her dread that Nicholas just might assault her one day. Sometimes the way he looked at her...She forced a smile. "Nicholas may do his best to exert power over me now and then, but I am confident he would never strike me. You mustn't think that way."

His eyes darted over her face before his worried gaze softened. "The mind can play horrible tricks on a man when he knows he is leaving his only daughter in the protection of another. I'm sorry. I am seeing things that are clearly not there."

Love for her father warmed Emily's heart, and she moved her hand to the crook of his elbow. "Let's go downstairs. All will be well. I don't want you to worry about such things when you have nothing to fear. Nicholas may be a rogue sometimes, but he is not a fool. The last thing he would do is cause me physical harm." Emily tugged at his arm. "He'll soon learn I'm not a woman to cower to that sort of behavior. Not even from my husband."

Her father chuckled. "I remember when I spanked you for climbing the apple tree in the garden. You were no older than four or five, but you looked at me with such venom…yes, I pity the man who takes you on in that way."

Emily grinned. "Yes, well, I have my father's spirit, do I not? Come, let us go downstairs." As they descended the stairs, Emily sighed. "The tobacco company is a business you and Nicholas's father, your best friend, wanted both your children to benefit from. You have to trust me that Nicholas will not have it all. As long as I draw breath, that will not happen, Papa. I promise."

"When Nicholas's father and I became partners, our dream was to pass a thriving empire to our sons…but alas, I was given a daughter. Albeit a heavenly one. I just thank God that you are now entitled to my half of the company even once you and Nicholas are married. Yet, it is my deepest wish that, in time, you will grow to love him and the business will remain intact, meaning your children, my grandchildren, will benefit accordingly."

Culpability for her gender and the worry she had caused her father pressed down heavy and unyielding on Emily's chest. She stared at his balding crown, once thick with dark hair as black as hers, and sought further words to reassure him. "Papa, look at me."

He met her eyes, and her heart hitched. The color at his cheeks grew sallower as the weeks and months wore on. Despite the physician telling him the inhalation of smoke would only strengthen the blockage in his lungs, Emily hazarded a guess the stub of a freshly smoked cigar smoldered in the drawing room ashtray.

She pressed a kiss to his weathered cheek. "You

have to trust me when I tell you all will be well. I am marrying Nicholas to ensure your legacy is not deleted from history with the stroke of a pen. I am looking after you, me, and any children with whom I might be blessed. Everything will work out as we agreed."

He smiled softly and patted her hand before gently leading her forward. They halted at the bottom stair. Nicholas was early. His voice was loud and his forced laughter far too jovial as he spoke to the footman behind the closed drawing room door.

Needing a moment to prepare mentally and physically to face him, Emily turned to her father. "Go on in. I'll be right behind you."

He ran his gaze over her face once more before he took her hand from his elbow. "You take all the time you need, my dear." With a quick smile, he turned and pushed open the drawing room door. "Ah, Nicholas. You are a little early."

The door closed behind him, and Emily approached the hallway mirror. Her maid, Annie, had buffed and preened Emily to within an inch of her life. Her hair shone glossy and smooth, the complex twists and curls adorned with scarlet feathers and pearl-tipped pins, a feat in itself. Annie could not have done more to raise Emily closer to Nicholas's extreme expectations if she tried. Knowing she looked her very best, there was little else she could do if her appearance remained unacceptable to him. After her mistake of impulsively interacting with Mr. Samson a week before, Nicholas had exerted control over her with complete noncommunication.

She must curb her compulsion to misbehave if she had any chance of making their union amicable. She blinked back tears of frustration and tilted her chin, staring defiantly at her reflection. The outcome at the auction might have flustered her father, but she did not regret her exchange with Mr. Samson in the slightest. The man had eyes the color of the ocean and a smile that sent shivers of excitement along her spine and, no matter how brief their encounter, she was grateful for it.

Emily pulled back her shoulders. She would soothe Nicholas's fury by being her most charming, her most happy, and most of all, her most malleable at the ball this evening. He so often thought himself the one in control in their relationship, but...Emily smiled, she really did beg to differ.

Exhaling, she made an about-turn and entered the drawing room. "Good evening, Nicholas."

Nicholas snapped his eyes to hers, and a surge of satisfaction warmed Emily's face when his wineglass paused at his mouth. His eyes widened, and a faint color darkened his cheeks. At least tonight she'd met his high standards. He stared for a moment longer, his gaze hungry, before placing his glass on the low table in front of him. He walked toward her, and Emily remained poised even though the lust that shone in the emerald depths of his eyes made her want to turn and flee the room. His heat was one that would certainly scald and scar rather than energize and excite. She concentrated on keeping her smile fixed in place.

He took her hands and kissed her cheek. "You look wonderful."

She dipped her head. "Thank you."

His gaze swept over her hair, her face, and the revealed orbs of her breasts. Emily slowly pulled her hands from his and swept past him toward her father sitting on the settee.

She sat beside him. "We are very much looking forward to this evening, aren't we, Papa?"

Her father's eyes shone with pride as he looked at her. "Indeed we are, my dear."

Nicholas cleared his throat. "Would you like a glass of wine, Emily?"

Thinking a little alcohol-based support might be in order for the evening, she nodded. "That would be lovely. Thank you."

He turned to the silver plate on the bureau, laden with glasses and a crystal decanter. He poured her drink, and their fingers brushed as Emily took the glass. When her eyes met his, Nicholas's flashed with knowing. Nerves washed through her blood. A dangerous aura surrounded Nicholas tonight, one she did not anticipate or understand. She sipped her wine, and its warmth was welcome against her throat. She cursed the tremble in her hand as she lowered her glass.

"Now then," her father said. "What is next on this evening's agenda? Ah, yes. I wonder if this would not be the opportune time to present Emily with your gift, Nicholas?"

Emily's smile strained. Another gift? Unease whispered through her as Nicholas came closer and slowly extracted her glass from her tightened grip. He placed her wine on the table with a predatory smile. Lingering for a moment, he whipped a scarlet velvet box from behind his back like a magician would the fanged jaws of a viper.

"Please accept this as a token of my endless devotion to you, my dear."

Emily lifted the lid of the box. Despite her

reservations about wearing such a jewel, a gasp escaped her. Lying upon a bed of creamy-white satin, the Heart of Kingston shone brilliant in its beauty as it sparkled and glistened beneath the candlelight.

"It looks even more beautiful now than it did at the auction." She pressed her hand to her chest. "I don't know what to say."

"Then say nothing."

She looked up. Nicholas's eyes shone with unexpected affection, and her heart skipped a beat. Every now and then, his childhood fondness for her shone in his eyes. Her shoulders relaxed a little. Could his frequent derision toward her be a façade to emulate his father's reputation as a ruthless businessman? Maybe the pressure of living up to the Milne name was a burden that grew heavier as the vastness of his inheritance increased.

"Thank you, Nicholas," she said quietly. "It's beautiful. Truly."

"May I?"

He held out his hand, and she passed him the box. With careful precision, he took the necklace from its bed and gestured for her permission to fasten it around her neck. She nodded and stood. When she heard the faint click of the clasp, it felt far too much like a ball being locked to a chain, and Emily closed her eyes. Nicholas's fingers lingered for an unnecessarily long time at her nape as nausea swirled inside her.

"There." His breath whispered hot against her ear. "Now you belong to me."

She stiffened before snapping her eyes wide open and spinning around. Angry words battled on her tongue, pinched and bit at the inside of her mouth like tiny daggers of poisoned injustice. Her fingers trembled when she touched the jewel lying on her chest.

"Indeed," she said, glaring at him. "Duly collared and kept."

A flash of color assaulted his cheeks, and affront raged instantaneously in his eyes.

Emily turned to her father. "Shall we make haste? I would hate to miss the start of the ball."

He rose unsteadily to his feet, and Emily cupped her hand to his elbow. They all moved to the drawing room door. The glimpse of the old Nicholas she'd grown up admiring clearly no longer existed. He wanted her and he had her. Hopelessness and anger waged a war behind Emily's rib cage as they entered the hallway, and at the appearance of her father's footman bearing their coats, he and Nicholas left her alone.

Emily stepped toward Annie, who waited patiently by the door holding open Emily's mantelet.

"Thank you, Annie."

The maid laid it over her shoulders. "Miss?"

"Yes?"

"The McKendrys have arrived asking if you, your father, and Mr. Milne would like to travel to the ball with them rather than taking Mr. Milne's carriage also."

"Well, I—"

"What a splendid idea." Her father beamed, coming alongside her. "I do so miss my friend Mr. McKendry."

Emily looked at Nicholas. His green eyes shone with triumph, and unease rippled along the surface of her skin. "Nicholas?"

A slow smile curved his lips. "As nice as Mr. and

Mrs. McKendry's carriage is, I would much rather escort you to the ball myself." He turned to her father. "If, of course, you haven't any objections, sir?"

Emily stared. Go alone with Nicholas to the ball? Trapped within his carriage where he could do and say whatever he liked to her without witness?

Her father looked from Nicholas to her and back again, a dark flush of color pinching his cheeks. "I will leave that choice to my daughter. Emily?"

Icy-cold perspiration broke out at the neckline of her dress. Her father's gaze was distrusting, Nicholas's challenging. Anger rose up behind her breast. How dare Nicholas so openly test her in front of her father? Well, if he thought he could intimidate her, he was wrong.

"I think that will be quite all right considering we are soon to be married," she said, firmly. "You go with Mr. and Mrs. McKendry, Papa. Nicholas and I will meet you at the Assembly Rooms."

Her father frowned. "Are you quite certain?"

She forced a wide smile. "I am."

Their gazes locked for a moment longer before her father exhaled a heavy breath. "As you wish, my dear."

Emily turned to Annie. "Will you help my father outside, please?"

She dipped her head. "Of course, miss."

Emily took Nicholas's offered arm, and they walked outside.

Her father was assisted into the McKendrys' carriage, and once it was a distance away along the cobbled street, Nicholas cleared his throat. Emily kept her gaze on the shrinking carriage until it was out of sight.

With a firm hand at her back, he steered her to his

carriage. "Shall we climb aboard, my love?"

Nicholas's family carriage was beautiful. Painted deep burgundy with gold edging and lanterns that glowed beneath the street's oil lamps, it was yet another public symbol of his inherited wealth. A wealth that would never be enough to ensure their happiness. Placing her fingers on the carriage door handle, Emily looked at the velvet black sky. It was a beautiful night. She should have felt excited, in love, yet the feelings inside of her could not have been more contradictory…

Swallowing hard, she ducked into the carriage. The interior was equally as luxurious as the exterior. The seats upholstered in plush gold velvet, the walls lined with a paler gold cloth around two huge round windows on either side, a smaller one at the back. It was fit for a princess, and it only reinforced the knowledge that her future stood on incredibly uncertain ground if she and Nicholas did not marry. Her father's physician's fees had taken the vast proportion of their funds, and all she had left was her share in the tobacco company. Without Nicholas's wealth and her providing him with heirs, everything her father had built could be lost. Frustration burned her eyes, and Emily ran her hands over the smooth softness of the seats, trying to gather her strength. From now on, she would do her utmost to make things more amicable between her and Nicholas. If his knowledge that she wasn't happy about the union was exacerbated any more, he might do anything to ruin her ambitions for a fairer future.

The carriage jolted and pulled away. They sat in silence as the horses clip-clopped through the cobbled streets toward the Assembly Rooms. Emily stared out the window, paying no heed to the spires of the passing

Bath Abbey or the couples walking arm in arm enjoying the late spring evening. Her mind whirled with a million and one thoughts and worries.

She needed to ensure she and Nicholas passed the next few hours with at least a modicum of enjoyment. All would be well if Nicholas accepted their marriage on a more even keel. He was a young man with a vision for more. Surely he would come to accept her need to be involved in their future decision making, past home and hearth?

Nicholas moved close enough that the heat of his thigh seared through the material of Emily's dress. Despite her best intentions for the evening, she stiffened.

"You really do look wonderful tonight." The soft tone of his voice filled the carriage. "Extraordinarily so. In fact, you quite took my breath away when you entered the drawing room."

Emily turned. Only sincerity showed in his dark gaze. Surprised, she forced a smile. "Thank you."

He smiled and faced front once more.

Beneath the amber glow of the evening light bathing the interior of the carriage, his handsome profile was difficult to ignore. His compliment surely meant he wanted the evening to be as much of a success as she did.

"I'm looking forward to this evening." She sat straighter in her seat. "It's been an absolute age since I danced."

His gaze wandered over her face before he touched his finger gently to her jaw. "And that, my love, is a shame because you dance so beautifully. I trust you will allow me the pleasure of your first?"

"I would very much like that."

She smiled even as tension flickered through her shoulders. She suspected an ulterior motive to his kindness but endeavored to keep up the façade of peace between them. She turned to the window. Her mind filled with the jealousy that the announcement of their engagement ignited amongst her peers. She'd thought it daft and entirely unnecessary bearing in mind Nicholas's recent mood changes, but when he behaved like this, a small part of her understood his appeal.

She let him take her hand when he reached for it.

"You know, many people will be watching us tonight." He drew gentle circles over her glove with his thumb. "You are considered very lucky to be my fiancée. I trust you feel blessed?"

Disappointment crashed into her heart like a herd of wild horses. She exhaled a heavy breath. "Oh, Nicholas, why do you insist on being this way?"

His smile dissolved. "What way?"

She waved her free hand in the air, looking to pluck the adjectives she needed from thin air. "So…superior."

He choked out a laugh. "Superior? Well, isn't that what I am to you, my love?"

Heat seared Emily's cheeks. "Maybe in the social world, but do you have to stress it when we are alone? Could we not just be Emily and Nicholas?"

"Do you not mean Nicholas and Emily?"

She pulled her hand from his and glowered. "Very well, Nicholas and Emily. Either way, I would like to enjoy a few moments with you without feeling you are the master and I little more than a puppet. We were once friends. We enjoyed each other's company. I never felt as though I had to bow and scrape to you."

"I make you feel that way now?"

She swallowed. "Occasionally, yes. We are to be married. I'd like you to respect me, at the very least."

He dipped his head. "I apologize. It is not my intention to make you feel that way."

Careful not to show surprise at his compliance, Emily felt a strange sense of waiting for the hammer pounding in her heart to fall. The seconds ticked by, and she cleared her throat. "Then let's say no more about it and try our utmost to enjoy the ball. I'm sure we'll have a wonderful time."

"I have yet to be convinced."

The hammer fell, and Emily's hackles rose. She clutched her fingers around her drawstring bag in a bid to curb her frustration. "Oh?"

He flicked his fingers across his trouser leg. "As we are confessing how each of us makes the other feel, I have a small issue I've been struggling with."

Not trusting herself to speak, Emily waited for him to continue.

He met her eyes, his gaze cold. "I sometimes suspect it is hard for you to be within ten feet of me, my love. You so often look as though you wish to flee from my company at any given moment."

Asking for God's forgiveness for her impending falsehood, Emily gave a small laugh. "There isn't anywhere else I would rather be than here with you. Now, can we please try—"

He lifted his hand with such swiftness, Emily flinched. He didn't grip her arm or her chin as she feared. Instead, he fingered the precious jewel around her neck.

"You need to understand I am not foolish enough to bestow gifts such as this without expecting some kind of remuneration."

The insinuation was rife. Her stomach lurched. "Am I not remuneration enough?"

His gaze snapped from the jewel to her eyes. "You are, if I have all of you. Partial compensation is not an option."

"I am not a bargaining tool, Nicholas." The remainder of her self-control snapped despite knowing she risked ruining the entire evening by arguing with him. She could not stand him treating her as though she was nothing more than a bag of horse manure with which to trade. "This constant struggle between us needs to stop."

A slow smile curved his lips. "Clearly you are not as compliant to our fathers' wishes as I was led to believe."

"Is that what you expect from me at all times? Compliance?"

His laugh was derisive. "Is that not what all men expect of their wives?"

"I will always do what is best for the people I love, but that doesn't mean I will bark and beg and roll over for you on command."

"Do you want to marry me, Emily?"

No! No! No! Bitterness rose in her throat. "I want us to be husband and wife, to build a life together. That does not mean I won't voice my opinion or occasionally disagree with you."

His smile turned wolverine. "You really have so much to learn. I wish, too, that we be husband and wife...in every way. Yet I simply see no pleasure in

31

your eyes when you look at me." His gaze drifted slowly over her face. "Even though I am well aware you are capable of looking at a man in a manner indicative of physical attraction."

She opened her mouth to ask what he meant, but her voice was silenced when he raised his hand and looked past her toward the window. "Ah, we are here. We will have to resume this conversation another time."

Panic pressed down on Emily's chest. Everything Nicholas said or did lately was shrouded with threat. Tension assaulted her neck and shoulders as the carriage stopped in front of the Assembly Rooms. She forced her trepidation aside and gathered her skirts.

"Why don't we push these silly disagreements away and instead be determined to enjoy ourselves?"

He stopped, his fingers on the door handle. "I concur entirely. Just so you know, I have seen your smile directed at one man in particular in a much more captivating fashion than you have ever once smiled at me. So be careful, Emily. Be very careful."

Perspiration struck cold along the neckline of her dress. "Nicholas, really. I have no idea of whom you speak. Shall we?"

His hand whipped out and gripped her wrist. "Of course you know. I speak of none other than your friend Mr. Samson." He tossed her arm away and pushed open the door.

Chapter Three

Emily stepped down from the carriage to be greeted by the excited chatter of the women and the raucous jibing of the gentlemen gathered outside the Assembly Rooms. Smartly dressed and elegantly coiffed, they stood around in a haze of jubilance, the distinct smell of rose water and cigars scenting the night air.

She stepped forward with her head held high and forced her hostile exchange with Nicholas to the back of her mind. She would endure the rest of the evening with a smile on her face and dancing angels at her feet. There would be plenty of time to worry about his further scolding tomorrow and indeed the day after that.

Arm in arm, they strolled into the antechamber where her father no doubt awaited them. She immediately spotted him. He appeared disturbingly older than his forty-five years, his body stooped where it had once stood straight, and pain contorted his expression as he focused on what a fellow guest said. When he turned and saw her, his anguished face softened. Emily returned his smile, her heart full of love for the man who only wanted the best for her, yet it also broke for what lay ahead for their impending futures.

Her father resumed his conversation with the gentleman standing to his side, and Emily glanced at Nicholas. His green eyes gleamed beneath the candles burning in the wall sconces all around them; his dark blond hair shone and his pale skin glowed pink with health. Yet his distraction showed in his shifting gaze as it moved around the antechamber, his jaw tight. Emily swallowed the words itching at her tongue. Having seen the same look on his face many times before, she sensed Nicholas was wary, on guard, waiting for something to happen. When Nicholas was nervous, it meant everyone else should be too. She wanted to reassure him all was well between them, wanted to make him believe their marriage would be a happy one. But how could she utter such things when doubts tumbled through her blood on an unending wave?

He abruptly turned, his face softening as he smiled. "Shall we go through to the ballroom?"

She smiled. "I'd love to."

An attendant took her mantelet, and then she and Nicholas walked arm in arm into the main ballroom. Emily admired the ornately carved cornices, high windows, and secluded gallery filled with suited musicians. Nicholas led her around the grand room, smiling and nodding hello to acquaintances. Prisms of light from the three enormous crystal chandeliers bounced from soft yellow walls. The Assembly Rooms reigned supreme as the perfect background for people to play the giddy game of socializing, courting, and remembering. If only she were there to watch rather than be watched.

"Ah, I see an acquaintance I must speak with." Nicholas's voice broke through her contemplation. "I will be just a few moments. Will you be all right standing alone?"

"Of course. You go."

He lingered a moment longer before giving a curt nod and moving away. As the minutes passed, Emily relaxed enough to watch the six or seven couples dancing, her foot tapping to the music beneath the curtain of her dress. When a waiter walked past, she lifted a glass of champagne from his silver tray and swallowed a delicious sip—but the bubbles promptly caught in her throat.

It couldn't be.

She snatched a harried glance at Nicholas. Thankfully, he was engrossed in a conversation with a gentleman she did not know. She risked another look.

Mr. Samson laughed raucously within a circle of men he entertained, their drinks forgotten in their hands as they listened in rapt appreciation. Emily's stomach swirled and her mind raced. She'd never been so absurdly pleased to see a member of the opposite sex in her life. Blithely forgetting her wisdom it would be better that she never set eyes on Mr. Samson again and for Nicholas not to detect her attraction to another man, she stared at the scoundrel's wickedly handsome face.

Her father suddenly appeared at her side. "Daughter? What on earth are you grinning at?"

With her eyes on Mr. Samson, Emily couldn't fight her smile. "Nothing, Papa. Nothing at all."

"I say, is that Mr. Samson?"

"I really couldn't say—"

Emily's words halted as Mr. Samson's gaze locked on hers. Her glass trembled. If he approached her, how would she hide her interest? He looked so regal, so handsome.

"Emily?"

She glanced at her father and back to Mr. Samson.

Her mind was numb but her traitorous body very much alive. "Why, yes, Papa. I think you might be right."

She failed to drag her gaze from Mr. Samson's. He looked so refined in a double-breasted tailcoat and matching trousers. His dark hair groomed, his stature proud. His mouth—that delicious mouth—was lifted with just a hint of a smile. His manner was so evocative, her toes curled inside her slippers. Emily shifted her gaze to the women casting continual glances his way. He was easily the most handsome and powerful-looking man in the room.

When she met his steady gaze once more, an illicit thrill shot through her very center. He looked only at her. He gave an almost indiscernible nod, that intoxicating smile still playing at his lips. Emily snatched her gaze away as panic erupted deep inside her. If Nicholas saw their silent exchange…

She needed to leave. Right away. She turned to her father. "We must go."

"What, but why?"

"I do not feel well…" The remainder of her claim died on her lips when the light around her fell into shadow.

"Well, how lovely to see you again."

Her stomach dropped. Mr. Samson stood so close beside her; she felt his heat. Her heart beat hard, but she forced herself to turn. His stunning blue eyes met hers.

"Mr. Samson, what a surprise."

"A nice one, I hope, Miss…?"

She swallowed against the dryness in her throat. "Darson."

His smile widened. "Miss Darson."

His blatant appraisal wandered from her hair to her

lips, and finally her eyes. "I am hoping you will allow me the honor of the next dance?"

Her father straightened. "Well now, I'm not sure…" He stopped and then his eyes took on a wholly different glint. "I think that is a wonderful idea. Don't you, my dear?"

Emily stared at him. What in heaven's name was he thinking? She opened her mouth to refuse when Nicholas stepped between them, huffing and puffing like a raging bull. "That, Mr. Samson, will not be happening."

As Nicholas's and Mr. Samson's eyes locked in silent battle, Emily's impending future played out in her mind. Who knew what would happen once she and Nicholas were wed? What if he never changed, and she failed to build a happy life for them? What if their children followed him in personality and put her through daily agonized torment and disappointment?

Careless abandon suddenly pumped through her veins. This was her final chance to dance with someone else as an unmarried woman. Mr. Samson faced her, and Emily's heart beat faster. What if another man never looked at her in the hungry, challenging way Mr. Samson was at that singular moment? What if she never again felt the sensations she felt under his unrelenting, provocative gaze? She drew in a breath, brushed past Nicholas, and took Mr. Samson's elbow.

"Why, thank you, Mr. Samson. I'd love to dance."

His slow and devilish grin as he led her away threw Emily's stomach into a frenzied loop the loop. The man was so undeniably exciting, she did not care one whit that she'd endure Nicholas's wrath later. She bit down on her bottom lip to stop her smile from spreading as they took their places on the dance floor.

Will stole a surreptitious glance at Miss Darson. From the moment she walked into the ballroom on Milne's arm, he'd wanted to talk to her. He watched them walk around the room, Milne with his nose in the air, Miss Darson like the elegant vision she was. They looked like a couple—an engaged couple. Will hated the way the scene made his stomach knot and his head pulse with tension.

When he'd left his lodgings, he had been clear in his mind that he was over his initial shock of Miss Darson's beauty and confidence and now knew what to expect from her. God, how wrong he'd been. She was dressed in red. The color of danger. His conscience screamed inside his head, warning him off, urging him to find another way to punish Milne without involving her.

His pull to the woman was unprecedented. Even the line of her jaw attracted him.

She met his gaze and the fire behind her huge coffee-colored eyes burned into his soul. Yet, they were tinged with a pleading that confused him. Did she want something from him? Had his attraction to her made him an unwitting pawn in her agenda rather than the other way around?

He pulled back his shoulders. His motivation burned like a brand on his heart, whereas Miss Darson led a privileged life and had everything a woman could want at her fingertips. The handsome, if morally repulsive fiancé, money, social acceptance…a home. His mother hadn't had any of those things, and Milne had taken even more from her. He'd stripped her of her dignity, and the man would feel the backlash of that even if it took Will's last breath to make it happen.

He cleared his throat. "Is everything all right, Miss Darson? You seem—"

"Happy? Empowered?" She gave a faint laugh. "I am, Mr. Samson. I am both of those things."

A strange and unexpected response. If he had doubted her before, Will was now certain she held an agenda. He shoved the screaming warnings to put urgent space between them into submission. Regardless of the dangers involved in getting her mixed up in his complex web of revenge toward Milne, she was too good an asset to waste.

She was beautiful and intriguing. Intelligence resided in her gaze as much as her wish for something more. It made her alluring, which, although not ideal, gave Will a stronger incentive to find out how he could make himself matter to her. Her desire could be the key to Milne's demise. If he could help her in some way, she might be inclined to want to see him again, and that, in turn, would consolidate her as the next step in his plan.

The music began, and Will sneaked a glance at Milne. He stared at Miss Darson, anger mixed with possession evident in the line of a jaw sharp enough to cut glass.

Satisfaction poured into Will's blood. She mattered to him. Nothing could be more perfect.

"Is something amusing, Mr. Samson?"

Miss Darson's soft but confident voice cut through Will's contemplation. He met her gaze and smiled. Her eyes were an open window to an inquisitive mind. The women of high society he'd met before left no mark on his memory or libido, yet Miss Darson stirred both.

He dipped his head. "I apologize. Your fiancé's expression makes for quite a distraction."

Faint color darkened her cheeks, and they joined hands as the dance dictated. A bolt struck his gut at the contact. Damn this magnetic allure to her. He focused on the steps and tried to ignore how the scarlet velvet of her dress and the shining jewel at her neck emphasized the pale perfection of her skin. She was truly breathtaking. The daring in her gaze only added a sexual temptation Will was sure she was blithely unaware of.

"Mr. Samson, you're staring."

Her voice jolted him from his hypnosis, and he cleared his throat. "I was thinking that my asking you to dance was made without thought or consideration to the aftermath."

She frowned. "Aftermath?"

Will tilted his head toward her father and Milne. "Your father looks vastly more pleased about us dancing than your fiancé does. I would hate to think I have caused you or him any discomfort."

She smiled. "It is only a dance, Mr. Samson. I am not at all uncomfortable. As for Nicholas, I'm sure he will not lose sleep over us having a mere dance."

"And your father?"

Her eyes clouded with apprehension. "Is dying. Believe me, nothing will make him happier than seeing his daughter do what she does best."

Will lifted his eyebrows. "Which is?"

Mischief lit her eyes. "The opposite of what I should."

Grinning, Will held her more firmly in his arms, enjoying how much their closeness must be riling

Milne. Her skin held the soft scent of roses, and Will breathed her in. She was slender and perfect in his arms, deceptively fragile as a porcelain vase. Yet he sensed Emily Darson to be far from weak. No lady of society could have her audacity, her teasing nature, without possessing nerves of steel. She was strong and sophisticated and hardly the type of woman to be easily duped. Only time would tell if he had the skill to steal her from under Milne's damn ugly nose.

The awareness of how comfortably she fit in his arms made Will's heart beat like a hammer. The look in her eyes exhibited her intelligence, and she'd admitted she was a woman who didn't always follow the rules. What if she turned out to be a challenge he hadn't prepared for? His smile faltered. It did not feel good to be in such an unusual state of self-doubt.

Her fingers tightened around his. "Mr. Samson, you really are the most preoccupied man I have ever met. Your preference appears to be glaring at my fiancé rather than engaging in conversation with me."

Will stood straighter and forced his focus. "I apologize. Your fiancé is quite a newspaper favorite. It is strange seeing him in the flesh rather than print."

She glanced at Milne, not a glimmer of fondness appearing in her eyes, before she drew in shaky breath and moved away from Will as she followed the dance's steps.

After a moment, she swept back into his arms. "Being under constant study like an animal at the zoo is not all it's made out to be."

"Do you not enjoy the attention of the media?"

Her eyes darkened with irritation. "Not in the slightest. I abhor people's gluttony of scandal."

He looked around them. She was right; gazes drifted their way from every direction. Was her life a constant state of scrutiny? Of course, in that moment, the risk of public exposure was far more dangerous to him than her, but the potential to ruin Milne made that risk endurable.

"Tell me about yourself, Mr. Samson." Her gaze was steady on his. "Better yet, tell me about your interest in Nicholas."

Damnation. He forced a smile. "I have no interest in Mr. Milne."

She gave a derisive laugh. "I beg to differ."

Damn, the woman was quick. "I speak the truth…it is in you I have interest."

A wave of surprise flashed in her eyes, before her gaze darted toward Milne and back again. Will bit back a smile. Clearly she wasn't quite the femme fatale she liked to convey, but then with a quick blink, her bravado fell back into place.

Her eyes shone with renewed interest, her confidence once more stirring his libido. If he were to crush his lips to hers, would she respond or reject?

"Why would you be interested in me? Have you no regard for decorum?"

He smiled. "Decorum?"

Another twirl and sweep. "Come now, Mr. Samson. You know as well as I, it is not considered proper to be interested in another man's fiancée."

His gaze fell to her lips, the soft lift at the corner of her mouth escalating his temptation to kiss her. Instinct told him she knew exactly what she was doing and had no shame in using her female wiles to get whatever it was she wanted—or needed.

The steps separated them, and he was forced to dance with a woman to the side of him. Will dipped and turned, his gaze hovering on the back of Miss Darson's head as she moved hand in hand with another gentleman. He glared. The man wore the expression of someone who'd won a thousand gold crowns at the card table. Jealousy flashed hot and unwelcome inside him until he noted the way she looked at the man. Will smiled. Clearly, the flirtation in her eyes was reserved for him and him only.

The tempo changed, and she whirled back into his arms. "Are you not as equally interested in me as I am you, Miss Darson?" he asked.

Her smile vanished, and pure panic flew into her eyes. "Of course not."

"Are you quite sure?"

She opened her mouth to respond but seemed to struggle to find any words.

He winked. "As I thought."

Will glanced toward Milne and her father. Milne looked fit to explode. His usually pale skin had reddened to the color of a fresh tomato, and his mouth was so tightly drawn, his lips were invisible. Will resisted the urge to laugh out loud.

"You're right, Mr. Samson. I am interested in who you are. Very interested."

Will faced her. Damn, he liked this woman. He liked everything about her. He smiled. "In that case, I'll enjoy getting to know you and you me."

He turned and flashed a wide smile at his adversary. Milne immediately stepped forward, only to be restrained by Mr. Darson's hand on his forearm. Interesting.

Miss Darson had turned to look at them too. "Something amusing, Mr. Samson?"

"I am merely wondering how long it will take Mr. Milne to return to his normal pallor. The man looks as though a vein might burst from his temple."

"As he continues to be a concern to you—which I very much doubt is genuine—don't look at him."

He faced her, and the need to kiss her grew more ardent. His gaze drifted lower, and his blood burned with desire. The neckline of her dress plunged low. The curve of her breasts showed just enough to be acceptably provocative. Agonizing. He needed to concentrate on the job at hand. This extraordinary beauty, who fit against him so perfectly, represented an open door, a way in. He cleared his throat. "Am I to assume by your indifference to Mr. Milne's study of us, he has displeased you in some way?"

Fascinated, he watched the happiness in her eyes evolve to wariness as her fingers tightened around his. "He is my fiancé. My happiness is always at the forefront of his mind."

Will studied her. Emily Darson was beautiful, intelligent, and quick-witted, but she did not wear the expression of a woman adored by her intended. She wore the expression of someone who'd had her mask ripped from her face to reveal the pain beneath. The tension between them grew; the music rang louder.

She snapped her gaze from his to look around the room. "You know, I surmised upon our first meeting that you were not all you appeared to be, Mr. Samson, and it seems I was right."

Will raised his eyebrows. "Not all I seem?"

"Why are you so concerned about the ins and outs

of my courtship?"

"Because I sense you want more than a conventional marriage."

She halted. "What?"

Damn it to hell. Why in God's name had he shared his true feeling with her? "The dance, Miss Darson."

She looked left and right as though remembering where she was and stumbled into her next step. The color in her cheeks illustrated her annoyance—and the truth. The marriage between her and Milne was entirely arranged. By no means unusual, of course, but if she didn't love him and Milne loved her…Will's gut knotted. Nothing could be more perfect.

"When you've quite finished staring at me like the cat who got the cream…" Her eyes burned with anger. "The end of this dance marks the end of any further interaction between us."

"Is that the way you wish it?"

Her gaze dropped to his mouth and lingered there, before she whispered, "What other choice is there?"

"There are always choices, Miss Darson." *God, she's beautiful.* "This does not have to end here."

Color spread from her collarbones to the shallow hollow at the base of her neck. His torment and the answering passion in her eyes were not a pleasurable combination but a revelation that somehow or other he cared about her happiness. A damn sight more than was safe.

"I'd assumed you to be well-mannered," she said. "But I was mistaken. You are an arrogant oaf. And of those, I have had my fill."

"Yet you've admitted to wanting to know more about me."

Their eyes locked. "What is it you want from me, Mr. Samson?"

Her eyes darkened to two pools of melted cocoa, and Will dropped his gaze to the creamy skin of her bosom once more. Oh, he wanted something, and right then it had nothing to do with Milne. He slowly raised his eyes to hers. He had to ensure she didn't forget him the moment she left the ball. "I want you, Miss Darson."

She paled. "What?"

"I said, I want you. You cannot deny the connection between us. I felt it from the moment I saw you at the auction. You winked at me, remember?"

The skin at her neck moved as she swallowed. "I did no such thing."

He raised an eyebrow and tried hard not to lower his lips to hers and devour each of her sweetly agitated breaths.

She glared. "Despite your best efforts, you will never pass for a gentleman."

Apprehension tip-tapped up his spine. Did she know? Had she already guessed his true status? He grappled for a witty comeback, a succinct response to alter her mindset or a declaration that would throw her into perplexity. Nothing came. She was intelligent, savvy, and far too astute.

They stepped back as the music slowed. She dropped into a curtsey, and Will bowed. When they rose, he held out his arm and she slid her hand into the crook of his elbow. It trembled. They walked across the floor, each step bringing her return to Milne closer.

Will drew in a breath. "You are right in your summary of me, you know."

She stopped, apparently oblivious to the rancor shooting in her direction from Milne's eyes. "I am?"

"It is highly unlikely I will ever be a gentleman or have the money to buy jewels such as the one hanging around your exquisite neck, but that does not mean I lack sufficient funds for a comfortable future. Of course, that may not be enough for you?"

Anger stormed in her gaze. "By saying that, you merely reinforce the short amount of time we have been acquainted and how little you know me. Money, inheritance is often more about legacy and loyalty. Sometimes if you walk away, you toss dirt in the faces of the people who strove for more before you were born. Do not stand in judgment of something you know nothing about."

Her anger was palpable and washed over Will in an undulating wave. She was full of passion and determination. She was strong. He looked over her head at Milne and her father. Judging from their body language, Milne was insistent on joining them, but her father had other ideas. His grip was ironclad on Milne's arm. Why was her father inhibiting him?

"I am not judging," he said, facing her. "I want to see you again."

She regarded him suspiciously before her gaze marginally softened. "Loyalty and fervor, Mr. Samson. That's what impresses me, not money or possessions. Keeping a promise is the most noble thing of all."

The tone of her voice implied something he didn't understand. "Meaning?"

She shook her head. "It does not matter."

"It does to me."

"Mr. Samson, please." Another glance at Milne.

"You must stop this. It was fun while it lasted, but now it's over."

Resisting the urge to grasp her hand, Will lowered his voice. "Tell me where you live."

"What?"

"Take a risk, Miss Darson. Tell me where you live."

The seconds ticked by like minutes, and then she pulled back her shoulders. "Royal Crescent. I live at Royal Crescent."

She strode from the dance floor, and Milne and her father rushed forward to greet her.

Will smiled as excitement churned like a tidal wave through his body. "Enjoy her while you can, Milne," he murmured as he strode for the exit. "Before long she'll have forgotten you exist."

Chapter Four

Emily frowned as her father paced another circuit around the drawing room. "Papa, please. Come and sit with me. It's only been three days since the ball. Do not let Nicholas irritate you so."

He halted and glared. "I beg your pardon?"

His cigar trembled between his fingers, and his breath rasped from lungs thick with the black stuff that was slowly killing him.

Her heart ached. "Every time I see you with a cigar, it makes me so scared for you. Please. Grind it out."

He shook the cigar in her direction. "This is the only pleasure I have left. Don't you dare try to take it away from me."

"Will you please calm yourself?"

"How can I? We have no idea when the man you are supposed to be marrying will see fit to honor us with a visit. Why does Nicholas feel the need to keep acting in such a juvenile manner?"

"He likes to feel in control." She waved her hand. "Pay him no mind."

"I don't care how he likes to feel. My patience to overlook his dramatics is stretched to breaking. This cannot go on."

Emily rose from the settee and grasped his hand. "I want you to enjoy your remaining time, Papa, not waste it worrying over Nicholas and his uppity moods."

He took two rapid puffs of his cigar, exhaling the toxic smoke in a thick plume between them. Dropping his hand, Emily whirled away in frustration. Damn Nicholas for putting her father through this.

"You know the reason for his absence, do you not?" Her father's tone was accusatory.

Emily squeezed her eyes shut. "Oh, Papa. Not again."

"I was wrong to encourage you to dance with Mr. Samson. God only knows where Nicholas will go from here."

"I am not afraid of him. He needs me to keep up the reputation he so badly wants as a successful man of business and family. Do you not see that? This is nothing more than a power play. Nicholas and I...we had an altercation before the ball. He doesn't like the idea I want our marriage on a more even keel."

"Oh, Emily. Are you still fixated on this belief that Nicholas will return to the relationship you had before the engagement?"

"Well, yes. If—"

"A man must be a man in his home. I completely concur with him on that level. He is the owner of a successful business, a man who people want to know, a man of influence. How on earth do you think he will feel to have his wife contradict him in public?"

Emily's cheeks burned with frustration. "I am not suggesting I would contradict him in public. I am saying between us, behind closed doors, I would like him to talk with me rather than bark at me, demanding I obey."

"But obey you must. It is the law of marriage. It is

a vow. It's no wonder Nicholas keeps disappearing for days on end. You clearly exasperate the man."

Humiliation quivered deep inside her, and Emily walked to the window, lest her anger show in her eyes. "It's time for a change."

Her father huffed a laugh. "Change will come soon enough, but I would rather go to my grave knowing you will be a good wife."

"As Mama was before me?" she snapped.

Silence.

Emily closed her eyes, shame flowing through her. "I'm sorry."

"Your mother had your fire." Her father's voice was quiet. "It got her killed."

She turned and opened her eyes. "I shouldn't...I'm sorry."

He shook his head. "Come here."

Emily walked into his open arms, and her father's breath brushed across her hair. "I know what you think you must do to be heard, but antagonizing Nicholas is not the way. Your mother was the epitome of compliance in the home. A true lady in every sense of the word. Gracious and loving, attentive and obedient. What she fought for outside of the home had nothing to do with our relationship."

Emily nodded. "I know. Nicholas is doing what he thinks is right." She pulled back from his arms. "I'll try."

He smiled. "Good girl."

"I just want more for my children than hopes of inheritance and arranged marriages. Society will not change while I am young enough to forge the life I crave." She slipped her hands from his and pulled back her shoulders. "But for my children, who knows? I might hate the fact money paves the way, makes acceleration easier, but it does. I will not forsake money that is rightly mine at a cost to my children, your grandchildren."

"If I haven't shown you prosperity comes from the fire residing here…" He pushed his fist into his stomach. "I hope one day you will meet someone who does."

Mr. Samson's face flashed in her mind's eye, and Emily stubbornly pushed it away.

"Papa, please understand what it is I want. More to the point, what I don't want."

"Which is?"

"To…to end up like Aunt Edith, for example."

"Aunt Edith? What does she have to do with this?"

"Well, for one thing, she is bitter and twisted by a life not unlike the life you suggest for me."

"Whatever do you mean?"

"She was compliant, was she not? She did not challenge Uncle David or curb his weaknesses for drink and infidelity. She kept quiet, remained a *good* wife. If that is where behaving as such leads, I refuse to follow in her footsteps."

"I am not asking you—"

"Her husband died and left her with nothing, Papa. She now lives alone, her children scattered around the country either dead or alive. I don't want that, Papa." She swallowed. "Neither should you."

His shoulders slumped. "Of course, I don't."

"Sometimes when Nicholas looks at me, I know his reasons for this marriage run deeper than the inheritance. There is something that pulls at him to make this marriage work. His ego was certainly damaged by my single dance with Mr. Samson, but I hope when he looks at me, he sees a good wife. Maybe sees that together we can make the business into something bigger than it already is." Hope dared to spark inside her. "I owe it to you and Nicholas's father to try, Papa, I know that. I will do my best, but without forsaking who I truly am."

He nodded and walked to the settee, collapsing his weight onto the cushions with an exhausted sigh. Emily swallowed the lump lodged in her throat. From now on, she would ease his every worry and concern until the day of his passing. She could not allow her father's final days to be tainted with contemplation and tension.

"There is nothing for you to fear. I promise," she said, firmly. "Nicholas will write or send a message soon, and I will deal with his reprimands then. I didn't hide my association with Mr. Samson. It was one very public dance, after all. He will come to see I have done nothing wrong."

"My dear, we both did wrong. I encouraged the dance, thinking Mr. Samson a handsome chap who could bring a smile to your evening. Little did I know what was to unfold."

Emily frowned. "What do you mean?"

"You, my dear."

"Me?"

He smiled. "It warmed me from the inside out to see you look so happy. For one beautiful moment, you were alive. Even if you were in another man's arms."

Emily's heart stopped. Was her enjoyment really that transparent? She laughed and waved her hand dismissively. "Mr. Samson and I spent most of the dance arguing. He is quite insolent."

Her father's smile widened. "Maybe he is, but you still liked him very much."

She opened her mouth to protest, but the words died on her lips. What was the use of denial when her body still tingled at the mere thought of him?

Her father sighed. "But the matter is no longer of consequence. Mr. Samson has gone, and now we can concentrate on your upcoming marriage."

His breath left his lungs on a rasp of exhaustion. Emily swallowed. Her father had witnessed the sensations Mr. Samson provoked in her, but he could not possibly have suspected the way he made her want to scream and shout, throw caution to the wind, and live with risk and chance. It was madness. Two short meetings and the man had yet to leave her thoughts for a single second.

It was little more than a heated attraction borne from the reality that she'd never be free to explore the way he made her feel. Heavens above, when Mr. Samson looked at her, she felt naked. Like he had the unseen power to make her clothes slip soundlessly from her body and pool in a heap at her feet. Arousal tingled through her, and Emily moved to the window. She would forever hold those beautiful feelings and wish them for her daughters, who she would ensure were free to marry men they loved, not men who held the power of their future in the palms of their hands—or worse, on signed pieces of parchment.

She gazed at the sunset as pink blended with the color of fresh peaches. She wanted to go out, breathe in the evening air. Claustrophobia threatened on such a beautiful evening.

Her thoughts returned to Mr. Samson and his dark blue eyes and so-often insolent smile. She shivered. His voice was deep and powerful, yet when they danced and he stood not four inches from her, the same voice softened to something infinitely more seductive. How she longed to hear it again. The man was a mystery. An intrigue.

Emily closed her eyes. Why did her life have to revolve around money and marriage when all she wanted was to find true love? Was she selling her soul for a piece of silver? A tear dropped to her cheek, and she swiped at it.

"Emily?"

She opened her eyes and turned. "Yes?"

Her father's brow furrowed. "Are you feeling unwell?"

Forcing a wide smile, she stepped from the window. She needed to get out of these four walls. "Not at all. Quite the opposite. Would you like to accompany me on a stroll around the park?"

He threw a perplexed look toward the window. "Now?"

"Why not? It's a beautiful evening, and we live in one of the most admired places in the whole of England. Why shouldn't we enjoy it at every hour? Dusk is falling, and the sky is the most enchanting color. Please say yes."

He waved her toward the door. "Take Annie with you and spare your poor ailing father the exercise. I am quite happy here with my paper."

She walked to him and pressed a kiss to his sunken cheek. "I'll not be long."

"Go on. Go on."

Emily left the room and rushed into the hallway. "Annie? Annie, where are you?"

****

Will stared at the damp-stained ceiling of his rented room and inhaled a long breath. He'd been busy in the three days since the ball but had not achieved enough to dampen the fire in his gut. He now knew Milne's father had died this last year leaving Milne partial heir to the Darson-Milne tobacco empire: three thriving factories situated in and around Bath that the two founders had built with a minimal amount of money and a hell of a lot of sweat and tears.

Having infiltrated the workers' lunchtime eating area outside the biggest of the three factories, Will learned over a sandwich and mug of tea how the staff had taken to Milne, their new boss, being at the helm. It seemed Milne couldn't put a foot wrong, shinier and more valuable to the staff than a damn piece of newly minted silver. He'd gone there expecting stories of tyranny or at least disregard for the men who worked for him, but no, Milne seemed to be keeping up his end of the bargain as far as his father's legacy was concerned. So, Will had looked into the second half of the whole. Emily's father. He was dying, leaving his daughter heir to the other half of the business. The rumor was that a marriage contract was drawn up to ensure the money remained in both founders' families. Further investigation led Will to discover just how trapped Emily was. If either party refused to marry, the willing party received everything. Milne and Emily each had solid motivation to marry the other.

Will curled his hands into fists. If they divorced, she'd be entitled to her half, but then what? How would they work together in harmony? Would she sell to him? To another? Or would Emily, a daughter who clearly loved her father, be forced to surrender her inheritance to a man she despised in order to survive with a modicum of happiness as a single woman? Will's vision turned red. Milne, in one way or another, would come out the winner.

He closed his eyes. His plan to seduce Emily meant she would lose everything she was entitled to if she broke off her engagement. He needed to leave her out of it. Find another way to hurt the bastard. But that also meant he would leave a woman who no longer served a purpose in his vengeance to a man who didn't deserve her—worse, would undoubtedly hurt her.

Emily Darson had haunted his dreams for the last three nights. He woke in the early hours with his arm slung across the bed as though he reached for her in the night. How could she be engaged to Milne? The thought of the scum touching her, talking to her—God, even looking at her—made Will want to vomit. He tightened his jaw and grappled to get his temper under control. The man was vermin. Shit on his damn shoe.

He'd stormed blindly ahead on his mission and by doing so hit a brick wall. His plan was messed up, no matter which way he looked at it and going after Emily would cost him dearly. Will rubbed his hand over his face. It was lust at first sight. It had to be lust. Anything else was inconceivable, but the truth was, her strength and humor, intelligence and wit, had somehow hooked him to her on an invisible chain. She challenged him with every syllable that tripped from her tongue, and she fit within the circle of his arms as though made for him. He would endeavor to find a way to make Milne pay, as well as save her from the fate of becoming his wife. But how could her entitled fortune remain hers too?

If he could release her from what bound her to Milne, it would go a long way toward soothing his guilt for deceiving her. To tell himself he was her savior was the only way Will could keep focused, keep planning Milne's demise. If the wheels he'd set in motion crushed him along the way, he would ensure Milne felt their fatal tread first.

He wandered across the few feet of space in his rented room and rested his hands on the peeling windowsill. The sky held the rosy hue of twilight. Beyond the roofs of the town houses, the magnificent treetops that graced the grounds of Victoria Park—which lay so close to Royal Crescent—called to him. He smiled.

"A perfect evening for a walk. Do you not agree, Miss Darson?"

He pushed away from the window and whipped his coat from the bed, putting on his hat, Will headed out the door.

Chapter Five

Will raised his hat to the stone lions that stood like sentries atop the nine-foot-high pavilions at the entrance to Victoria Park. On the short walk there, his mood lifted from subdued anger and frustration to one of buoyant optimism. He would continue working on his relationship with Miss Darson until the solution to his problem became clear. Which it would. The answers always came…if you bided your time. Will pulled his coat together tighter and marched ever closer to the perfect place from which to observe Royal Crescent. All he wanted was to ascertain which house among the renowned semicircle of Georgian residences belonged to the Darsons. Surveillance of a target was an invaluable part of a successful outcome.

He needed to be vigilant not to be seen too soon or too often.

"Good evening, young man. Everything all right?"

Will jumped at the sound of a booming male voice to the side of him. Straightening, he touched the brim of his hat. "Absolutely, sir. Just taking in the beauty of Bath at twilight."

"Indeed. Indeed." The man nodded toward the Crescent. "The houses never fail to impress."

"They're magnificent."

The conversation lapsed as Will followed the man's gaze across the park toward Royal Crescent and wondered when the architect, John Wood the Younger, designed it, if he had any idea it would be considered one of Bath's architectural masterpieces. Despite the semicircle of houses being finished over a hundred years before, people still held it in high regard, and Emily living there spoke volumes as to the worth of her father's tobacco company.

Will scowled. She deserved her half. He cast a surreptitious glance at the man beside him and cleared his throat. "I understand Darson of Darson-Milne tobacco lives there. I was lucky enough to meet him and his daughter at the Assembly Rooms last week. Do you know the Darsons? Lovely people."

He laughed. "Everyone knows Oliver Darson, sir. A great man. Such a shame illness has struck him so harshly."

"Yes, he struggled somewhat at the ball. Is there nothing to be done?"

The man stared at the houses, moving back and forth on the balls of his feet. "Alas, I believe his lungs are the problem, and they say it is only a matter of time. I often see the physician entering the property."

Will followed his gaze as his heart beat faster. "They live at number 22, I think Miss Darson told me."

"No, no, number 24, sir."

Will bit back a smile. "Ah."

"Anyway, I must be off. I only came out to stretch my legs. My wife will be wondering where on earth I am." He held out his hand. "Nice to meet you."

Will took his hand. "You too, sir. You, too."

The gentleman walked away, and Will's grin broke. Number 24. With his hands clasped behind his back, Will walked on with an air of nonchalance. He came to an opening in the trees that served as the perfect vantage point to view that particular house. Some way or other he would take Emily from Milne without her losing her inheritance. He frowned. There had to be a way, and the sooner Milne understood Will intended to pursue him like a cat after a rat, the better.

His mother's voice came into Will's head, reminding him if he let Milne take over his life, his adversary had won. He heard her begging him to release the bitter resentment from his heart lest he die a cold and lonely man. She had dreamed of him married, a successful entrepreneur with children playing at his feet and a wife at his side. Will squeezed his eyes shut. His mother had harbored such romantic dreams, but when hunger had struck and they neared the end of their rent money, she uttered not a word when Will rushed out and returned with pocketfuls of stolen booty. She tutted and clipped his ear, sending him to his side of their rented room to get on with practicing his letters, but despite her chastisements, tears of relief glittered in her eyes at sight of the bread, fruit, and fresh milk he'd pilfered. She'd eked them out to last as many days as possible.

Will snapped his eyes open as a raggedly dressed street urchin bolted out of nowhere and shoved him backward. He sped past Will with no fear of recrimination or remorse.

"Hey, what do you think you're doing?" Will cupped his hands around his mouth. "Get back here."

He took a few long strides forward, intending to give chase when a nearby cacophony of panicked female screeching resounded.

"Help! Oh, please, someone help us!"

Will broke into a sprint and raced along the path. A few yards ahead of him, a woman lay on the ground, her skirts pulled above her knees revealing flesh-colored pantalets, her bonnet tilted atop her head. A younger woman was crouched down beside her, sporadically comforting her or shouting for help at the top of her lungs.

Will dropped to his knees beside them. "Ladies? Are you all right?"

The woman sitting on the floor clutched her ankle. "Annie, please. Calm yourself. I will be perfectly fine in no time."

Will concentrated on her ankle. It was swelling with each passing second. Without thinking, he gently eased his thumbs along the tender flesh, checking for any breaks.

"I say…" the woman objected.

"It's all right, miss. Nothing appears to be broken, but an ice pack will help with the swelling. Let's get you up off this cold ground." He met her eyes and his heart stopped. "My God, Miss Darson."

She snapped her eyes from her ankle to him. "You!" Her face colored, and she slapped his hands from her legs. "Don't you dare touch me. Drop my ankle at once."

Will's heart kicked back into place as he grinned. He raised his hands in mock surrender. "I apologize. I was just trying to help—"

"Yes, by mauling me."

"I was hardly mauling you."

Her eyes flashed with indignation. "Yes, Mr. Samson, you were. Now, thank you for your interest, but my maid and I are quite capable of returning home unaided."

Will looked in the direction the boy had fled a few seconds before. "Did that young lad who passed me like a cannonball do this to you? If he did, I won't rest until I track him down and hang him by his underpants on a lamppost outside the Theatre Royal."

The young girl giggled. Will looked up and winked. Her face immediately flushed red. He returned his attention to the beautiful and disheveled Miss Darson as she moved to get up.

"Whoa, whoa. What are you doing?" He held his hand to her leg once more. "You cannot possibly walk."

She glared. "Of course I can. Do not mistake me for a silly woman who isn't capable of looking after herself." She looked at the girl. "Annie, if you take my hand—"

Will cupped her elbow. "Miss Darson, please. Let me help you."

"I am perfectly all right. Annie?"

The maid grasped her other elbow, and Miss Darson trembled, her voice shaking whenever she spoke between grimaces. Will's stomach tightened with an emotion he daren't contemplate. Her hair hung in tendrils from beneath her bonnet, and the side of her face was streaked with mud, yet all he saw was her wonderful dark eyes and voluptuous figure...and a determination that was entirely her.

"Please, miss. Let this man take your arm," her maid pleaded, her eyes wide with panic. "What on earth will Mr. Darson say if I tell him a gentleman tried to assist you and we refused his help?"

"It is me who is refusing his help, not you. Father will only reprimand me, so stop your fretting and help me forward."

Annie straightened. "No. I will not."

"Annie, you will do as I ask right this instant. What on earth is the matter with you?"

Will cleared his throat. "Miss Darson, clearly your maid—"

She snapped her gaze to his. "Did I ask your opinion?"

"No, but—"

"Then let me deal with my maid as I see fit." She faced Annie. "Well?"

Will looked at the ground lest she see his smile. He had the sudden urge to whip her into his arms, march across town, and toss her into the famous healing waters. His smile widened when he thought of her sodden clothes clinging provocatively to her curves…

Annie's voice cut short his fantasy. "Pardon me, miss, but you know that's not true. Mr. Darson will say I haven't looked after you properly, and then where will I be? He'll send me to bed with docked wages, and I need that money to help Mama—"

"All right. All right." Miss Darson lifted a hand. "Enough."

She met Will's eyes over Annie's head. Her reluctance to even look at him could not have been more clearly etched on her face. Her eyes narrowed, and her jaw tightened. "Fine. Mr. Samson, would you be so kind as to assist me home?"

He bowed. "It would be my pleasure. It is barely more than a hundred yards to the Crescent, so I'll carry you safely home in no time."

"You will do no such thing, sir." Her eyes flashed with warning. "I refuse to allow you to pick me up like a bag of meal—"

Will swept her into his arms, and her words died on her sharpened tongue. Annie hurried to rearrange Miss Darson's skirts over his arms to protect her decency. Will glanced at the maid. Judging by the amused glint in her eye, Annie was enjoying her mistress's state of indisposed surrender as much as he was.

Miss Darson, on the other hand, struggled against him, her eyes alive with venom and shock. "Put me down this minute. I swear my father will hunt you down and shoot you dead when he learns of you manhandling me this way."

Will lifted an eyebrow. "And what of your fiancé? Surely, he'll wish to pummel me more? Or is Milne weaker than a dying man?"

"I do not mention Nicholas because woe betide you if he should hear of this."

Will laughed. "Woe betide me? I am quaking in my boots, Miss Darson. Absolutely quaking, I tell you."

Before she could say anything else, Will strode forward, carrying her across the grass toward the Crescent, hoping she'd soon exhaust herself of pummeling his chest and swinging her booted feet back and forth. For such a slender woman, she was anything but fragile. Twice he almost dropped her when she reached around and painfully pinched the flesh at his shoulder blades, and three times she called him names that no lady of her status should know, let alone utter.

His back smarted and his shoulders ached by the time they finally reached the pavement around the Crescent.

"Oh, thank goodness." Annie hurried ahead of him. "Quickly, Mr. Samson. This way. This way."

Will followed the maid up a short walkway to a painted black door bearing a brass knocker and letterbox shining beneath a polished lantern. Annie opened the door and rushed inside, holding it open for Will and the tussling tigress in his arms to enter.

Miss Darson's thrashing abruptly stopped. "Are you smiling, Mr. Samson? Is there something about my assault and your subsequent caveman brutishness that amuses you? Because let me tell you this—"

Ignoring her, he turned to Annie. "Drawing room?"

The maid nodded, hiding what he was sure was a smile behind her fingers.

He winked at her and followed the direction she pointed. "Miss Darson, I promise you there is nothing the least bit amusing about being attacked by the person you are actually trying to help."

"Then why don't you put me down before I take a handful of your crowning glory and yank it out by the roots?"

Will stopped and stared into her eyes. Somewhere in the back of his mind, he was aware Annie watched them and knew it likely the girl would scream her head off if he took advantage of her mistress, yet Miss Darson's face hovered inches from his…

"You wouldn't dare."

The warning didn't come from Annie but Miss Darson, her tone so low it could have been deemed a growl. Will blinked. She'd read his damn mind!

He swallowed and inwardly cursed the heat singeing his face. "Pardon me?"

Her eyes shone with triumph. "I know exactly what you were thinking, and if you wish to use your lips on some poor unsuspecting female in the future, I suggest you learn to close your eyes. They're a mirror to your despicable soul."

Will opened his mouth to retort. To toss something clever and witty in her direction but snapped it closed. Fine. She'd won that round, but there was always round two.

He dragged his gaze from her beautiful brown eyes. "Shall I lay you on the settee?"

"No, you can lower my feet to the floor. I have been telling you since we left the park, I am perfectly capable—"

"The floor it is."

Will abruptly put her down, and she swayed unsteadily backward, then sideways, before he swept her back into his arms, silently cursing his pathetic attempt at exerting his male authority over her. Irritation simmered in his stomach as he marched across the vast expanse of the room and gently laid her on the cushioned settee.

Their gazes locked until Annie cleared her throat. "I'll...um...fetch Mr. Darson. He should be told what has happened."

She hurried out, and Will turned to survey the room.

From the heavy drapes at the window to the, not one but two, crystal ashtrays and half a dozen porcelain figures lining the mantel, it was obvious the Darsons had a pretty penny. Was this house and its contents the sum of it? Or was he wrong about Miss Darson and she was just another money-hungry socialite willing to marry for money in order to keep her in the manner she was accustomed?

Emily hated the way her breath hitched, and her

skin still burned where Mr. Samson had touched her. Even now she couldn't drag her gaze from the breadth of his shoulders as he surveyed the room. The contrast of his dark hair against his white shirt collar drew her eyes again and again. She couldn't believe a stranger, a man of Mr. Samson's size and physical stature, was in her home when she was alone and unchaperoned.

It was incredibly unnerving and, if she were honest, more than a little exciting.

He abruptly turned, and warmth rushed to her face. If he noticed her staring, he didn't acknowledge it. He came toward her, his intense blue eyes on hers. Heat flared in places she'd only really become aware of since knowing him. Her mouth dried. The man moved her in ways that would make her father throw him out in an instant had he known.

His gaze wandered over her face, his brow furrowed. "Are you feeling better?"

"Yes. Much. Thank you."

He smiled and lowered to his haunches. "Good."

His eyes were dangerously level with hers, so she looked at his mouth, assuming it somewhat safer territory. She was mistaken.

Emily snapped her eyes back to his. "You can leave now." *Why am I whispering?*

They continued to look into each other's eyes, and no matter how much she wanted to break the moment, she was caught in an invisible trap.

"You have a nasty bruise forming on your cheek." He lifted his hand as if to touch her face but instead it fell to his leg. "Did the boy do that to you?"

She raised her fingers to her cheek and winced. "No, I must have knocked my face when I fell."

"Just as well." He pushed to his feet and the moment broke. "Because if he had as much as laid a finger on you…"

Trepidation knotted Emily's stomach, making her lightheaded. Who was Will Samson? Was he dangerous? Was she insane to allow him entrance into the house? Right then, he looked capable of knocking the boy into next week, whereas a moment before…Emily shivered; he looked capable of pulling her into his strong arms and kissing her with skilled and gentle persuasion.

"He was a boy dressed in rags," she said, pleased that her voice sounded so calm. "No doubt running from trouble. It's quite all right. I'm sure I'll live."

His study of her was intense, and her heart beat a little harder. Will Samson could be a powerful man. Yet not powerful like Nicholas—powerful in a perfectly honorable way. God help her. She felt protected. Cared for.

His stare turned soft and apologetic, and her undeniable attraction to him rose unwanted once again. "I appreciate you have a good and, no doubt, generous heart, but the boy should be held accountable."

She looked at her hands as she tightly clasped them in her lap. "What does it matter? We have little way of finding him. Bath is a big place with lots of corners. Considering my father's current state of health, it might just be the death of him if he was to hear any suspicions of me being hurt at someone else's hands. I hope you will support my wish not to further upset him."

"How will you explain the bruise?"

"Leave that to me. I'd appreciate it if you do not contradict me when I retell tonight's events to him."

His jaw locked. Emily waited. It was imperative she win this battle. For all her problems and challenges ahead, her father remained paramount in her consideration—and would until the day he died.

He raised his hands in a gesture of surrender. "Agreed. I will respect your wishes with regard to your father."

Relief slumped her shoulders. "Thank you."

"But I still maintain the lad should be thrashed for making you fall in the first place."

She turned from his gaze as a shameful thrill ran through her. The look in his eyes was possessive, virile. Almost as though she was his. She moved and her breath caught as pain shot through her wrist and shoulder.

"Let me help you." He came forward and then hesitated. "Do you mind?"

He gestured toward her back. Emily's heart beat faster. What choice did she have but to let him touch her again? She shook her head. He slid one arm behind her and offered his other arm for her to grip. Feeling weightless in the powerful circle of his arms, he lifted her into a more comfortable position. She lay back against the pillows, their faces barely inches apart.

"You looked flushed." His hands were still upon her. "Shall I ask Annie to bring some water?"

His breath whispered across her lips, and Emily flicked out her tongue to wet them. Her mouth was as dry as a desert. He followed the gesture with his eyes and tension crackled. "No. I'm quite all right," she managed. "I'm sure she will soon return with Papa. Why don't you take a seat while we wait?"

He moved to an armchair a few feet away, and

Emily released her held breath. "I try my hardest not to judge people's actions without knowing their motivation. That boy could have tried to take my bag for money to feed himself or an elderly relative, maybe his expectant mother. There is poverty and disproportion all over this city and—"

"We have all been hungry, Miss Darson, but never in a million years would I have hit a woman over a missed meal."

Emily stared, and he looked to the floor. Realization dawned, and she was reminded how little she knew the man who now sat with her, alone in her drawing room. "You have known what it is to live on the streets?"

"I do not wish to talk about it."

Her mind raced with a million and one suppositions and questions. He intrigued her, fascinated her. Mr. Samson was a man of the world, not one of social class and privilege, but a man who could teach her things. Real things. Things that mattered. She swallowed. What was she thinking? She must stay loyal to her father's legacy and keep every option and opportunity open for her children. Thoughts of what a man like Will Samson could or could not teach her were deplorable, and shame flooded her senses.

The seconds passed. After what felt like minutes, he raised his head. His eyes shone like sapphires beneath the candlelight. Angry. Passionate. "I have known what it is like to have no idea when I will eat again, and I have never raised my hand to a woman. It's important to me that you know that."

Before she could respond, the drawing room door flew open, and Emily was forced to swallow her curiosity.

Her father hobbled into the room as quickly as his weakening body would allow. "Emily, my love." He came toward her with his arms outstretched. "What in heaven's name happened?"

He bent over to embrace her, and Emily's gaze met Mr. Samson's over her father's shoulder. A muscle flickered in his jaw as he stared ahead.

Looking away, Emily eased her father back and held his hands tightly in hers. "I'm perfectly all right." She smiled. "Thankfully, Mr. Samson rushed to my and Annie's aid like a hero from one of my romantic novels you detest so much."

"What if he hadn't been there?"

"What is the use of ifs, whats, or maybes? All is well, and we should thank Mr. Samson and ask that Malcolm take him back to his lodgings."

She sensed Mr. Samson's gaze on her but kept her eyes firmly on her father. It was best he left and she never saw him again. Every moment she spent with him, the more he piqued her interest, and that spelled nothing but trouble.

Her father offered Mr. Samson his hand. "I don't know how to thank you, sir. My daughter is everything to me. If anything were to happ—"

"Now, now, sir." He clasped her father's hand. "She is safe, and I only did what any other decent man would've done had he been there."

"Well, at least have a drink with me so I can thank you properly."

Emily stilled. *No, no, no!*

Mr. Samson briefly met her eyes, and a small smile twitched his lips. He dipped his head. "You are most kind, sir."

Her father beamed. "Excellent. Annie? Would you be so kind as to bring some wine?"

Annie curtsied. "Of course, sir."

Her father turned to Emily. "My dear? Will you join us?"

Emily's nerves heightened. She wanted Mr. Samson gone but forced a wide smile. "That would be lovely."

Annie left to get the wine, and hopeless resignation swept through Emily when her father cupped his hand to Mr. Samson's elbow. He led him to the fireplace out of her earshot. She must see Mr. Samson as a charming stranger. A man she'd met on a few occasions. She could not be drawn to him without letting down her father, Nicholas's father, even Annie, Malcolm, and the rest of the staff who relied on her for their future wages. Her hands were tied, and having Mr. Samson near pulled the twine that bound her tighter than ever.

Her father turned, and his smile vanished. "What is that upon your cheek?" He touched his fingers to the tender spot as though she were made of porcelain. "Emily?"

She gently drew her father's hand from her cheek. "My face must have hit the ground when I fell. It's nothing. Now, if Annie hurries along with the wine, we can share a quick glass with Mr. Samson as a thank-you, and then he can be on his way. I am quite sure he doesn't wish to be delayed any longer."

"I'm quite happy, Miss Darson."

Emily shot him a glare, and he winked. Heat warmed her face. Yes, the man needed to leave. She pushed to her feet, and he immediately came forward to assist her.

"I am quite all right, thank you." She faced her father. "I think I will retire, Papa. I have become very tired all of a sudden."

"Of course, my dear. Of course. I will summon Annie."

Mr. Samson coughed. "I think it best we leave that drink after all, sir, and let Miss Darson rest."

"There must be something I can do to repay you. Will you take a cash reward maybe? Or maybe join us for dinner tomorrow evening?"

Emily froze. Hadn't her father already acknowledged how dangerous it was for her and Mr. Samson to be in the same room together? Yet now he saw fit to extend an invitation for the man to dine with them. Her mind whirled with excuses, proclamations, anything to stop such a thing coming to fruition.

Mr. Samson's eyes locked on hers. "That is most generous, sir. Thank you."

Emily glared. The man positively enjoyed himself! Enough was enough. She had to stop this. She looked from her father's melted chocolate gaze to Mr. Samson's sapphire one, and a strange sensation clutched painfully at her heart. Two men so different, yet instinctively, she felt they would be all she needed in a different time and place.

"I am sure Mr. Samson is accepting your invitation merely to be polite, Papa. He must have a million and one preferable things to be doing than spend tomorrow evening with us."

Mr. Samson's eyes glittered. "On the contrary, there is nothing I would enjoy more."

Her father chuckled. "There now. It is decided.

Shall we say seven o'clock?"

Mr. Samson bowed. "Perfect."

He looked at her, his face etched with undisguised glee. Emily's cheeks burned, and her chest tightened and just for the need to do something, anything, she poked her tongue out. His smile widened to a grin. Had she lost her mind? Sliding her hand from her father's arm, she sat back down on the settee, sucking in a breath as her bruised behind touched the seat.

Her father's and Mr. Samson's voices faded into the background. Was her father no longer concerned about Nicholas's opinion? After all, his ire at her dancing with Mr. Samson would be entirely eclipsed by outrage once he discovered Mr. Samson had dined at their home.

Her father's voice cut through her befuddled mind. "I will ask Mr. Milne, my daughter's intended, to join us for dinner, too."

"Of course, sir, it will be a pleasure to see Mr. Milne again."

"Indeed. I'm sure he'll want to thank you for coming so bravely to Emily's rescue."

Helpless desperation scratched at Emily's insides as she sat in stupefied horror. What was she to do? The implication of her alarm couldn't be ignored. She could not stand by and allow Mr. Samson and Nicholas to be in the same room together.

Mr. Samson left her father's side and came close enough for Emily to see flecks of gold in his eyes. Infinitely conscious of every part of her body, her mouth drained dry. Attraction hummed between them on a tangible thread.

"I wish you a good night's sleep, Miss Darson." He

lifted her hand to his lips. "I hope you feel better tomorrow."

He dropped her hand and walked from the room with her father. Silently, she raised the hand Mr. Samson had kissed and pressed the faint moistness of his mouth to hers. She was in the direst of situations yet could not wipe away her thoroughly treacherous smile.

Chapter Six

The next day Emily awoke late. The midmorning sun filtered through a narrow gap in the drapes, spearing a ray of light across the bedspread that stopped directly at her heart. She stared at its point, and superstitious apprehension jangled her nerves. It was a sign. A sign that could be read in one of two ways—each as terrifying as the other. It could be the tip of the dagger that would slowly and painfully kill her upon her marriage to Nicholas or else the fated tip of Cupid's arrow if she dared explore the way Will Samson made her feel whenever he looked at her.

She squeezed her eyes shut and groaned into the silence of her bedchamber. Her entire life, she had been destined to marry Nicholas. A boy she trusted growing up, maybe even admired, but when his father died leaving him alone in the world, Nicholas changed. Sometimes she saw flashes of the boy who made her laugh, who cared if she scraped a knee or struggled with her reading, but when she grew into a woman, his interest in her became feral and financial. Neither held appeal nor attraction.

She opened her eyes. Now Will Samson had come along and sent her focus into a spinning mess of emotional confusion. Emily swallowed against the hard lump lodged in her throat. How could she ignore these feelings? Her attraction to the man with eyes bluer than the ocean was too strong. He shifted her attention from expectation and priority, vanquished her belief of an adequate life with Nicholas. Instead, he turned her fantasies to things far more explicit. When he looked at her, she felt invincible. When he smiled at her, she wanted to laugh, and when he touched her, she wanted to...

She smoothed her fingers over the hills of her sensitive breasts as she stared at the gathered gold material of the canopy above her, erotic images filling her mind. Her fear of being in Mr. Samson's company was justified by her secret desire, but another part of her felt he was the answer she was waiting for. Emily shivered. The knowledge in the heat of his gaze told her to trust him.

Yet, had he not suggested exactly what he wanted from her at the ball? When she had been in his arms, the desire for his kiss heated her very core. Now thoughts of doing more than sharing a simple kiss rushed over her body with a desperate longing. To have one wild night...a forbidden night of intimacy with her hair loosened of its pins and her body free to follow its desires.

The harsh rap at the door sent Emily's heart leaping into her throat. "Who is it?" She quickly sat up and smoothed the bedclothes straight in nervous agitation.

"It's Annie, miss. It is nearing ten o'clock."

Emily relaxed back against the pillows. What did Annie know of lustful thoughts? Even if her guilt was written on her face, Annie would not comprehend it.

Emily fixed a welcoming smile in place. "Then you'd better come in."

The door opened and Annie entered, a breakfast tray expertly balanced along her forearm. "My, you look in a good mood today, miss."

"The sun is shining, and I feel a little shoe shopping might be the order of the day."

Annie lifted her eyebrows.

Emily swallowed. "Why are you grinning at me like that?"

Annie's eyes glittered with delight.

Emily straightened her shoulders and pulled on what she hoped was a stern expression. "Annie, stop that right now."

Her maid placed the breakfast tray over Emily's legs and busied herself pouring milk into a teacup. "I'm thinking Mr. Samson's saving you last night might have stirred up some feelings, is all."

Emily cleared her throat. "We may have become close over the years, Annie, but I will not tolerate insolence."

Annie whirled away from the bed, her hands outstretched. "I knew it." She turned in circles around the bed until she came to a stop on the other side. "He is so handsome I would have been ordering you to have a sight test if you hadn't seen it. Those eyes! I swear I nearly swooned when he winked at me. What a rogue! So funny and strong. When he lifted you into his arms—"

"Pull yourself together this instant." Emily bit back her smile and turned her attention to the breakfast tray lest Annie notice the humor in her eyes. "Mr. Samson is a gentleman visitor to this house, and I will not have you fawning over him like a lovesick child." Emily picked up her fork and speared a piece of bacon.

"Furthermore, you should not have been staring at him long enough to notice his eyes."

"Yes, miss."

"The man already regards himself as something special. Let alone enduring stares from my maid when he comes here."

"No, miss."

Something in the arbitrary compliance of Annie's demeanor alerted Emily to an ulterior opinion. The bacon dangled from the fork's prongs as she studied her. "What are you up to, Annie St. Clair?"

Annie lifted her shoulders. "Nothing." She swayed back and forth on the balls of her feet with her hands clenched behind her back, a hint of a smile at her lips.

Lowering her fork onto the tray, Emily lifted her teacup to her mouth to keep her smile hidden. After a purposely long moment, she returned the teacup to its saucer with a faint clatter. "You know I've been thinking about him, don't you?"

Annie's grin lit up the room, even though the curtains were still drawn. "Isn't he divine? I know you are engaged to Mr. Milne, and there is little to be done about that but...Oh, miss, how Mr. Samson looks at you."

Emily's heart jolted. "Looks at me?"

"Surely you see the softness in his eyes, the way he runs his gaze over your face...and figure when you're not looking." Annie clasped her hands against her apron-clad bosom. "A man who looks at a girl like that could lead her to the ends of the earth."

"Nonsense."

"I speak the truth. I know for a fact Mr. Darson noticed him watching you. I swear it."

Disappointment dropped like a stone into Emily's stomach. "If you think that, then you are wrong. If my father noticed, he would not have invited Mr. Samson to attend dinner with us this evening."

"I know what I saw."

"You're mistaken. Mr. Samson's interest in me is nothing of the romantic sort or otherwise. He is simply a man who has come momentarily into our lives and will no doubt disappear again very soon."

Annie shook her head, her hazel eyes gleaming. "I am never wrong about these things. My mam says I've got an intuition for it. I predicted every one of my three sisters' love affairs, and now they are each married with children."

"Well, this time your intuition is completely off the mark. If Nicholas were to catch even a whiff... What on earth is the matter now?"

Annie stared at Emily with her eyes protruding as though they'd grown stalks. "Mr. Milne."

"What about him?"

"I almost forgot."

"Forgot what?"

"He's on his way."

Emily laughed. "See? Wrong again. It's this evening he is coming."

"No, miss. It's now. This afternoon."

Emily frowned. "This afternoon? But Father sent a message for him to come this evening."

"I know, but the post came this morning, and Mr. Milne has written of his arrival this afternoon. The correspondence must have crossed in the post."

Trepidation clutched Emily's insides, but she forced a laugh. "Will you take that ridiculous look of horror from your face? Mr. Milne's coming here should not distress you. It is I who hasn't seen him since the ball…not that I feel horror. I feel pleased." Emily put the tray to the side of her and whipped back the covers. "It is time I was dressed."

"What about your breakfast?"

"I have quite lost my appetite. Everything will be quite all right with Nicholas this afternoon, I'm sure. The sun is shining. We can take a walk."

Concern shadowed Annie's eyes. "What will he say when he sees the bruise upon your face? I fear he will be more upset by its imperfection than its implication."

She brushed past Annie to the dressing table and looked in the mirror. The bruise had developed overnight and now reflected back at her in all its rainbow glory.

Pressing her fingers against it, Emily winced. "You're right. I look as though I have been brawling in the street. This will give him ample ammunition to further distress Papa about what he deems my insolent behavior."

"We'll find a way to make it less obvious. If I—"

"Ooh, why does he have to be so superior? He knows I will no sooner back out of the marriage and lose Father's money to him, than he would lose his father's to me." Tears of frustration burned Emily's eyes. Why did she feel more trapped than ever before?

"There is nothing for it, Annie. I must take whatever Nicholas throws at me. All that concerns me is easing my father's worries of how Nicholas will treat me when we are married and he is no longer here to look after me. I know he wants us married, but I also see how his concerns are exacerbating his illness. He is struggling so much with shortness of breath and fatigue. I swear I saw him attempting to conceal a bloodied handkerchief from me yesterday."

"What?"

"Exactly. He is dying, Annie and, on top that, he is entirely convinced Nicholas will treat me no better than a dog once I am legally his. How Papa can even think I would tolerate such treatment is beyond me, but I will not allow his fears to add to his distress. Not when he is so very weak."

"Of course, and all I can promise is that I will do all I can to protect you, but I worry even I won't be able to stand up to someone of Mr. Milne's size."

Emily stood and took Annie's hand in hers. "Nicholas will hurt neither you nor I. Not ever. That's a promise."

A devilish light burned once more in Annie's eyes. "I bet a bruised cheek wouldn't lessen Mr. Samson's feelings for you. In fact, I bet fifty pounds your entire body could be black and blue, and he would still take the most glorious pleasure in it."

Emily laughed as goose bumps erupted on her arms. "Will you stop? If Papa or Nicholas were to catch wind of your fantasies, there would be hell to pay." She dropped Annie's hands and walked to the window and snapped back the drapes. Yanking up the sash window, Emily leaned out and inhaled great breaths of fresh air to cool her face and still her hammering heart.

For all her bravado to Annie, she was afraid what Nicholas's reaction would be when he saw her. Even though he'd never been violent toward her, a suspicion he would want to blacken the other eye felt warranted.

And not because he would feel anger over her injury as Mr. Samson had, but because Nicholas would only think of how her looks affected him.

She turned back into the room and helped Annie get her armor…clothes…ready for the day ahead. An hour or so later, wearing a pale lilac dress that was a particular favorite of Nicholas's, Emily walked into the drawing room to await his arrival. The room was alight with the early afternoon sun, the yellow walls adding a bright and happy ambience. She sat on one of the winged armchairs and then stood. Sat again and stood. She couldn't stop the tension running through her veins. If Nicholas caused a fuss about her face when she could have been killed, then he was even less of a man than she cared to give him credit for. Her hands shook. She would tell him exactly that and face his ensuing wrath regardless. He should be relieved by Mr. Samson's presence, not angered.

Wheels crunched outside the window, and Emily hurried to it. The carriage door opened and Nicholas stepped out. He paused on the pavement and glanced left and right along the Crescent like a king of all he surveyed. Unimpressed by his self-importance, Emily stepped from the window just as the drawing room door opened and her father ambled in. She took his elbow and steered him to his favorite chair. "Come and sit down, Papa. Nicholas has just arrived."

"Ah, the man at last graces us with his presence."

Further words dissolved on her tongue as the drawing room door opened a second time and Annie stepped into the room and curtseyed. "Sir, miss, Mr. Milne."

Nicholas swept past Annie as though she wasn't

there, marched straight to the center of the room, and grasped Emily's father's hand. "Good afternoon, sir. I hope I find you in fine spirits on this beautifully sunny day."

Emily's stomach tightened. His happy demeanor was wildly disconcerting. If she knew Nicholas at all, that was exactly the feeling he wished to provoke. His green eyes glistened as he smiled. Foreboding tip-tapped its warning up the length of Emily's spine when he gave an abrupt turn and focused his attention on her. She pulled back her shoulders as he came toward her, leaving her father in his wake with a theatrical sweep of his jacket.

"Emily." He opened his arms wide before bending at the waist and grasping her hand in his. He pressed a firm kiss to her knuckles and looked up. His smile vanished. "My God, what happened to your face?"

Emily stole a glance at her father as he made his way across the room. His progress was slow, but she waited for the feel of his hand at the small of her back. She still needed her father, as any daughter would, when faced with danger. His fingers dug into her waist in encouragement.

She cleared her throat. "I was accidentally pushed to the ground by a young boy in the park yesterday evening."

Nicholas's gaze darted from her face to her father's and back again. "By a boy? What are you talking about?"

"Annie and I went for a walk. It was such a beautiful evening, I wanted—"

He turned to her father. "Please tell me she did this without your permission?"

Her father stiffened beside her, and Emily's hackles rose. How dare he speak to her father in that way and tone of voice? She opened her mouth to admonish him, but her father got there first.

His voice was colder than Nicholas's. "Emily does not need my permission to walk out with her maid."

"Why ever not? It is the evening. She is alone—"

"Have you met Annie? She would lay down her life for Emily."

Nicholas huffed out a laugh. "Clearly not. Look at her."

Her father's hand dropped from Emily's waist, and he stepped nearer to Nicholas. "Don't you ever refer to my daughter as 'her' again, do you hear me? Her name is Emily. A beautiful name bestowed on her by her dead mother. Use it."

Emily's breath caught in her throat. Her father trembled with anger, and his sunken cheeks were red with fury. Despite the words burning her tongue, she pulled her lips tightly closed knowing this was an argument her father was perfectly capable of ruling.

Nicholas pulled his lips back from his teeth in a grimace. His eyes flashed and his hands fisted at his sides.

Emily's heart picked up speed. If he so much as raised a hand to her father…This was the side of her father she desperately missed. The man he was before he ailed and his breathing became difficult and his chest tight. This was the man who raised her to be strong and compassionate, caring yet firm. Tears hitched like glass in her throat.

Nicholas finally broke the tension. He faced her, and Emily held firm beneath the frigid coldness of his gaze. "I apologize. I did not mean to be abrupt nor rude."

Emily dipped her head. "Clearly it has shocked you to see me—"

"I assume your attention was turned elsewhere when this happened. You look...deformed by this blemish."

Emily stared. "Deformed?"

"Yes. Deformed."

Unable to trust herself, Emily looked to her father to take up the conversation lest she say something she would regret.

He shook his head, a smile of disbelief playing at his lips. "Well, if that is the way you feel, Nicholas, it would probably be for the best if you walked away from my daughter, don't you think?"

Nicholas blanched. "What?"

"Emily is a beautiful young woman. Any man would want her." Her father turned to face her. "I am quite sure when society learns of Nicholas's decision to annul the engagement, my dear, another man, a worthy man, will eagerly propose."

Emily stared, her mouth dry. Where on earth had this come from? Had he lost his mind? Her heart swelled with love. He was provoking Nicholas to walk away, to end their engagement and hence, everything would be left to her. As proud as she was of her father, she had to stop him. If Nicholas thought for one moment her father was attempting to dupe him, heaven only knew what he would do.

"Papa, stop this. All is well. Nicholas did not mean what he said. He is just shocked by the bruising. Are you not?"

The two men locked eyes as they would horns. The room fell into shadow, and even though Emily hazarded a cloud had passed over the sun, she shivered beneath its implication. Nicholas's cold green eyes bored into her father's with such animosity, she wanted to lunge forward and slap him.

At last, he stepped back. "I apologize. To you both."

Emily released her held breath. "Apology accepted. Papa?"

Her father glared at Nicholas a moment longer, before he grunted and turned away. Emily's heart sank when he drew a cigar from a box on the low table.

"Father, would you mind taking your cigar into the garden? It is a beautiful day. Nicholas and I will take tea together, and I will tell him of our dinner plans tonight to thank Mr. Samson."

"What?" Nicholas's voice was like a cracking whip. "Mr. Samson is coming here? Tonight?" His eyes were narrowed to slits.

Heat sprang to Emily's cheeks, and she cursed the fact that the tone of his voice made her heart jump. "I will explain everything in a moment—"

"You will explain now."

Anger exploded like a firecracker behind her rib cage. Her restraint splintered, and her determination rose. She took a step closer to him and her father clutched her arm, but Emily paid no heed.

"I'll explain, Nicholas. Very clearly. It is quite possible Mr. Samson saved my life yesterday evening, and in the way of a small thank-you, Papa invited him to dine with us." She stared directly into his blazing eyes. "Surely you would like to thank him for coming to my aid?"

Seconds ticked by as his eyes bulged, and his color darkened. He glared. "Absolutely."

Her father cleared his throat and released her arm to snip off the end of his cigar. "Good. Now we are agreed, I will leave Emily to explain this evening's arrangements."

He pressed a kiss to Emily's cheek and silently ambled from the room. As the door closed, she squeezed her hands tightly together in front of her. "Before I explain anything about Mr. Samson, Nicholas, I want to remind you my father is dying. It is a sad state of affairs when a man upsets his future father-in-law at any time, let alone when he is in such a weakened state."

He looked to the floor. "I know that; you need not remind me."

Emily stared at his bowed head. His voice wavered when he spoke, and now his breath shook as he inhaled. When he raised his head and met her eyes, Emily swallowed her gasp. His eyes glistened with unshed tears. He looked positively distraught.

Emily stepped back, shock cooling her temper. "Nicholas?"

His gaze shifted to the bruise on her cheekbone. "The state of your face frightens me."

"Frightens you?"

"I love you."

Her heart stopped, and her tongue felt too big for her mouth. "Nicholas, you do not—"

He smiled softly. "You're surprised. Clearly my feelings are far from reciprocated. That is understandable."

Panic and guilt, confusion and despair tumbled around inside Emily's mind as she struggled to find the words to respond. "Nicholas—"

"Say nothing." He leaned forward, gently placing his lips against the bruise on her cheek. "No one will ever hurt you again. I will see to that. You are mine, Emily. Forever."

She froze despite the warmth of his breath upon her skin. He straightened and took her hands in his. His eyes were now dry of tears, his mouth drawn once more into a wolverine smile.

"I worry all the time, you know. I worry about you, me, our future together, but more than anything, I am in a constant state of fretfulness that I am missing something that's right there in front of me."

She trembled. "Missing something?"

He lifted his hand to her face, and his mouth twitched. He clearly enjoyed her discomfort.

He took a fallen curl lying at her cheek between his thumb and finger. "Indeed, my love. I think you are up to something. I think you've the audacity to take me for a fool."

She swallowed and forced a smile. "I would never do any such thing. Our marriage is written in stone. I will not…"

He gripped her hair so tightly, the stretched follicles stung at her scalp. She bit back a whimper as he leaned close.

"Then tell me why the hell Mr. Samson will be sitting at your father's dining table tonight? Precious Emily."

Chapter Seven

Will studied Milne over the rim of his wineglass. The Darson dining room hummed with tension. Despite having arrived promptly at the designated time, when Will walked into the house Milne's booted feet were already comfortably established beneath the table. The sight of him had been disappointing. He'd so looked forward to watching the expression on Milne's face when he entered his fiancée's home and found Will talking in soft tones to her, his lips barely inches from the smooth skin of Miss Darson's exquisite neck...

He stole a glance at her across the table. She looked ravishing in a gown of midnight blue; a pendant of the same color nestled at the cleft of her bosom. The dress molded her figure in the most enticing way yet was perfectly suitable for dinner at an upper-class table. The woman had no idea of her allure. Will took a drink in a bid to cool the fire inside him.

So far he'd barely said a word to her or Milne, because Oliver Darson seemed intent on monopolizing his attention. Will took appraisal of the not-so-happy couple as the man mumbled away beside him. Something had shifted between Miss Darson and Milne. He had no idea what, but it showed in the stiffness of her shoulders and the way Milne tilted his chin whenever he looked at her.

Unease rolled through Will's gut, and he turned his

Rachel Brimble

attention to Mr. Darson. He didn't want Miss Darson or Milne to know he'd spotted a change. A change that came from God knew where—but he'd find out one way or another.

Annie entered the room carrying a tureen, and Oliver Darson clapped his hands together. "Aha, the soup. Marvelous."

Will sensed Emily's gaze on him and turned. Her cheeks flushed pink, but she didn't look away, her gaze unreadable. The heat between them was palpable, so extraordinarily strong, he vowed to use the intensity of it rather than question it. Her dark brown gaze had lost its luster, her mouth its mischief. She was astoundingly beautiful—even with the overly rouged cheeks she'd colored in a clear attempt to tame her injury. Something bothered her, her fire extinguished.

Will's gut tightened as foreboding fueled inside him.

Was it ever a good thing to feel so drawn to a person? Surely it would end in disaster if something blazed too hot for either person to handle. Certain the attraction on his part was bound to his desire to hurt Milne, Will suspected the same could be said of Miss Darson. After all, she was with the bastard to ensure her inheritance remained in her family. He didn't blame her but longed for a way to give her liberty without sacrificing what was rightfully hers. It made him sick to his stomach to think of Milne gaining such a woman because of legacy rather than love.

Will picked up his soup spoon despite his vanished appetite and managed a couple of sips, before stealing a glance at Milne, who stared into his bowl, a muscle twitching methodically in his jaw. Satisfaction spread through Will's gut. The man was far from happy.

This is just the beginning, my friend.

He cleared his throat. "I am glad to see you looking so much better this evening, Miss Darson."

She hesitated, her spoon hovering above her bowl for a second before she lifted her chin and met his eyes. "Thank you, Mr. Samson. I am much better and grateful you were there."

Will smiled, hoping it would encourage a curve of her beautiful lips. "It was nothing. What man would miss the opportunity to sweep a beautiful woman into his arms?"

Milne flung his spoon into his soup bowl, and the silver clattered sharply against the china, spattering a shower of purée over the white tablecloth. Miss Darson flinched.

"Are you purposefully provoking me, sir? Or just astoundingly rude?"

Will tightened his grip around his spoon, fighting the urge to get up and slam his fist into Milne's face. "If I have in some way offended—"

Milne's face darkened to scarlet. "How dare you insinuate any kind of physical or romantic entanglement with my fiancée. You know Miss Darson and I are to be married, yet you talk to her in a manner that is insulting to me and your hosts."

Will glanced at Miss Darson. She sat ramrod straight, her spoon dripping liquid into her bowl unnoticed. He then turned to her father. Oliver Darson's eyes were alive with interest, his cheeks flushed. Keeping his face impassive, Will turned to Milne.

"I completely understand your jealousy, sir, and I apologize for provoking your insecurity. It won't happen again."

Milne's face darkened from scarlet to purple. "How dare you. I have no reason to be jealous. Miss Darson is mine, is she not? You are merely a man who made our acquaintance a few days ago and now finds himself treated to a meal as a sign of goodwill for doing absolutely nothing."

Miss Darson gasped. "Nicholas, how can you say such a thing? Of course Will...I mean Mr. Samson did something."

Milne turned his glare on her, and Will closed his fist around his napkin, every nerve in his body hitching to high alert. If he so much as raised his voice to her...

"He did nothing. If he had, we wouldn't be forced to look at that ugly bruise on your cheek, would we?"

The sound of the word "ugly" being directed at her fanned the flames of Will's anger. It burned hot and fast, bubbling his blood to boiling. The man had beaten Will's mother. Beat her and left her battered body to languish upon a hardwood floor. Now he tossed an accusation of imperfection at the most perfect woman Will had ever met. His vision turned red at the edges, and he inhaled a long steadying breath in an effort to regain his equilibrium.

"Maybe my timing was too late to prevent Miss Darson from being assaulted, but I think you are wrong that I did nothing," Will said, quietly.

"Meaning?"

"Meaning, Miss Darson was distressed and shaken. I brought her home. Back to where she feels happy and safe, loved and cared for."

"What of it? Any passerby would have done the same thing. You sit there like a puffed-up know-it-all.

You're an arrogant fool."

Will's heart beat like a drum, and his knuckles ached where he clutched the napkin instead of Milne's throat. The silence was such that the clock above the fireplace sounded clear, ticking by the seconds of unspoken retaliation. Will dragged his gaze from Milne and glanced at Emily.

Her cocoa brown eyes pleaded with him not to react.

He dropped his napkin onto the table. How was he supposed to refuse her?

Oliver Darson broke the silence. "Gentlemen, please. This is not the evening I had in mind when I invited Mr. Samson here. Emily has been through enough without being witness to a bear-baiting."

Will's shame further fueled his ill feeling toward Milne. The poor man was dying, for crying out loud. "Sir, I apologize. There will be no further cross words."

Oliver Darson turned to Milne. "Nicholas?"

Milne continued to glare, and Will glared straight back. It was time he revealed himself as an adversary for his fiancée's affection. That would be enough to irritate Milne for now. If Will had his way, the man would eat dirt before he laid a finger on Miss Darson or any other woman from that moment on.

"Fine." Milne's jaw tightened. "I apologize, too."

Emily's father cleared his throat. "Good. Gentlemen once more then. As far as I'm concerned, Mr. Samson saved Emily's life, and you should think the same, Nicholas. In fact, I would like to see you thank the man as I have."

Will's lips trembled as he fought his grin. The glee in Oliver Darson's gaze could not be mistaken, and

Will had no doubt the man was thoroughly enjoying himself.

Milne's hand shook as he reached for his glass. "Then I will do so now. I thank you, Mr. Samson." He took a hefty mouthful of wine. "I thank you from the bottom of my heart."

Will's smile broke. "You are more than welcome, sir. It was my absolute pleasure."

"Right then, are we ready for our second course?" Oliver beamed. "Annie? If you would be so kind."

"Yes, sir."

Annie cleared their soup bowls, expertly stacking them one on top of the other.

Oliver chuckled. "You know, I am confused as to why we haven't made your acquaintance around town, Mr. Samson."

Will's stomach knotted, but he kept his smile locked in place. "Indeed, sir."

"Are you new to Bath? First the auction, then the ball, and now coming to Emily's rescue. It seems our paths were destined to cross."

Will concentrated his gaze on Oliver. Was this normal dinner conversation? Or was Miss Darson's father as wily as Will suspected, despite his deteriorating health? The time had come to further his plan. Will picked up his wineglass and took a fortifying mouthful as three sets of eyes studied him.

"I have been in town just two weeks, yet consider myself incredibly fortunate to have met both you and your daughter...and, of course, Mr. Milne, seeing as I know nobody else here."

"Nobody, sir?" Oliver raised his eyebrows. "In the whole of Bath?"

"No, I'm here on what I had hoped would be a short mission, but unfortunately, the quick resolution I prayed for is yet to come. And now my funds are running low, forcing me to reconsider my options if I am to stay longer. If I do not find somewhere cheaper than the room I am currently renting, I will have no choice but to return to my hometown of Bristol before I've accomplished what I came for."

Milne slapped his hand on the table. "Ah, at last. The truth comes out."

"Nicholas, for goodness' sake." Miss Darson's voice cut across the room.

Will slid his gaze to her, and his heart soared to see the fire once more in her eyes. They were almost black with anger.

"Have you not already commented on the lack of quality in Mr. Samson's clothes? That he couldn't bid enough on the Heart of Kingston? Doesn't the fact he came to my rescue yesterday mean anything to you? Do you still judge him on whether or not he meets your material standards?"

Their gazes locked, and Will's heart picked up speed. Knowing what Milne was capable of doing with his hands, especially to a woman of Miss Darson's size, made his body tremble. It did not matter her gumption; the man was an animal, and Will struggled to maintain restraint. He had to continue with the masquerade. If he failed, he stood to lose the chance of living a life free of resentment and hatred. He stared at Miss Darson. A chance of having true love in his life one day.

Milne glared, his cheeks ruddy with rage. "You have no say in this, Emily. No say at all. How I speak to Samson has nothing to do with you."

The skin at her throat shifted as she swallowed, before she snatched her gaze from his and stared blindly across the room, her jaw set.

"Well, Samson," Milne demanded. "Nothing to say?"

Guilt gnawed at Will's conscience as he glared. He hadn't been there for his mother or every woman Milne had likely hurt in the last two years. The only way his fury would be purged from his blood was either by Milne's death or incarceration.

Emily abruptly stood and the scrape of her chair across the floorboards sliced the silence. "I'm sorry, but I must be excused." She tossed her napkin onto the table. "I've quite lost my appetite."

"Sit down!"

Milne's yell reverberated around the room, and Will fisted his hands on the table.

Emily's cheeks flushed as her body visibly trembled. Will's heartbeat accelerated. She couldn't leave. He needed her there. He wanted her there. If she wasn't in the room, God only knew if he'd have the strength to resist punching Milne to the floor.

Will stood. "Miss Darson, please. If you leave, then I will, too. I'd like to explain what has brought me to Bath. Your father has been good enough to invite me here, and now I wish to answer his questions. Please. Won't you sit down?"

Her gaze darted over his face and lingered at his lips. He longed to touch her, take her hand, anything to make her understand Milne would never hurt her while he still had breath in his body. Now, more than ever, he vowed to find a way to ensure she didn't have to marry the cad.

"Please."

Slowly her gaze softened, and a blush colored her pallor. She dipped her head. "Fine. I'll stay...for a little while."

Will glanced at Milne as he sat. The man continued to glare at Miss Darson.

Will coughed. "To further explain, sir."

Annie came in the room carrying steaming plates. Will smiled his thanks as she placed his dinner of beef and potatoes in front of him and continued to talk as the young girl made her way around the table.

"I make an adequate living as a painter, but it leaves little over for luxuries. Therefore—"

Milne laughed. "Painter? As in portraits?"

Will snapped his gaze to Milne's. "As much as I love that kind of work, sir, I earn a more reliable income by painting houses, boats, or wherever else I can find work."

Oliver Darson nodded. "And your work is of a good standard, Mr. Samson?"

Will confidently held his gaze. "Exceptional. So I'm told."

"Well, that's just excellent. Excellent. I admire a man who makes his own way in life. You should be proud of your vocation. You are what I call the salt of the earth. A man willing to get his clothes dirty and his hands cut." He glanced at Milne. "A man intent on making his own fortune rather than relying on others to give it to him. You, sir, are what this country is built on."

Will dipped his head. "Thank you. Alas, it seems my hard work does not provide the funds I need to stay here and achieve my mission."

"What is this mission?" Miss Darson asked.

"I am in Bath looking for my nephew." The ease of the lie tripping from his tongue didn't sit lightly in his conscience when she looked at him, her huge brown eyes wide with interest. "He disappeared just after his tenth birthday, two weeks ago. He fled my sister's farm in Bristol and has yet to return."

"Bristol is miles from Bath." She frowned. "Surely you do not think he could have traveled all that way alone?"

"I dearly hope he has. The alternative that he has not made it to the city alive cannot be considered."

Her cocoa gaze turned soft, and she reached out as if to touch him before dropping her hand into her lap. She blushed, and guilt mixed with desire inside him.

She picked up her water. "I am quite sure he is alive and well."

"Thank you, Miss Darson. That means a lot to me."

She smiled.

Will turned his attention to Oliver Darson. "We are pretty sure he would have fled to Bath because finding his fortune here one day was all he ever spoke of. He was fascinated by Pulteney Bridge, the Abbey…" He gestured toward the window. "The fabulous architecture at every corner. He said he felt he belonged here." He turned to Miss Darson. "I understand that, too, now I'm here." He quickly faced her father. God, how he longed to kiss her. "Would you know of anywhere I could stay, sir? Somewhere cheap?"

Mr. Darson studied him for a long moment, and Will concentrated on keeping still under his scrutiny. After the longest time, with Will's nerves stretched, Oliver slapped his hand firmly on the table, making his wine shudder. "You will stay here. With us."

Emily's intake of breath echoed around the room. "Papa, whatever are you thinking? Mr. Samson couldn't possibly—"

"Nonsense, Emily. Of course he can. We have plenty of room. I cannot think of a better or more perfect solution."

Will's stomach knotted with triumph. "Mr. Darson, that is really—"

"No." Milne pushed to his feet and slapped his hands on the table. "How can you expect me to stand by and condone such a thing, sir? Another man living in the same house as my intended? I will not allow it."

Emily's father sighed heavily, not even meeting Milne's livid glare. "Don't be so melodramatic. Have you not already expressed the clear opinion you don't care for Emily's going out at dusk? Raised concerns about the areas she frequents on her outings with Annie? Well, this is the perfect solution."

Will stared, confusion marring his thoughts let alone Milne's. What was he talking about? How would his staying there affect Miss Darson's outings? He stole a look at her. Her eyes were wide, and her mouth dropped open. She stared at her father as though he'd sprouted another head.

Will cleared his throat. "I don't understand, sir."

"Neither do I." Milne huffed. "What are you talking about?"

The old man smiled. "If Mr. Samson stays here, I can ask him the great favor of accompanying Emily on her outings in exchange for free bed and board. That way, neither you nor I have to worry about her safety when we are unable to accompany her."

The curse that emitted from Emily's mouth quashed the last shred of Will's self-control. He grinned as Milne looked on as though Mr. Darson had stuck a rather lengthy stick right up his future son-in-law's backside.

"Emily Margaret Darson," boomed Oliver. "I should ask Cook to swill your mouth with castor oil."

She leaped to her feet, her face bright red. "Mr. Samson cannot possibly stay here. Nicholas is right. Whatever will the neighbors think to see me riding out with a strange man at my side? The whole town knows Nicholas and I are betrothed."

"Exactly. Which is why I, you, and indeed Mr. Samson can carry out this arrangement free of social consideration. Need I remind you, daughter, you are sporting a particularly large bruise on your face, your favorite walking dress is ripped at the hem, and you have scratches on your legs? I refuse to risk anything like that happening to you again."

She snapped her gaze to Will.

He wiggled his eyebrows, and her face burned a deeper red. His body burned with elation. Oliver Darson had taken his plan forward two steps in one fell swoop. Now that he had infiltrated the family home, he was another step closer to seducing Emily…or, at least, helping her find a way out of her marriage contract. His smile wavered. If that's what she wanted, of course. He hadn't even asked her.

She twisted her eyes to Milne. "Nicholas, say something. This is incredible."

Silence.

She stamped her foot. "Nicholas!"

He started as if woken from a dream. "Yes?"

"Are you happy Mr. Samson is to escort me on my excursions? To drive me around town? The two of us together where everyone can see us?"

Milne's sallow complexion paled further, fury burning like wildfire in his eyes. Tension skittered across the surface of Will's skin, and his smile dissolved. The man's rage permeated the air.

Oliver Darson gave a dismissive wave. "Emily, leave Nicholas be. It does not matter that he's fallen into a rare state of no opinion. You will do as I bid until I am in a box. When I say Mr. Samson is welcome to stay here and guard your well-being as a means of earning his bed and board, so be it. The arrangement will ease my mind, while giving Mr. Samson further time to search for his missing nephew. Now, let's eat."

He watched Emily's bowed head for a moment before she scowled at him, her eyes shining with challenge and her jaw tight. He grinned. This would surely be his most enjoyable masquerade yet.

She put down her fork and dabbed at her lips with her napkin. "Are we really supposed to believe you have no ulterior motive to being here, Mr. Samson? That you did not orchestrate this to happen from the moment we met?"

Will stared, his self-satisfaction dissolving. Damn, she was good.

His smile faltered. "What do you mean? My nephew—"

"Emily, that is quite enough." Her father snapped his head up. "Mr. Samson is now a guest in our home. I raised you to show more respect to visitors."

Will met her unwavering gaze. She didn't so much as turn to her father. "I merely wish Mr. Samson to prove my suspicions wrong, Papa."

He slowly laid down his fork. "Your father's offer for me to stay here is a generous one and I would desperately like to accept, but if you feel uncomfortable…"

"The last thing you make me feel is uncomfortable, Mr. Samson." Her glare intensified. "I am merely concerned about other people's perception of the situation."

She lied. He made her uncomfortable. The way her eyes darted to his lips, the flush at her cheeks, and the rapid shift of her throat as she swallowed gave her away. She felt the connection between them. He was certain of it.

"I will merely do as your father asks," Will said, quietly. "If anyone outside of the house thinks it inappropriate—"

Her father laughed. "Believe me, Mr. Samson. There will be no problem. Any busybodies with something to say about how I ensure my daughter's protection can speak to me directly. Now, enough of this debating. I have made up my mind."

The room fell into silence as they ate. Will's mind whirled. Did Miss Darson suspect his motives? Maybe she knew something. What if she was the first person he underestimated? He studied her.

"Please understand my nephew is alone in one of the busiest cities in England. It near kills me each hour he is missing. To have somewhere to stay for the most gracious of returns is something I am immensely grateful for. You have my word, I will honor your father's request with the utmost decorum."

She steadfastly met his gaze. "Yet despite your

concern for your nephew's well-being, you sit here enjoying our food as darkness falls and he could be out there somewhere walking the streets."

Will lowered his head. "There is nothing more I can do tonight. I struggle every day when I have to give up searching and wait for the morrow's sunrise."

She laughed dryly. "If my beloved nephew or cousin or even dog was missing, I would scour the streets until my eyes refused to remain open."

Heat burned at his cheeks, as a flash of victory gleamed in her eyes.

Irritation simmered in Will's gut. "You're wrong, Miss Darson."

Her eyes gleamed brighter. "Oh?"

"When darkness falls on a city, the last thing you want to do is advertise the fact that there is a young boy walking the streets alone and afraid. There are men out there who search for these boys every single night. They don't see a young boy, desperate and alone; they see cash in every inch of his body."

Her smile wavered, and the light in her eyes died as his words snuffed out her glee. "That is a horrible thing to say."

Guilt twisted inside him as she paled, but it was a case of fighting for survival. He took a drink of wine. "Horrible but true. I am desperate to find him without increasing the danger he is in. If I ask too much, or come in contact with the wrong person, I publicize he's alone."

She looked to her plate and Will turned his gaze to Milne. Milne stared straight back and said nothing.

A few moments passed before Miss Darson pushed to her feet. "I'm sorry, but I must wish everyone good night. Suddenly, I wish for nothing more than my bed."

Will stood, as did Milne and her father. Will's gut clenched when Milne took her hand in his. "On reflection, your father is right. This is your home, and you are his most precious possession…as you will soon be mine. I am sure you and I can manage to comply with his wishes until such time as we are married, can we not?"

He didn't wait for her answer but, instead, lifted her hand and briefly touched his lips to her skin before brushing past her. He stood in front of Mr. Darson and held out his hand. "I bid you good evening, sir."

Oliver nodded and took his hand. "Emily is all I have, Nicholas. I will not risk her being hurt. Having Mr. Samson with her, when you are not, will ease my final days."

Nicholas arched an eyebrow. "You will far outlive Mr. Samson's stay, I am sure, sir." He turned to Will, his mouth curved into a sly smile. "After all, I am sure Mr. Samson wishes to find his nephew in the quickest possible time and return him to his mother forthwith. Am I right?"

Will nodded. What the hell was this turnaround about? "Absolutely."

Milne's smile widened, and he turned back to Emily's father. "There you are. I expect our gracious visitor to be gone as quickly as he arrived. Now, I must go." He gave a curt nod to Miss Darson, her father, and then Will. "I bid you all good night."

He made for the door and disappeared into the hallway. Miss Darson stared after him before she turned and approached her father. "Good night, Papa."

"Good night, my child." He pressed a kiss to her

cheek before lowering his weakening frame into his chair. "We will talk more in the morning."

Will drew in a breath. It was time for him to leave, too, before anything else could be said or done to ruin this new opportunity. First, though, there was just one more thing...

He coughed. "I think I will say good night as well. The evening has been quite eventful." He looked to Mr. Darson. "I am grateful for your food and hospitality, sir, but feel it best I allow Miss Darson to retire as she sees fit. Would it be all right if she sees me to the door, sir? I would like to reassure her I will do my utmost to ensure people fully understand I am only accompanying her as a companion and nothing more."

"Of course. I will leave you in Emily's fair hands. Leave your lodging address on the table by the door, and I will see you are picked up at midday."

Will bowed. "Thank you, sir. You have no idea how much this will help me."

Miss Darson gestured toward the open door. "Shall we?"

"After you."

With a final nod to Mr. Darson, Will followed Miss Darson from the room. She held her head high and her shoulders rigid as they walked through the hallway in silence. When she curved her fingers around the handle of the front door, he covered it with his. Hers stilled, and she stared at their joined hands.

Her skin was warm and soft beneath his; the scent of her hair flowers in springtime as it wafted beneath his nose. "Miss Darson? Will you not look at me?"

As though his voice broke an invisible spell, she whipped her hand from beneath his and spun around.

Will didn't immediately meet her gaze. He took the pleasure of lingering over her open mouth, higher over the loosened strands of her thick dark hair. Her bosom rose as she inhaled, her exhalation escaping softly from between her lips.

"Is there something you wish to ask me?" The tone of her voice would have sounded infinitely superior but for the quiver residing just beneath it.

He met her eyes, knowing full well she saw his hunger. "I think you incredibly beautiful."

Her eyes widened, and he mentally willed her to move away, to open the space between them and berate him for flattering her like a lover in her father's home. She did not. Someone needed to take control of what was happening between them, and as time moved on, it seemed less and less likely it would be him.

She tilted her chin and held his gaze. "You should not be saying such things to me when you know there is every possibility you are to be alone with me every day until you find your nephew. I'm engaged to Mr. Milne, and even though he did little to fight this situation this evening, his patience will soon wear thin. He has a temper you'd be wise not to provoke further."

"Is that so?"

"Yes, so you can continue to wear that self-satisfied expression all you want, I know what he is capable of, and you do not want to be on the receiving end of it."

Will's smile dissolved as a stab of anger swirled hot and fast inside him. "What do you mean, you know what he is capable of? Has he struck you?"

She stepped back. "No, of course not."

"Are you telling me the truth?"

"Yes."

Will studied her. He would kill Milne as soon as dawn broke if he found he had ever hurt her. Seeing fear in her eyes, Will forced his anger into submission and pushed back the hair across his brow. "I apologize for my brashness, but I've told you before that I won't tolerate a woman being struck by a man. Not even a man who supposedly loves her."

She huffed out a dry laugh. "Oh, never fear, Mr. Samson. Nicholas does not love me." She brought her hand to her mouth. "I shouldn't have said that." She threw a glance toward the closed dining room door before meeting his eyes once more. "I am just one of the hundreds of women held by the chains of an arranged betrothal. There is no love between Nicholas and me. Our union was decided before I was barely eleven years old."

"Why are you telling me this?"

Color rushed to her face, and she laughed nervously. "I have no idea."

Will met her smile. "I will endeavor to at least try not to upset Mr. Milne any further."

"Thank you. Our fathers signed a deal many years ago, and neither Nicholas nor I will concede to breaking it. This is my truth and that is his. You being here and…implying things…will make the situation harder for me to bear." She looked to the floor and shook her head. "I've said enough. You should leave."

He gave in to his earlier instinct and gently lifted her chin. Tears shone in her eyes, and a stab struck far too close to his heart. "You deserve more, Miss Darson. A woman as beautiful, kind, and passionate as you deserves the world."

He dropped her chin and turned, yanking the door open and striding outside. The blast of cool night air fanned his cheeks but failed to appease the fire raging in his blood as he stormed along the cobbled street and out of her possible sight.

Chapter Eight

Emily cast another hurried glance at the carriage clock sitting on her bedroom mantel. She fastened the button on her glove and whirled away from the fireplace to look at Annie.

"I feel so nervous. This is ridiculous."

Annie smiled. "Mr. Samson is merely a man, miss. A man with eyes that make a girl shiver, but a man all the same."

Emily glared. "This is not funny. Whatever will people think? I can't believe Papa has orchestrated this. We will be riding through Bath."

"In a carriage. No one needs to know."

"Mrs. Cambridge's sewing circle will know."

Annie gave an inelegant snort. "Who cares what they think? They never agree with anything. Whiners and moaners, the lot of them."

Emily frowned. "Annie…"

Her maid looked to her feet. "Sorry."

Pulling back her shoulders, Emily endeavored once again to beat off the nerves fluttering in her stomach and the anticipation bursting in her heart. This evening would be her and Annie's first excursion with Mr. Samson. Just the thought of being seated near him in the carriage sent a bolt of anticipation through her.

"Come. Let's get this over and done with."

Annie walked ahead of her onto the landing, and

they were halfway down the stairs before Emily noticed Mr. Samson talking to her father at the front door. It was clear by their stature, they were waiting for her. She continued her descent. There was little use denying how much happier her father looked secure in the knowledge she and Annie wouldn't be going out unaccompanied.

She stopped beside them. "Are we ready to go?" She smiled in the hope it hid the tangle of nerves sweeping through her and kept her gaze steadfastly on her father rather than Mr. Samson. "I will not be home late, Papa." She kissed his cheek. "Even though I promised to help Mrs. Cambridge with her sewing circle this evening, the ladies are all of a mature age, so I'm sure they won't be chattering beyond half past nine."

He squeezed her gloved hands. "Take your time, my dear. You haven't even ventured as far as the shops since Mr. Samson has been staying here." A knowing gleam sparkled in his eyes. "In fact, I was beginning to worry you might be avoiding going out altogether."

Emily's cheeks flushed hot. "Don't be silly. Now, you have an early night. Annie gave Malcolm strict instructions to look after you." She finally met Mr. Samson's eyes and her stomach executed a spectacular loop the loop. It did her focus no good to have such a handsome man as an escort. She inclined her head. "Mr. Samson."

He smiled. "Miss Darson."

Emily tilted her chin and walked outside with Annie close behind. Carrington, the family's chestnut mare, stood at the carriage's helm, impatiently clacking her hooves on the cobblestones. Emily smiled her thanks to the footman as he helped her into the carriage, and she sat as close to the window as possible before spreading her skirts about her. Annie sat down beside her followed by Mr. Samson who, of course, elected to take the seat directly opposite. The carriage pulled away with a jerk, and Emily purposely trained her gaze on the passing houses as they exited the Crescent and traveled down the street toward the circle of residences known as The Circus.

Mr. Samson's gaze burned hot on her cheek, but she refused to look at him. Until she had clearly established in her mind how to get through this outing, Emily didn't trust herself to speak firmly or with authority.

"Miss Darson?"

She turned and her heart kicked at the sight of his soft smile. "Yes?"

"Is everything all right?"

Emily stared at him before she released her held breath and a little of the tension left her rigid body. Although unsure of what she expected to see in his eyes, it certainly hadn't been sincere concern. He was a man after all. Didn't all men consider women a possession? Something to do with as they willed? Shame warmed her cheeks. Rubbish. Mr. Samson was unlike any man she'd ever met.

"This," she said. "It's…unconventional."

"Unconventional?" He grinned. "It's insane."

A burst of laughter tickled her throat, and she met his grin. "My father is a law unto himself. There rarely rhyme or reason when it comes to what he thinks is right for me. In business, though, everything is well thought out and considered."

"Matters of the heart rarely follow a logical path." He stared at her with one brow raised. "Wouldn't you agree?"

Emily stared into his eyes, her attraction to him betraying her. She looked once again to the window. "Indeed. My father has been a widower a long time, and he's raised me with the same opinion of what is best for me as any other man."

"Meaning?"

She turned. "Meaning, he doesn't look at my life as mine to do with as I wish. He wants me to be happy, but he wants me to be looked after, too."

His smile dissolved. "Isn't that what you want?"

"To be happy, yes, and I honestly believe the only route to that happiness is having the option to look after myself, Mr. Samson, but, alas, the option is nonexistent."

"Is this about your marriage contract with Mr. Milne?"

Heat flooded her face, and she cast a hurried glance at Annie, who quickly looked to the floor. Why had she shared so many personal details with him? "Somewhat, yes. I wouldn't want my father's legacy to go anywhere but to his grandchildren, so the contract is right and just."

He frowned. "Is that truly how you feel?"

She flinched. "Mr. Samson, I really do not think—"

"I'm sorry." He held his hands up in surrender. "It's none of my business."

He leaned back in his seat and faced the window.

Further words of explanation battled for release on her tongue. Her billowing tenderness demanded he turn to look at her, open his ears to her words, and accept that her future was not her own to determine. "My father is dying, Mr. Samson. I want…I must do right by him or else never forgive myself."

He turned. "I understand."

"Do you?"

"Yes. We owe everything to our parents who love and do their best for us. That I know above all else."

Even in the semidarkness, Emily recognized the undeniable respect and fondness in his gaze as he clearly thought of someone she could not know but longed to. What was this feeling deep inside of her wanting to trust a man she'd barely known more than a couple of weeks? Whether by design or destiny, Mr. Samson became forever more intriguing to her impudent nature. He challenged her, encouraged her to fight rather than attempting to pacify her as every other man had before him. His appeal was dangerous, and now he lived in her home.

She had to find a way to get rid of him or risk her marriage to Nicholas becoming a bigger and more hateful proposition than it already was. The minimal trust and respect she'd had for the man she grew up with wobbled more and more precariously with every passing day, and she feared Nicholas's reaction should she disappoint him. She swallowed the tears that lodged in her throat and tilted her chin. She'd face her future as her mother faced her death. With dignity and courage.

The carriage hit something in the road and lurched Emily forward. With a gasp, she clasped her fingers to Mr. Samson's knee to prevent herself from tumbling to the carriage floor. Realizing her position, she attempted to snatch her hand away, but he grasped it tight.

"Tell your father of your concerns, Miss Darson."
He stared deep into her eyes. "It will undoubtedly give
him more reason to fight his illness."

Emily's heart beat wildly. "What concerns? I am
perfectly content."

He shook his head, his green eyes blazing with
passion. "No, Miss Darson. Content is the last thing you
are."

She snapped her gaze to Annie, who stared back at
her, seemingly entirely enraptured by the conversation.
"You barely know me," she said, attempting a glare at
him. "Do not assume—"

"If your father must die, let him pass knowing you
are still entirely alive. That whatever he has done or
regrets doing has not broken your spirit. That you will
go on to be the woman you were meant to be."

Fear clutched at her heart that this stranger seemed
to know so much of what she thought and felt. "What
do you mean by that?"

"Your marriage contract. Your father is not happy
about it."

She opened her mouth to retort. To call him rude.
Insolent. Yet, pride seeped from her body as her
mother's beautiful face filled her mind's eye. She shook
her head. "So much has happened to him. You don't
understand."

"Then tell me."

The need to suddenly confess everything, to lay the
burden on his shoulders, rushed to the surface. She felt
such incredible trust in him. Nicholas would never
show an inch of Will's compassion. Sadness flooded
her senses.

Emily turned to the window. "I can't."

"Emily, please."

Her heart leaped at the sound of her Christian name uttered so softly on his tongue. And worse, it severed the fragile thread holding her common sense in place.

She looked at Annie, and her maid eagerly nodded.

Emily's heart beat faster. She had to talk to him. "My mother was murdered. I will always do my utmost to ensure my father's life does not pass in vain also." She eased her hand from his. "I should not be telling you this."

The carriage halted, and seconds later the door opened. Light from the lanterns outside illuminated the interior. Not waiting for Mr. Samson's assistance or anyone else's, Emily alighted from the carriage, leaving Annie and him to follow.

****

Emily stood with Annie in the hallway of Mrs. Cambridge's house and stared out of the open front door. Usually, in a bid to keep her father from sending out a search party, Emily rushed home the moment the meeting came to an end. Tonight she remained immobile. Mr. Samson waited outside, and she had no idea what she would say to him when her every instinct told her he was unlikely to let her admission about her mother go by without further discussion.

Her fellow members wished her good evening as they passed, their good wishes doing nothing to move her feet forward.

Annie touched her arm. "I think it best we make our way home now, miss."

Emily remained frozen to the tiled floor. "I can't."

Annie moved from her side to stand in front of her. Emily stared past her to the open front door.

"Miss, look at me."

"Hmm?"

"Mr. Samson will have the manners not to mention your mother again. He's a gentleman."

Emily jerked her gaze to Annie's, her paralysis broken. "No, he isn't. What gentleman would push and push a lady until she told him such intimate details about her life as I have told him?"

Annie frowned. "I wouldn't say he pushed you exactly."

"Miss Darson?"

At the sound of Mr. Samson's voice barely two feet away from her, Emily whirled around, her heart pounding. "Do you not possess even an ounce of etiquette, Mr. Samson? It is extremely bad form to sneak up on a lady conversing with her maid."

Amusement shone in his eyes. "I apologize... again."

"What do you mean again?"

"I always seem to be apologizing to you, do I not?"

Emily pulled on her gloves, her gaze intent on the task rather than on him. "Maybe you should start thinking why that is."

"Maybe I should."

"Like now, for example. You should not be inside the house. This is a private residence, and you are here as a chaperone. I cannot imagine the hostess invited you in."

"Oh, but she did." He turned and tipped his hat to Mrs. Cambridge.

Emily followed his gaze. The mistress of the house stood at the door, bidding farewell to members...with her attention trained on Mr. Samson more than on them.

Her blatant disregard for her guests was indefensible. Emily's throat burned with something that could easily have been deemed as jealousy. The older woman's eyes were positively hungry with desire, and if her tongue wet her bottom lip anymore, it would droop to the floor beneath the weight of her lustful saliva.

She huffed out a breath. "Well, I see you are as capable of manipulating the older generation as you are me. But then, I already knew that from the things you have managed to persuade my father into saying."

He smiled. "I find Mrs. Cambridge's attention extremely flattering, considering I am not part of your set. What they say about the upper class is clearly not true."

"And what do they say?"

"You are toffee-nosed snobs. People who'd never deign to be seen walking within five feet of someone below their class. Unless that person was in your employ, of course."

Insult burned hot in her chest. "I have never heard such utter nonsense in my life."

"I'm not suggesting you should be blackened with the same brush, Miss Darson. In fact, I am so confident such snobbery isn't in your nature, I've asked your driver to take Annie home so you and I can take a leisurely walk back to the Crescent...alone."

She blanched. "I beg your pardon?"

"I have asked your driver to take Annie home while we walk."

Emily looked to Annie and back again, cursing her sudden inability to speak. She swallowed in an attempt to get her tongue functioning. "You expect me to walk home alone with you?"

He nodded, his eyes bright with challenge. "Why not? Your father trusts me to look after you, and it's a beautiful evening."

The walls closed in on her as the chatter of the ladies surrounding them grew in pitch and volume. Was he insane? If people saw them, they would assume...but then, would they not assume he was a relation? Everyone acquainted with her knew of her engagement to Nicholas. If they didn't know her, people would surely assume they were just another married couple taking an evening stroll.

She looked into his devilishly handsome face, her gaze tracing the contours of his infuriating mouth before flitting back to his eyes. Excitement burst like a breaking balloon in her chest. Oh, what a thrill to be out after dark with a man other than Nicholas or her father! Her heart raced and her imagination soared. She could do this. Of course she could.

The night air came through the open front door and whispered across the floor, shrouding her with its potent liberty. Her appetite for adventure halted. If they were alone, he would ask about her mother.

"I don't think that's a very good idea."

"No danger will come to you, if that's what concerns you."

The heat in his gaze could not be denied. A strange sensation tugged at her chest and deep between her legs. "What if you are the danger, and I cannot see it?"

His gaze fell to her lips, and the sensations intensified. "Trust me."

She turned to Annie. The girl's eyes were wide enough to roll right out of their sockets, mouth agog. Emily bit back the sudden urge to laugh out loud and pulled back her shoulders, her decision made. "I will be walking home with Mr. Samson, Annie. If you could be so kind as to inform Papa."

The girl blinked, and she immediately erupted with a smile the width of her face. "Of course, miss. Take your time, miss. I'll allay your father's worries and get him to bed. Never fear. You take your time now."

She turned on her heel and rushed from the house as though her bloomers were on fire. Emily stared after her, grinning like a fool.

Mr. Samson touched his hand to the small of her back and gestured toward the door with the other. "Shall we?"

Emily smiled. "Indeed we shall."

The two of them walked forward with their heads held high and passed Mrs. Cambridge and the women surrounding her. Emily bit down on her bottom lip to stem her smile at the satisfying sight of their wide eyes and open mouths. With every step they took away from the house, Emily became more aware Mr. Samson had yet to remove his hand from her spine. Soft heat simmered there, radiating outward and upward, warming her bones and making her stand tall and proud. It was a new experience, being so conscious of a man's closeness, of the way her shoulder barely reached the middle of his upper arm.

"I hope you are not too upset with me for sending your driver on without us." His voice broke through the evening quiet. "I wanted to talk to you privately and saw no other way of making that possible."

"What is it you want to talk about?" Emily stared ahead, grateful her voice sounded as it usually did rather than being tinted with the shrill squeak of the nervousness she felt inside.

"Mr. Milne."

Emily halted, and his hand fell from her back. Her sinful excitement vanished. "Nicholas? What about him?"

"I wish you were not so determined to marry him."

"Who I marry has nothing to do with you. I barely know you."

"Don't marry him."

Emily stepped back. The look in his eyes was unnerving. It was as though he implored her to walk away from Nicholas with absolute conviction. Unwelcome suspicion gripped her. "Who are you, Mr. Samson?"

"I'm…just a man looking for his nephew."

"Then why do you care who I marry? You are a temporary visitor to my home. Nothing more, nothing less, and your concern confuses me."

"It confuses me, too, but I care about you. More than I should."

Heat pinched at her cheeks, and her stomach knotted with treacherous longing. "Why are you doing this to me?"

"I just want you to see you don't have to commit your life to a man who speaks to you the way he does…who I fear will be capable of much graver things as time goes on."

The memory of Nicholas's gaze when he caught her by the hair crashed into Emily's heart and mind. She swallowed and looked past him. "I am a big girl, and despite my father's overprotectiveness, I can look after myself." Irritated and frustrated, she forced herself to meet his gaze. "I do not have to explain myself to you. You are insufferable. We happened to meet at the auction house, and somehow you have come to be escorting me around town. You, Will Samson, are not a man to be trusted."

"Yet, here you are alone with me on a darkened street."

Emily swallowed, her heart beating fast. "What of it? You do not scare me."

"Then tell me what does."

Their eyes locked, and she admonished herself when her gaze drifted lower to his mouth. Why did she keep doing that? She raised her eyes. His gaze burned straight through her, scorching her deep inside. She had to do something, say something. The tension between them was too much to bear. She had worked tirelessly to uphold her commitment to both Nicholas and her father; yet with Mr. Samson, she had become trapped in an entirely different way. Each as unwelcome as the other.

"Emily?"

The sound of her name on his lips sent a shiver through her. Forcing a wry smile, Emily lifted an eyebrow. "Are we addressing each other on a first-name basis now... Will?"

He returned her smile. "I think we are. At least in private."

She laughed. His tone was rife with insinuation. "You really do consider yourself quite the man about town, don't you? The ultimate rascal? Is that what you want? To cause a scandal?"

He held out his arm. "I'll risk scandal if you will?"

Emily's heart hitched. How could she refuse such a challenge and not lose face with the man? He was a rascal of the highest order. She struggled to grab hold of her gathering panic. With Nicholas, she felt threatened when her heart beat this way; with Will it felt exhilarating.

Smiling, she tucked her hand into the crook of his elbow, and he winked. Emily's stomach promptly turned all the way over, and she laughed. Really laughed. He joined her laughter, his eyes shining in the most charming way as he laid his hand ever so gently over hers.

They walked a few yards in silence, and Emily tipped her head back to look at the emerging stars and crescent moon. It was a beautiful night, and her heart beat lighter than it had in weeks. The thought of her impending marriage threatened at the periphery of her mind, and she stubbornly pushed it away. Not now. Later. There would always be time later. Will's arm was strong and sturdy beneath her palm. She was safe. They continued forward, and Emily breathed deeply. She wanted to talk to him the same way she had in the carriage. Somehow, he pulled this innate need from her without saying a word; it was frightening but quietly reassuring at the same time.

"My father blames the Women's Society for Mama's death."

He turned and their eyes briefly met before he looked ahead once more, his grip on her fingers tightening ever so slightly.

"She was an active member," she continued. "I suppose it's where I get my passion for right and wrong." Further words lodged in her throat, and the road ahead blurred.

He stopped as though sensing her distress. "Emily,

if you do not want—"

"I do."

His gaze held soft concern, and the last of her hesitation melted.

She inhaled a shaky breath. "My mother and five other women were holding a very visual campaign around the city center when it happened. They stood on crates and shouted for support. Waved makeshift banners urging women to let their voices be heard."

He smiled softly, his teeth white in the semidarkness. "Definitely from whom you inherit your spirit, I see."

She briefly met his smile. "While female spirits are often dampened…my mother's was extinguished. It was deemed an accident, but she was murdered that day."

"Murdered?"

"A group of gentlemen saw fit to heckle my mother and her comrades before attempting to remove them from the entrance of the Pump Rooms. They were manhandled from their crates while people stood around doing nothing to help them." She stopped, drew in a calming breath as habitual anger simmered inside her. "My mother stumbled and fell, cracking her temple violently against the cobblestones. Her death was instantaneous."

He squeezed his eyes shut. "My God."

"I've been told when her blood seeped onto the stones, the noise went from anarchy to silence in a matter of seconds."

"I am so sorry."

Tears sprung into her eyes. He understood her pain. His empathy came through in the softest nuance of his voice. Instinctively, Emily sensed his grief, too.

Without thinking, she lifted her hand to his jaw. "Will?"

He opened his eyes. They burned like two blue flames in the darkness.

"Have you lost someone, also?"

His jaw tightened beneath her palm. "Yes."

"Who?"

His gaze flittered over her face, before he blew out a breath. "My mother. She was a good woman whose life was cut short unnecessarily, too."

He eased her into his arms. Shock and the awareness she shouldn't be doing this, shouldn't be seen in a man's embrace, but the thud of his heartbeat against her ear kept her there. She closed her eyes and listened to the roar of his blood. The rush of it filled her with equal measures of sadness and pain, strength and fortitude. This was wrong. She should stop, pull away, open the space between them and create a necessary barrier, but the feel of his hand smoothing her back in comforting circles drew the last ounce of fight from her. Even as her tears slid warm down her cheeks, she didn't move away.

"Emily?"

"Yes?"

"Does Milne kiss you?"

Her heart leaped into her throat, and she straightened in the circle of his arms. "Surely you do not expect me to answer that?"

"Does he?"

Her body trembled. The street was dark and deserted. She stood alone with a stranger's arms about her. "No." The word tripped from her mouth before she could catch it. "I know he wants to. I see it in his eyes."

His gaze dropped to her mouth. When he met her eyes, the desire she saw so often in Nicholas's was reflected in Will's—but in an entirely different, nonthreatening way. A wonderful new sensation pooled like liquid heat in her stomach. A sensation that made her silently plead for him to crush his lips to hers...

He bowed his head until his lips hovered barely an inch from hers. "May I?"

Perspiration broke out cold on her forehead as her gaze darted from his eyes to his mouth to his eyes once more. "Will..."

His mouth covered hers, and with gentle persuasion, he opened her mouth, provoking her response. The illicit place between her legs throbbed, and her nipples tingled in the most delicious way. Her eyelids grew heavy and closed; her fingers slid onto the hard breadth of his biceps.

Their lips savored and devoured. He eased his tongue inside her mouth, and he swallowed her gasp. Shock gave way to yearning, and Emily kissed him deeper, held his arms tighter. She wanted his touch, wanted him to discover her—and as much as those wishes terrified her, for one blessed moment, Emily did not think and, instead, she surrendered.

Chapter Nine

Will leaned his elbows on the roughened stone ledge of Pulteney Bridge and stared into the brown-green depths of the River Avon. The June sunshine dappled the water with sprinkles of silver as people walked along its banks toward the Parade Gardens beyond. As the church clock crept closer to midday, the area grew busy with maids hurrying along on errands and mothers gossiping as their children tossed stones into the water.

It should have been a scene worth painting. Yet, the reason for Will being there cast the scene in ugly gray.

The villain of the piece appeared at the steps leading to the walkway at the water's edge below him. Will squinted and pursed his lips tightly together. Milne slowly descended, his head held high, his ever-present cane theatrically flicking outward as his booted feet touched each step.

Will shook his head. "You pompous ass."

Milne continued to stroll along the side of the river, raising his hat to certain individuals whom he deemed worthy of acknowledgment. Others were ignored, despite their genial nods. He walked with the air of a man in control, a man who had the entire world at his feet.

Will smiled. *Not for much longer, my friend.*

Will pushed away from the ledge and strode along the road, keeping his gaze on Milne. Eventually, he'd have to come back up to street level. It had been almost two weeks since Will had left his rented room above a barbershop in town and moved into the Darson household. Five days since he'd kissed Emily. He wet his lips as he remembered how hers had tasted. Soft and as sweet as the freshest apricot, but when her tongue had met his so eagerly...Will swallowed. How he'd not taken her there and then he'd never know.

Drawing in a long breath, he forced his focus back on the man who continued to walk around thinking it was his right to marry a woman like that. Will's gut lurched. He'd told himself over and over again since their kiss to walk away, to find another avenue to pursue that would ultimately result in Milne's ruin. To keep his distance from a woman who haunted him day and night. Yet, he could not. He refused to take the risk of leaving Emily open to Milne's danger and have him hurt her. The woman was beautiful inside and out and, even though Emily would never be his, he intended to ensure she didn't waste her life with a bastard like Milne.

Will quickened his pace as Milne made his way toward the steps leading up from the riverside to street level and forced himself to concentrate on the day's mission to orchestrate a separation between Milne and Emily forever.

Milne emerged onto the street and stopped. Will focused his attention. Milne's eyes narrowed as he looked about him, his nose lifted as though sniffing the air like the mongrel he was. Will moved behind a flower stall. The pretty young girl working there lifted a bucket of Queen Anne's lace onto an overturned crate and spotted him. She looked him up and down in open appreciation. Will flashed her a smile. Her cheeks turned rosy before her mother came up behind her and scolded her for daydreaming. Will's smile widened when the girl smiled back at him and poked her tongue out at her mother's turned back.

He turned. Milne was headed straight toward where Will hid. He shot back against the wall behind him, his heart beating fast. "Shit."

Milne walked past.

Waiting a beat, Will exhaled his held breath and followed. Milne stopped every now and then to peer down his nose at a stallholder's wares, predictably unaware of anyone but himself. Feigning interest in an earthenware pot in a stall a few feet away, Will pulled down the brim of his hat and hunched his shoulders. After a moment, Milne moved on and after another fifty yards, entered a side street.

"Hello then, where are you off to?" Will quickened his pace.

Milne trekked farther along the street, sporadically casting furtive glances over his shoulder. On the third occasion, Milne halted, his nose lifted to the air once more. Will ducked into a doorway and pressed his back against the wood. He squeezed his eyes shut as his pulse pounded in his temple. Had Milne seen him?

He counted to five before leaning out from his hiding place. Milne had walked on, his gait now a manic trot. Will grinned. With Milne's height and weight, but lack of physical fitness, he bore the uncanny appearance of a gibbon with a stake shoved up its backside. Will came out of the doorway and followed Milne as he skulked out of the side street and into another. Unease stirred Will's blood. Maybe Milne knew he was behind him and thoroughly enjoyed having the upper hand.

Suddenly he came to an abrupt stop, and Will hunched down behind some discarded boxes left on the curbside. If Milne confronted him, Will would have no choice but to give him the short and to the point punishment he'd had in mind when he first arrived in Bath. He curled his hands into fists. Retribution was often a dirty job, but he wasn't averse to getting his hands dirty for a good cause.

He risked a peek around the boxes. Milne was bent at the waist, catching his breath. A slow smile curved Will's mouth. It felt good to see the bastard vulnerable. The man spent far too much time hiding behind an upper-class veneer, trying to show the world he had no weaknesses.

Milne straightened and stared in Will's direction for a horribly long time before he stepped to the closed door in front of him. He rapped his cane against it three times in quick succession. After a few seconds, the door opened. Neither the person at the door nor Milne spoke; he just walked inside and the door slammed closed.

Will cursed. He had no way of knowing who was in there, if they were male or female, young or old. Standing, Will removed his hat and swiped a hand across his brow. His mind whirled. Milne's financial security was dependent on his marriage to Emily. As far as Milne was concerned, the marriage would go ahead no matter what. Which surely meant whatever or whoever had brought the son of a bitch to the seedier side of town must satisfy Milne's other hankering. Lust.

Rage stabbed at Will's chest. Clearly Milne still paid for the services of prostitutes. He closed his eyes. His mother wasn't a prostitute. He refused to see her that way. She gave her body so Will could eat fresh food and sleep in a warm bed. She was a mother.

He opened his eyes and willed his breathing to slow. If Milne left one woman beaten and bloody, it was guaranteed he'd do it again. The image fanned Will's motivation for revenge to fever pitch. Heat spread through his blood as he glared at the closed door. Why would a leech like Milne change just because he had one of the most wonderful women Will had ever met as his fiancée?

Bile rose in his throat as Emily's exquisite face blurred with his mother's swollen and bloody one. Milne had neither moral ground nor conscience. He needed to be squashed underfoot like vermin. The truth that there were more women out there beaten and left for dead roared through Will's conscience. He should've tracked Milne down years ago. He should've gone after him no matter his mother's protestations. He covered his face with trembling hands.

He could not lose control and risk being hanged. He'd promised his mother his neck would forever stay attached to his body, and on that he would deliver. As for the promise not to avenge her beating? He'd kept his fingers crossed behind his back for that one.

Female companions willing to share their special type of company could be found at nearly every street corner in certain areas of Bath, and someone with Milne's wealth could pick and choose. Will lowered his hands and stared at the closed door. Why had Milne come here? Did this run-down, filth-ridden part of town singularly cater to his perversions? Did the woman behind the door provide a special service?

Will fought the need to bash the door down with his bare hands. He needed to put some space between himself and Milne, but at least it was a start that he'd discovered a place Milne visited. Pushing to his feet, Will walked back along the street as memories of his mother thrashed around inside his head like a macabre collection of picture postcards. Milne would never ask or care why the women he exploited did what they did. He would never consider the hardships they suffered to have no option but to stoop to the level of taking a man's penis inside them over and over again. The piece of shit would view them as nothing more than a means to satisfy his desires.

Angry tears burned the back of Will's throat. His mother sold herself only when she saw no other choice. Discreet, proud, clean, and softly spoken, his mother was a woman admired and respected. Even by the men who visited her. As a boy, he'd been confused by her visitors, yet happy to have a full belly and unafraid of any who spoke gently to her and kindly to him.

The noises of the busy main street interrupted Will's reverie and he blinked. Tired to the marrow of his bones, he slumped to the ground, unable to face the crowds. His blood roared in his ears, and he pressed his fists to his temples to block out the shouts and cries of the street traders. The real noise—the noise scraping away at his soul—would not stop until Milne paid for what he'd done and continued to do.

Will stared back down the street toward the closed door before standing. As he battled with the decision to sprint back there and smash his way inside, the sound of a coin clinking to the ground at his feet stole his attention. The boy standing in front of him could have been Will fifteen years before. His jet-black hair was spiked in all directions, his clothes clean but ragged, his bright blue eyes shining with knowledge beyond his years.

"What you doing, mister?" The lad picked up the coin and flicked it into the air. He caught it deftly and enclosed it tightly in his hand. "You lost or something?"

A smile tugged Will's lips. "I'm having a little look around. That all right with you?"

The boy grinned, his teeth showing as a white slash through his grime-covered face. "You're thinking of paying a little visit to Laura, ain't you?"

Will glanced toward the door. "Is that her name? The woman who lives in the house with the milk jugs outside?"

The boy's smile faltered, and his eyes narrowed. "You ain't here to cause her no hassle, are you? She's lovely is Laura."

" 'Course not." Will tugged at his jacket lapels. "Do I look like the type of gentleman who'd ever harm a lady?"

The boy looked him up and down and sniffed. "You don't look like a gentleman."

Will grinned. "You've got some spunk for a little one, haven't you?"

The boy shrugged. "Have to, don't I?"

"Here." Will reached into his pocket. He pulled out a sixpence and held it between his forefinger and thumb in front of the boy's face. "What can you tell me about little Miss Laura in exchange for this?"

The lad eyed the coin like it was a gold nugget. "That depends if you want to know about Laura or the halfwits who go in to see her."

Will respected the boy's integrity. He gave a slow nod as though considering his proposal. "Let's start with the halfwits, shall we?"

The boy reached for the coin, but Will snatched it out of reach. "Information first."

His new friend scowled and stuffed his hands into his pockets. "What d'ya want to know?"

Will tilted his head in the direction of the mystery residence. "A man went in there not more than fifteen minutes ago. I want to know how often he's here and how long he's been coming to see her."

"What did he look like? Judging by the way you're dressed, you'll likely be more interested in the stuck-up toff than the geezer with six little 'uns terrified of making it seven."

Will bit back a smile. "Who's the toff?"

He crossed his arms. "Well, now, information on someone of that stature might cost you a bit more."

"No, it won't."

The boy pulled back his shoulders. "It might."

Will forced a glare. "No, son. It won't."

Color flushed high on the ragamuffin's cheeks, and he uncrossed his arms and raised his palms in surrender. "Fine, fine. No need to start flexing your muscles. A kid's got a right to try, ain't he?" He glanced down the street. "He's here every month around this time. He likes Laura, but if she brings a mate in to cover for her, he takes one of them. He ain't fussy."

Will followed his gaze. "How long has this been going on?"

"About a year, on and off, I reckon."

"He's only here once a month?"

"Yeah, I'm guessing it's when his posh whore's got the ladies' monthly and he don't want that on his whatsit."

Will snapped his head around. "His posh whore?"

The boy's eyes gleamed. "Ah, you didn't know he had two on the go? If you want to know more, I'm going to have to insist—"

Will tossed him the sixpence. The kid caught it without blinking. Will drew out a second one and held it up. "It's yours if I like what you say."

The boy grinned. "Oh, you'll like it, all right."

Will's blood pumped faster.

The boy sniffed and ran the sleeve of his torn jacket under his nose. "He's got a mistress he keeps in her finery up on Milsom Street. People say she's been servicing him since he was a teenager. Bit sick if you ask me. He's stupid over her. Not in love or anything, but he's got a nasty reputation for wanting things that are his to stay his, if you know what I mean. So rather than let her go, he set her up for his exclusive pleasure."

"He's known this woman since he was young?" Emily came into Will's mind. She said she and Nicholas had known each other since childhood. Did she know the woman he kept as his mistress? Did she know he had a mistress? His stomach lurched with revulsion. How could Milne want any other woman than her?

"Oh, yeah. She works in the milliner's. Keeps her reputation decent. Load of crap, ain't it?"

"She's part of his social set?"

"To a point. Her wealth don't stretch to that of him

and his fiancée, but it means—"

"Wait. You know about his fiancée?"

He laughed. "God, yeah. She's the most beautiful woman you'll ever see." He gave a wolf whistle through his teeth. "She has masses of thick black hair. I bet it reaches to her waist when it ain't all pinned and fussed with. And her body? Man, what I wouldn't give to be left alone with her for an hour."

Will couldn't have agreed more, but he forced a scowl on his face. When he spoke, his tone was laced with anger. "How have you seen his fiancée?"

The boy frowned. "I don't live in a bloody cave, mister. I venture into town every now and then. Those toffs can be generous with their donations to a lad on the street once they've got the liquor in 'em."

"You've seen her with him?"

"Yep, her and the mistress at the same time sometimes."

Shock kicked Will in the stomach. "What?"

"Yep. He gets off on it, I reckon. That beautiful woman ain't got a clue her future husband goes out dancing with both her and his whore in the same damn room."

Will tossed the second coin, and the boy snatched it in the air. "Cheers, mister. Good doing business with you."

He moved to walk away, and Will caught his wrist. "You don't tell anyone I was here asking questions, you hear?"

The boy winked. "No problem."

Will released him, and his informant walked in the direction of the town center. Milne was exposing Emily time and again to public humiliation, and she had absolutely no idea. She might have told him there was no love between them—but he couldn't imagine for one minute, she would ignore the risk of public ridicule. The woman's demeanor screamed of self-respect and the fire in her eyes was testament to her tenacity. Will's heart twisted. It was that strength, more than anything, which drew him to her. They were kindred spirits. He squeezed his eyes shut. Damn, he could not think of her that way. Not now, not ever.

He turned and joined the throng of people milling along the town's streets. Whatever happened next, Will now possessed another vital weapon in his budding arsenal and would soon be equipped to obliterate Milne and expose who the man really was for all of society to see. *Good God, I'm going to strip him down and let the vultures pick him bare to the bone.* A few more bits of evidence and the contract of marriage to Emily, and Milne's succeeding fortune, would be washed clean away.

Surely, if he could prove Milne's infidelity, the inheritance would be Emily's in full?

****

Emily stared at her father across the breakfast table. The morning sunlight lit the dining room and her mood. Overly buoyant since her and Will's kiss, she had struggled to keep her face devoid of happiness for the past week. It wasn't right that she was this happy about kissing a man other than her fiancé, but she couldn't contain the thrill of it.

It made her feel alive that she had so carelessly exposed herself to risk. In that moment, she wouldn't have cared if Her Majesty Queen Victoria had seen them. She bit back a giggle. Deep inside she was alive—truly alive. The kiss meant that, for now, her entire being was not made up of preparing to sacrifice her life for her children's future.

Her smile slipped as she dipped her spoon into her boiled egg. For all the happiness Will brought her, she needed to ensure he didn't accompany her into town today. She lifted her fingers to her lips as she had a million times since their kiss. She'd avoided him and suspected he avoided her. She'd not left the house, so there had been no reason for his company before now.

Today she needed to go to town. She hadn't seen her friend Katherine for so long, and neglecting their friendship was a bad thing when soon she would need her company to fortify her once she was married. She shivered.

"Emily? Are you cold?"

She forced a wide smile. "Not at all, Papa."

Emily took a bite of egg as her father turned to his buttered toast. After a moment, she took a deep breath. "I need to go into town today, Papa."

"Ah, well in that case, I need Will to purchase me some cigars. I don't like the thought of a lady in a tobacco shop."

She slowly lowered her spoon to her plate. "I was hoping you'd let Annie and me go alone today. I'd like to go to the haberdashery for some ribbons and then meet Katherine for tea. She'll hardly relax with a strange man at the table."

He met her gaze. "No."

Emily frowned. "Why ever not? I will not be alone. The three of us will be perfectly safe."

"No."

"Papa, please. You are being entirely

unreasonable."

"You know the rules. I will not risk you to further assault. My mind is made up. My physicality is faltering, and I want Will with you."

"This is madness. I will be quite safe."

"Are you arguing with me?"

Determination pulled back her shoulders. "Not arguing but asking. Please. This trust you have in Will is based on nothing more…Papa?"

Her father sucked in a loud breath, and his fork clattered onto his plate.

Emily leaped to her feet, her heart beating fast, panic a boulder in her throat. "Papa!"

Her father's arms flailed outward, sending his teacup spilling across the table. His face grew dark red, and a vein bulged at his temple. She rushed forward, sending her plate and egg toppling to the floor unheeded.

Her father started to choke in earnest.

"Papa! Oh, no. I'm so sorry. Papa, please." She slapped him on the back, again and again. "Why do you insist on eating and shouting at me at the same time?" Her attempt at humor did nothing to lessen her panic. She couldn't lose him. Not like this.

Emily darted her gaze to the closed dining room door. "Annie! Annie, help me. Someone help me!"

Grasping her father's arm, she yanked and pulled him from the chair to his feet, her arms trembling from the strain and perspiration breaking out on her skin. What was she to do? Tears threatened as her father's coughing halted, and the skin around his mouth turned blue.

"Help me. Please. Somebody!"

The doors crashed open, and Will came rushing in. "Emily?"

"Will, help me. He's not breathing."

He strode forward and yanked her father from her arms. He whirled him around and slapped him hard on the back. Her father's lips grew darker.

Emily could hardly bear to watch. "Will, please. Do something."

He ignored her, his face shone white with concentration. Emily lifted her hand to her mouth as he pulled her father's ailing frame against his muscular one and counted to three before bringing his hand down hard between her father's shoulder blades. She cried out.

"Come now, Mr. Darson, be a gentleman," Will panted. "One, two, three."

He slapped his back again, this time so hard her father stumbled forward violently, but Will held him fast. A lodged chunk of bacon shot from her father's mouth, and Emily watched in horrified silence as it flew through the air before ricocheting from the mirror above the fireplace with a resounding ping.

Her father's gasps of breath and hacking cough filled the room as Will guided him to his chair and grasped his bony shoulder. "Not the best way to start the day, if you don't mind me saying so, sir."

Her father dabbed a napkin to his mouth as the coughing subsided. "That was quite a trick you performed there. I feel like such a fool."

Will swiped a trembling hand over his face. "Would now be a good time to confess I had no idea what I was doing?"

Her father managed a small laugh. "Indeed not. I

am grateful all the same."

With her hysteria back under control, Emily came forward and threw her arms around her beloved father's neck. "I thought I'd lost you."

He pressed his lips to her temple. "Now, now, my dear. Didn't I tell you I will not be leaving this earth until I see you in your wedding dress, eh?"

Emily's stomach lurched. Her wedding day to Nicholas loomed less than two months away, and the prospect became ever more unpleasant. She painted on a smile and turned to Will. "Thank…"

Her gratitude froze on her tongue. She had been so blinded with panic when he came bounding into the dining room, Emily hadn't noticed how he was dressed. Heat assaulted her cheeks. Clearly, he'd returned from riding. Had she shouted loud enough for him to hear her in the guest room upstairs where he'd been changing? She jerked her gaze back to her father in order to think straight. "I don't know how I will ever repay you."

Even with her back turned, the sight of Will's bare, muscular chest and torso shone bright in Emily's mind. Add his bronzed shoulders and dark smattering of hair at his navel which disappeared behind the buttons of his riding breeches and she was entirely lost. The familiar and insufferable pull at her center gave another untimely tug.

She cleared her throat. "I'll summon Annie and get you straight to bed, Papa. You need to rest."

"Rubbish." He gave a dismissive wave. "I choked, nothing more. Now I would like everything to return to normal. Let the event be forgotten. Now about you and Annie going into town today—"

Emily waved her hand. "I am not leaving you after

what just happened."

His steely gaze met hers. "Yes, my dear, you are."

"But—"

"As I almost died, you can concede to my wish of having Will accompany you." His eyes gleamed with triumph.

Emily's mouth drained dry. Now what was she to do? Her father had her exactly where he wanted her. She shot him a glare. "That's emotional blackmail."

He laughed. "Indeed it is." Her father looked over her shoulder and beamed at Will, his eyes so soft with fondness, he might have been looking at his son. "I insist you take the morning off from scouring the streets for your nephew, Mr. Samson, and take Emily into town. I will send Malcolm out asking questions about the boy. Who knows? Another person asking after the fellow might nudge people into taking his absence seriously."

Helplessness curled into a ball inside her as Emily stared at Will who frowned at her father. "I really don't think I can do that, sir," he said. "Every hour that passes is another hour when he could've been found."

Her father shook his head, and Emily scowled. The man was struggling not to smile. He was intolerable. Yet her heart swelled with love for him. If she ever doubted from whom she inherited her cunning…

"Nonsense." Her father waved his hand once more. "As long as someone is looking for the boy, what does a couple of hours of your dedication matter? I insist. Every day you've been here, we've hardly seen you. Now you will take Emily out, or else I might have to reconsider our arrangement."

Trepidation—or anticipation—crept up Emily's

spine and she resisted the urge to bolt from the room. She and Will hadn't been alone since their kiss. What if it happened again? The fact she didn't trust herself to resist him spoke volumes. She forcibly locked her gaze on Will's. "Today could be the day you find the boy. Isn't that right, Will?"

He stared for a long moment before the frown left his brow, and his eyes shone with enjoyment—a look she was beginning to love as much as detest. Her stomach executed a loop the loop that weakened her knees. Damn him.

He exhaled a heavy breath. "On the contrary, I have exhausted every avenue I can think of, and taking a day to reflect might be just what I need to evoke some new ideas."

Emily swallowed her scream. The man stood half dressed in her dining room and now expected to escort her into town. Her lips tingled with the memory of his kiss.

Her father slapped his knee, making her jump. "Excellent. Emily wishes to purchase some ribbons and such for the wedding, isn't that so, dear?"

Her eyes remained locked with Will's. "I wish to pay a visit to the haberdashery and then on to see my friend who works at the milliner's on Milsom Street. The excursion will undoubtedly bore you to tears, but if Papa insists—"

"The milliner's?" Will's soft smile dissolved, and the humor in his gaze became avid interest.

Emily frowned. "Yes. Is something wrong?"

His Adam's apple bobbed two or three times before he spoke. "No, of course not."

Suspicion lit like a spark in her mind. What in the

world was he up to now? If she'd doubted Will's story about a missing nephew before, it had just become ten times stronger.

She smiled. "I will see you out front in half an hour...if that allows you enough time to get properly dressed, of course."

He grinned before giving a slight bow. "It most certainly will."

"Very well then."

She brushed past him.

If the man thought her afraid of being alone with him again, he was sorely mistaken. Furthermore, if he thought she would swoon if he touched her again, he was wrong about that too.

Excitement and daring rushed through her, and Emily turned. "Do you know, I've quite changed my mind. Time is of the essence after Father's upset. I'd like to get into town and back as soon as possible. So there is no need to change from those breeches and boots, I find them...quite acceptable." She stared openly at his chest. "However, a shirt might be a good idea to save Mrs. Cambridge's heart if we should see her."

Turning, her grin equally as wide as his, Emily strode from the room and shut the double doors behind her. Releasing her held breath, she called for Annie before racing upstairs in an entirely unladylike manner.

Chapter Ten

The ride across town from Royal Crescent to
Milsom Street was a pleasant one. Pleasant, but quiet.
Emily struggled in vain to keep her gaze from Will's
muscular thighs as much as she did from wondering
what caused such a reaction in him when she
announced her intention to visit the milliner's. Casting
a surreptitious glance at his profile, her stomach rolled
with excitement. He was unfairly handsome. She bit
back her smile. As dangerous as her attraction was,
Will Samson possessed a lightheartedness that made
her feel wonderful. Good times and laughter radiated
from his eyes in a silent promise every time he looked
at her. It felt so good compared to the feelings
Nicholas's eyes evoked in her. Entrapment and misery.
Never anything more.

Emily turned her gaze to the safer view of the
passing shops and houses. It was a glorious beginning
to June with the sun high above them, its rays warm on
her face. The weather filled her with renewed optimism
she hadn't felt since the bitterly cold month of February
when Valentine's Day had brought a frantic call for the
physician when Emily suspected her father's barking
coughs and wheezing were the symptoms of the terrible
influenza epidemic attacking Bath.

She had not been prepared for the real diagnosis
when the doctor had taken her hand in his and warned

her his illness was connected to years of working in the tobacco factory, plus the innumerable cigars her father had smoked over the years.

Tears pricked hot behind her eyes, and Emily inhaled a shaky breath, pushing the negativity to one side. She would enjoy today. Her father had orchestrated it, after all. He wanted the best for her and clearly thought a day with Will was what she needed. Who was she to argue? She took in the stares pointed in their direction, the curious eyes and furrowed brows, and unashamedly basked in the attention.

It pleased her if they knew her and wondered why the stranger she danced with at the ball now drove her so openly through town. Or if they didn't, it pleased her she and Will made a handsome enough couple to cause people to stare in such a manner.

The feeling of potential scandal was joyously liberating. Every part of her life was planned with propriety and necessity in mind, and Nicholas had ensured their betrothal was common knowledge the moment he put the ring on her finger, thus cutting off any chance of fun and abandonment.

With Will at her side, she would enjoy a day of misbehavior. Emily smiled. As the days wore on and the wedding date neared, a strange power was gathering strength within her. Her plan to meet with Katherine was not based on the sole mission of hats and tea. Emily had much more strategic plans in mind, even if she hoped today her nonsensical but deep-rooted suspicions would be proven unfounded. If they were, there was no doubt Katherine would become a trusted confidant and ally during her enforced marriage. But, if her suspicions were correct, then she would have lost one of her oldest friends…

Sensing Will's gaze on her, Emily turned.

He smiled. "Happy?" His gaze revealed pleasure—at least that was what she hoped.

She arched her eyebrow. "How long have you been looking at me instead of the road?"

"Long enough to want to know what is going on in that fine and pretty head of yours."

"I was thinking how much I am enjoying the scandal we're causing."

"We're causing a scandal?"

She smiled. "Why, yes. Look around. See how the people stare at Miss Emily Darson, Nicholas Milne's fiancée, no less, riding in broad daylight with a handsome stranger. My reputation will be in tatters."

His beautiful eyes sparkled with mischief. "Handsome stranger?"

She nonchalantly lifted her shoulders. "You rank above the gargoyles of Bath Abbey."

He pulled his face into a comical insult. "Thank you for the compliment."

"You're welcome."

Laughing, he glanced about him and lifted his hat to two young ladies walking arm in arm on the street. They giggled and nodded discreetly back.

Emily coughed as jealousy sparked inside her. "After your heroic rescue of my father this morning, I decided to cast aside my reservations about you."

"You have reservations about me?"

"Of course. You have all the characteristics of a rogue."

His eyes grew wide, and he pressed a hand to his heart. "Me?"

Emily laughed, her heart soaring deliciously. "Yes, you, but today is a new day for me. I am not going to care what people think. I value your company, and today I will enjoy myself."

His gaze wandered over her face, lingering at her lips as a muscle leaped in his jaw. "Do you value it enough to allow me to kiss you?"

Her heart stopped, and fear skittered along her nerve endings, lifting the hairs on her arms. "You wouldn't dare."

He leaned closer. "Are you saying that because you do not want it or because we shouldn't?"

Her chest rose and fell with each ragged breath, and a tingling erupted deep in her stomach. "Will, stop it." She looked around her as panic coursed through her veins. "Right now."

He laughed and Emily stared ahead, her skin hot with traitorous longing for his touch, her lips aching with want for his kiss. She'd thought of little else but him for days and was clearly capable of losing her head around him, and for all her bravado, she was afraid. She always told herself that no one was capable of controlling her. Will wasn't telling her what to do or even implying what she should do. Yet, just a moment before, he had been in complete control of her, whether he knew it or not.

Was she losing control? Her worst fear brought out by a stranger. She glanced at him. But how could fear feel this good? She thrust her gaze to the street. People talked. People gossiped, and despite wanting to enjoy their limited time together, she couldn't afford to risk Nicholas recognizing her regard for Will. If he did, he could easily go after him, and goodness only knew what would happen.

She swallowed the bitter taste of loss. "We have to be careful, Will."

His smile dissolved. "I was only teasing—"

"Were you?" With her heart thundering, the question tripped from her tongue before she could trap it within. Her tone was undeniable. She didn't want him to tease her; she wanted him to want her even if they could never act upon it.

His gaze darted over her face, before he looked ahead of them, his jaw tight. "I would never do anything to frighten you or taint your reputation."

Emily trembled as relief relaxed her shoulders. He hadn't denied the attraction pulling between them on a tangible thread. He liked her. As a person—and a woman.

"No one can ever know we kissed," she said, quietly. "If Nicholas were ever to learn of it, I dread to think what he would do to you...or me."

He turned and his blue eyes sparked with determination. "You have nothing to fear on that score. If he finds out—which he won't—I am perfectly capable of taking care of myself and you. I will never let that man hurt you. Ever."

She smiled as warmth encased her heart. "You say that as if you are to be in Bath a lifetime. You are leaving soon. Nicholas isn't."

For the first time in her life, Emily's fight for independence wavered. It felt so right to imagine Will as her great protector...but he would soon leave and then she'd face Nicholas's newly revealed temper alone. A fact she didn't relish, but neither did she entirely fear it. The man made her angry enough to fight for her right to her own life with every last ounce of her being.

"Then I promise while I am here, nothing will happen to you."

Tension radiated from him, and Emily pursed her lips tightly closed. Now was not the time to protest or argue. The hard set of his jaw and the crease between his brows showed his inner frustration. The notion he cared for her was enough. She needed little else from him. To have known Will Samson and the way he made her feel would be stored in her memory for a long time after he left. He made her feel she was amusing and desirous rather than tiresome and uncooperative as Nicholas so often referred to her.

He cleared his throat. "I do not regret our kiss for a single moment...but I accept it will be detrimental to both of us if it were to happen again."

She swallowed the lump of disappointment lodged in her throat. "Exactly."

"Milne is not the reason, though. What could he really do? Refuse to marry you?" He huffed out a breath. "Is that really such a concern to you? I think not."

She glanced at him. "It angers you...this lack of love between Nicholas and me. You cannot be ignorant of the number of loveless marriages that exist in this world. None of us can. They're everywhere."

His jaw tightened. "You deserve more than a life married to a man like him. Just because the bruise fades from your face doesn't mean he won't replace it."

Their eyes met, and the rage in his stare ignited hers. "This isn't about choice, or lack thereof. Don't you see that? I'm not happy, but don't mistake that for naïveté."

"You think there isn't a choice? Your fathers drew up a contract. That doesn't mean it cannot be broken. It strikes me your father regrets its creation more than you do."

"He might well look like he does now and then, but deep down, he knows as well as I do that I must marry Nicholas to ensure the full financial inheritance he built with Nicholas's father comes to his grandchildren in the future. If I fail to marry Nicholas, it will all become his, and everything my father worked for will go to whatever children Nicholas might have with someone else. I can't sit by and let that happen, Will. I won't."

"Money is not a family's legacy. Unconditional love is."

Anger pinched hot at her cheeks. "It's my unconditional love that makes me willing to sacrifice, willing to compromise. I would live in poverty if it meant freedom to think and speak, but this isn't about me. What right do I have to make that decision for my unborn children?"

"Milne is scum. He will ruin your life." Will pulled on the reins, and the horse slowed to a stop outside the milliner's. "I will prove it to you if it's the last thing I do."

Passion whispered over the surface of her skin as her suspicion about Will reignited. He had so much rage toward Nicholas, too much certainty about a man he supposedly met two weeks ago.

He moved to stand, and Emily clasped his hand. It trembled in her grasp.

"You know him, don't you? You know Nicholas."

He stared at their joined hands.

"Tell me, Will. Are you truly in Bath looking for your nephew? Or are you here for something else entirely?"

He looked up, and Emily stared deep into his eyes, her heart beating fast in anticipation he might tell her something she wasn't certain she wanted to hear. "You are so carefree, so full of laughter until the moment Nicholas is seen or mentioned. Then this look overcomes you."

"What look?"

She swallowed. "As though you could kill him."

He stared for a moment longer before he jerked his hand from hers and swung abruptly from the gig.

Emily trembled. She played with fire provoking an answer from him, but she had to know. Whether she wanted it or not, Will filled her thoughts night and day, and the anger inside him ran deep. The thought he suffered alone made her want to put her arms around him and ask him to share his burdens with her. He marched around to her side and offered his hand. She gathered her skirts and slid her gloved hand into his.

Once her feet touched the pavement, he released her hand and offered his arm instead. "I will be gone from your life soon enough, but before I leave, I'm determined you will see other possibilities than marrying Milne. He is not the man to provide the wings you need to fly as high as God intended."

Her heart shifted. He believed in her. Thought her capable of more than being a wife to a man like Nicholas. He stepped toward the milliner's with his jaw set and his stride determined. Emily walked beside him, the words she wanted to say scalding her tongue. He pushed the shop door, and they stepped inside.

The sight that greeted them forced Emily's heart into her throat and her hand from Will's arm. "Nicholas! Whatever are you doing here?"

Nicholas and her friend Katherine leaped back from the counter as though they'd been struck. Will stiffened beside her. A silent, pregnant moment ensued before Nicholas stepped toward her, tugging at the bottom of his waistcoat, his chest puffed out like a caricature gibbon.

"What am I doing here? Shouldn't I be asking you the exact same question, my dear?" He tossed a glare at Will. "And with Mr. Samson, no less."

Emily looked to Katherine. She remained immobile behind the counter, clutching her darling little daughter, Aimee, to her chest. "Katherine? Are you all right?"

Her friend nodded, her face pale. "Of course. It's lovely to see you."

Emily's senses leaped to high alert, her suspicions even more so. Katherine was far from all right. She turned to Nicholas. "I'm here looking for a new hat. As you so helpfully pointed out to me last week, my purple one is fit to be thrown in the River Avon. Why are *you* here?"

His chest expanded farther. "Not that I owe you an explanation, but I was looking to buy you a new hat as a surprise."

He lied. Emily glanced at Katherine. Her eyes were wide with fear as though Emily might reach out and strike her. Something was profoundly amiss. Afraid her friend might swoon at any minute and send Aimee toppling to the floor, Emily swept toward her and grasped Katherine's trembling elbow.

She smiled. "Don't look so worried. Nicholas and I

wouldn't be ourselves if we were not having cross words. Isn't that so, Nicholas?" She tickled little Aimee under the chin. The child giggled. When no answer came from Nicholas, she turned. "Nicholas?" Nicholas tossed a glare at Will before approaching the counter and possessively sliding his hand to the base of her spine. Emily's stomach clenched.

"Indeed, my love." He stared at Katherine. "Now, where are those hats you were about to show me, Miss Carter? I trust your opinion implicitly seeing as you know Emily so well."

Katherine flinched. "I'm sorry?"

"The hats, my dear girl. You were about to retrieve some new designs from the back room when Emily entered the shop and ruined my surprise."

Katherine blinked, and then a bright smile lit up her face. "Of course, of course. The hats. I'll just put Aimee down somewhere safe to play. Yes, that's what I'll do. Excuse me one moment."

She disappeared through a curtain behind her. Emily frowned. She was about to demand Nicholas explain his atrociously bossy attitude with her friend when a movement to her other side caught her attention. She turned.

Will grinned at Nicholas in an exaggerated—and provocative—way.

Emily glared. "Will? What is the matter with you?" She hoped her irritated tone belied her sudden attack of nerves. There was no mistaking the anger and distaste in Will's eyes. She looked from one man to the other. The last thing she wanted was a showdown in such a public place. "Will? I asked you—"

"Are you quite sure about that, Milne?" Will stared

past her to Nicholas.

Dread dropped like a stone in Emily's stomach. Surely he wouldn't start an altercation after what they'd said to each other during their journey? Clearly her feelings didn't matter to him. Nicholas would undoubtedly challenge the fact she held Will's arm when she entered the shop soon enough, and now Will saw fit to torment him into an argument.

Emily faced Nicholas, and any possible words promptly lodged in her throat. His emerald eyes glowed like jewels.

"Am I sure about what, Samson?"

The atmosphere crackled with tension.

"Are you certain the shopkeeper who is busy in the back putting your..." Will shook his head. "Apologies, I mean *her* child down to play, was really about to show you some ladies' hats?"

Emily whipped her head from one man to the other as though her neck were made of rubber. Will implied Aimee was Nicholas's child. Her heart raced. The same thought had occurred to her time and time again, and it was what she'd hoped to confirm one way or the other by coming there. Even though Katherine had sworn Aimee was the result of a hasty engagement to a man Emily had never met—a man who subsequently disappeared without trace—Emily had never really believed her. Her friend's life had barely changed before or since her pregnancy. Something that was far from normal considering the sharpened knives of those who loved to gossip.

Katherine had always seemed so protected...

She needed to know, once and for all, if that protection was because of Nicholas.

Of course, if Aimee was his child, there was little she could do about it, but she refused to let Nicholas go on thinking he had secrets safely hidden from her. He would learn she was not stupid, and she would confront him accordingly.

Nausea whirled inside her. The worst thing about it would be Katherine's betrayal. A friendship ruined. Yet another thing she held sacred in her life Nicholas would've destroyed. Nicholas being unfaithful and fathering an illegitimate child had little bearing seeing she held no romantic feelings toward him. It would be Katherine she'd lose.

Nicholas moved his hand from her back and pinched his fingers into her waist. His anger palpable. "Well, of course she was. Do you always have to act like such an imbecile, Samson? For the life of me I cannot see what Emily's father thinks he is achieving by—"

"Only I cannot see a single item on this counter." Will waved his hand, undeterred. "Or maybe you only entered the shop a moment before us?" His tone dripped with accusation.

Emily momentarily forgot her concern about an altercation breaking out between them and, instead, waited for Nicholas's reaction to Will's insinuation.

She tipped her head back to look at him. "Have you been here long, Nicholas?"

He snapped his glare from Will to her. "Long enough to tire of the sight of these four walls...and the desire to buy you a present."

His pallor had paled to the color of window putty.

"Has something happened between you and Katherine?"

"Don't be so ridiculous."

She glanced toward the curtain through which Katherine had disappeared. "If you upset our friends, we risk being solely reliant on each other's company. I don't imagine either of us favors that outcome, seeing how things are growing considerably distant between us."

Katherine re-entered the room before Nicholas could respond. Her friend's cheeks flamed like two red tomatoes, marked by silver streaks showing she'd cried.

Striding forward, Emily took Katherine's hand. "I'm sorry if Nicholas has been brusque with you. You are my friend, and I expect you to be treated as such."

Katherine cast a quick glance toward Nicholas, then Will, and finally back to Emily. "Everything is fine, honestly. Mr. Milne always shows me the greatest courtesy."

Will sniffed. "I'm sure he does."

The tone of his voice grated on Emily's nerves. She was not prepared to stand there while he did nothing but throw out thinly veiled accusations. She turned. "If you have something you want to say, Will, then please just say it."

Please, Lord. Don't let him say it. I want to speak to Katherine alone. Not here. Not like this.

He opened his mouth to speak, but Nicholas released her and strode forward, making Emily stumble backward. He stopped toe-to-toe, eye-to-eye with Will, fury burning in their eyes.

"Gentlemen, please," Emily said, firmly. "There is no need—"

Nicholas jabbed his hand into the air, cutting her off. "First, I am not happy my fiancée sees fit to call a man she has barely known more than two weeks by his Christian name. Second, I can't help thinking you suspect me of some kind of wrongdoing with regard to Miss Carter."

Will smiled. "If you were really here buying Miss Darson a gift, I'd have no problem with you at all. If she were mine, I'd buy her gifts every day."

Emily's gasp merged with Katherine's. Emily flushed at Will's fearless confession, and her body tingled with excitement to see him not so much as flinch to have Nicholas standing so close to him.

"I should thrash you." Nicholas spat the words through clenched teeth.

Will's smile dissolved. "But you won't. It's not in your nature to strike men, is it?"

"What the hell is that supposed to mean? You do not know me or anyone else in this town, Samson. You are a nobody. A nobody who is supposed to be looking for his nephew. Yet you seem to spend most of your time alone with my fiancée."

Will tilted his head toward Emily. "Look at her, Milne. Does she appear distraught her father has demanded it so?"

Heat burned Emily's cheeks. "Stop this. Both of you."

Will met her eyes, and the anger burning in their royal-blue depths made her shiver. He had absolutely no intention of stopping. Or maybe he didn't know how. Fury came from him in waves, ricocheting from the walls around them.

His gaze shot back to Nicholas. "Why don't we all show a little integrity here?"

Emily froze. What was he doing? He knew what it

would do to her reputation, let alone Nicholas' unpredictable temper, if he suspected anything between them. If Nicholas learned of their kiss, she and Will would never share another. Despite her insistence, there would be no repeat of it, suddenly that was her biggest fear.

She took a step forward. "For goodness' sake, what on earth do you think you are achieving by behaving this way?"

"It's time for some honesty. Time you told your fiancé how you really feel."

Anger, disappointment, and hurt burned inside her, the ache at the center of her chest testament to just how little she knew this man she'd come to like too much, too soon.

She blinked back the tears that pricked her eyes. "How I feel is I want you to keep your nose out of my relationship with Nicholas. It is none of your concern."

His dangerous gaze bored into hers. "I'm not sure I can sit by and watch you—"

"That is exactly what you'll do. This is my life, is it not? You have yours, and you will soon leave Bath, God willing, with your nephew. You will no longer know me or anything about me, so you will stop this right now."

Emily trembled, her heart hammering and her throat hurting from the threat of tears. Nicholas stood ramrod straight, his face scarlet with anger and his lips white. His hands were fisted at his sides.

Emily looked to Katherine. "I am sorry to have ruined your morning, Katherine. We shall leave you in peace. I have nothing else I can say, except sorry."

Her friend stood pale and immobile, her gaze

trained on Nicholas. Bitter anger roared in Emily's breast. Anger toward Will, her father, her mother for dying so young, but most of all for her impossible situation. All the frustration, hurt, and desire to have more to live for whirled inside her on a gathering storm. She would not surrender to the scene Will demanded. It would do no one any good. When they were alone again, she would tell him the unforgivable effect his outburst would have on her reputation. Worse, her belief he understood her, maybe even cared about her, was washed away forever.

She turned toward the door, but Nicholas whipped out his hand and gripped her arm so tightly her pulse beat against his fingers. "We are not leaving until Mr. Samson explains his accusation."

Emily yanked her arm in an attempt to free it. Nicholas held tight.

She pulled again to no avail. "Let go, Nicholas. You're hurting me."

His manic gaze shot to Will. "Come now, Mr. Samson. If you think you know something, spit it out."

Murderous rage glowed hot in Will's eyes. His teeth clenched and bared like a vicious animal.

Nicholas stepped back when Will brought his face close to his. "Take your hand off her, or so help me God, Milne, I will beat you into next week."

Seconds beat out, their unified breathing the only sound in the small shop before Nicholas finally dropped her arm.

Emily stared at the two men facing each other, reciprocated hatred etched on their faces. She had to do something. She stepped between them and faced Nicholas because his eyes were the easier of the two to address. Will saw too much of what was inside her. Nicholas did not care.

"This masculine parade needs to stop. Please take me home, Nicholas."

Will touched her arm. "You cannot leave with him knowing what you do."

She snapped her head around. He spoke of Aimee. She saw it clearly in the blue of his eyes, the furrow at his brow. Aimee was Nicholas's child. Emily swallowed the bitter taste in her mouth and held his gaze. "As I told you before, my relationship with Nicholas is not your concern."

Disbelief followed by disappointment flashed across his gaze. "You want me to turn away? To look in the other direction?"

She tilted her chin and cursed the tears behind her eyes. "Yes." Dread that he'd turn away and never look at her with interest, respect, or desire again surged through her, but the need for distance between him and Nicholas was paramount. Why did he not see what his actions did to her plans for a secure life for her children? How their marriage kept her father's life work intact? Silently, she begged him to trust her, to understand. If Aimee was indeed Nicholas's child, the blame fell on him, not Katherine. The poor girl looked terrified. Too terrified undoubtedly to refuse Nicholas anything. Nicholas disgusted her—Will the opposite. If there was any other way…but the thought of everything her father gave her being taken by Nicholas made her sick to her stomach. The longer Will was in Bath, the more of a distraction he became.

Will shook his head. "This is insane."

She swallowed. "That is your opinion."

"Emily, for the love of God—"

"Will, please."

"Enough!" Emily started as Nicholas's yell shattered the tension between her and Will and Katherine let out a cry. "Get the hell out of here, Samson. Now."

Emily stared at Will, praying he heeded her wishes. "Please, just take the gig back to the Crescent. My father's insistence you escort me around town is not the way things should be. Nicholas is my fiancé, and I should only be seen with him."

Nicholas snorted. "You heard her. Leave. Clearly her father's dying is affecting his common sense. If you do not realize that, then you are a bigger fool than we already thought."

Emily's pulse beat hard as she waited for the axe to fall, for Will to carry out his threat and punch Nicholas to the ground. She closed her eyes, not wanting to witness it, but footsteps across the tile floor and the ring of the bell above the door sounded instead. She opened her eyes. Will had done as she asked.

Chapter Eleven

Emily clenched her trembling hands tightly together in her lap, her heart beating an erratic tattoo. The interior of Nicholas's carriage had never felt so claustrophobic. His driver slammed the door on them, and the seconds ticked by in fraught silence until the carriage jerked away from the front of Katherine's shop.

She wished Nicholas would just get on with whatever he wanted to say. His theatrics were becoming intolerable, and her impatience was wearing thin. If he thought for one minute she was going to sit silently while he ranted and raved, he had a surprise coming. There was every possibility Aimee was his child, and there was every possibility when they returned to Royal Crescent she would find Will had gone for good. Both likelihoods added fuel to the already raging fire inside of her.

She cleared her throat. "Nicholas, will you please say something."

His glare bored down on her. "You want me to say something?"

Emily straightened her spine and kept her gaze level with his. "Yes."

"Fine, if you want to do this now, we will. I will not stand for it. Neither would my father have."

"You will not stand for what?"

He squeezed his eyes shut. "You know exactly what. Samson." His eyes snapped open and blazed with anger. "Our marriage contract does not state at any juncture I should tolerate third-party involvement."

In an attempt to still her temper, Emily shook her head. What did he consider Katherine if she were the mother of his child? A figment of their imagination? "You are giving far too much credit to Mr. Samson by calling him a third party. He is a guest in my father's home, nothing more, nothing less. Another week or so and he will be gone."

Nicholas narrowed his eyes. " 'Nothing more, nothing less,' she says. I am not stupid, Emily. I see the way he looks at you."

A flush of satisfaction pinched her cheeks, and Nicholas's scowl showed he'd seen it. She huffed out a laugh and looked through the window at the passing town houses. "Don't be ridiculous."

He gripped her wrist, and Emily turned. His face was flushed, and a vein throbbed like a lightning bolt down his forehead. "Do not laugh at me."

Fear burst behind her rib cage, and she swallowed. It would be foolish to further anger him. If he were to strike her, his driver would undoubtedly turn as deaf as a doorpost. "I'm sorry, but the notion that Mr. Samson is interested in me…" She slid her wrist from his hand, relief shuddering through her when he released her without a fight. "It shouldn't anger you even if it were true. It should make you proud to have me on your arm. To show the world I am yours despite another's admiration."

A flash of what could be deemed as jealousy shot into his eyes, turning them almost black. He tipped his head back, and the rare laugh that emitted from his open mouth sent a shiver down her spine. The sound was eerie in its execution. Dangerous.

"You are quite the clown, my dear." Nicholas dipped his head, his gaze hot and intense. "There is clearly a need to sidestep manners and just say what I see."

Emily smiled, in the hope she took his laugh for humor, rather than intimidation. "What do you mean?"

"You, my dear."

Her smile faltered. "What about me?"

"How you look at him."

The laughter was gone, his tone icy-cold. Emily's smile froze. Her mind blanked of all thought.

"Nothing to say for once." Nicholas smiled. "Well, then what I suspect must be true. You have feelings for Samson."

Say something. Anything. Lie. Deny.

Emily cleared her throat and plucked at a nonexistent piece of lint on her skirt. "I really do not like what you are suggesting. If you are accusing me of some sort of dalliance with Mr. Samson, you are insulting me." She met his gaze directly. "Is that what you are suggesting?"

Their eyes locked in silent battle as the sounds of the street filtered through the window. Emily gathered her resolve. He would not win this battle. She'd done nothing wrong. Well, if she excluded her and Will's kiss, of course.

"Fine. I do not suggest a dalliance." His jaw tightened. "However, I will no longer tolerate the man's presence around you. I demand he leave your house immediately. I am a patient man, but you must deem me without a backbone if you think I will consider that man staying there another day. If we return to your father's home and find Samson there after our heated exchange at the milliner's, he clearly has no respect for your wishes and your thoughts are wasted on him."

My thoughts...oh, if only you knew the depth of my thoughts as far as Will is concerned. "His concern is for his nephew. Not me. Father will want him to stay until the boy is found."

Nicholas glared. "Rubbish. I wouldn't be surprised to learn the boy doesn't even exist. I do not trust Samson as far as I could throw him."

"Maybe so, but Papa will not like being told who he can or cannot invite to stay in his own home. Until such time as he passes, it is his decision who stays there and for how long. As you have already said, neither of us knows for certain Mr. Samson has not gone of his own free will, so I think we are wasting our breath discussing him."

Nicholas narrowed his eyes. "If we find him gone, will you be pleased or saddened? That is the question."

Emily turned to the window once more. "Mr. Samson has done nothing wrong beyond this afternoon's events. For that outburst, you are both equally guilty of putting poor Katherine in the most awful situation. If he is gone, then so be it. We will all get on as we were before."

"So you still do not see he is trouble?"

Emily drew in a shaky breath and turned. "There is trouble at every corner of our society, Nicholas. We face it when it comes and then try our best to put it behind us. I refuse to waste any more time talking about this. You talk of respect, so please, extend some to my father. If Mr. Samson returns and wishes to stay, and Papa would like it so, and we would both do well to accept that. Also, he saved my father's life this morning."

"What?"

"He was choking on some food, and Mr. Samson managed to dislodge it. Can you really imagine my father banishing him from the house after that?"

His green eyes blazed. "Fine."

"Fine?"

"Fine. I will say no more of it. Clearly my hands are tied."

Emily fought the trepidation that raised the hairs at the nape of her neck. This was far from over. Nicholas never gave in to anything he didn't want to happen. The realization that he would no more walk away from his inheritance than she would burned bright and clear. She stared ahead lest Nicholas detect the shiver of fear that swept over her.

He shifted beside her. "I have one more question."

Sending up a silent prayer for strength, she met his eyes. "Yes?"

"What am I supposed to say to my peers when asked why a man I know nothing about is escorting my fiancée about town?"

Emily tilted her chin. "You will tell them the truth. That I was hit to the ground in the park, and when neither Papa nor you are able to accompany me, Mr. Samson does so at Papa's request."

"I see."

Unease rippled across the surface of her skin. He wore the expression of a cat poised to strike. Her heart picked up speed.

"So, if Mr. Samson returns, your father intends the scoundrel escort you for as long as it takes him to find his nephew…or us to marry. Correct?"

She nodded. "Yes. I believe that's what he said."

"Hmm. Well, then, there is only one solution should we find Samson there when we get back."

"Which is?"

"We are not set to marry for another two months. Even if we assume this boy is real, it could take weeks to find him. If he's not already dead."

Emily flinched. "That's a horrible thing to say."

Nicholas lifted his shoulders. "We do not know Samson, my love. He may not have any family. He could be a criminal. Have you not considered his past?"

No. Just his future. "Of course I have, but one cannot accuse people of things. He has done nothing to make me fear or dislike him and until such time—"

"You are happy for me to be ridiculed for my lack of control over you."

Anger washed through her veins. "You are sadly mistaken if you think I will stand by and let you control me, Nicholas. Do we really have to keep having this conversation?"

He glared, two spots of color darkening his cheeks. "It seems we do. This is not the way things were done in my father's household, and it is not the way they will be done in mine. My father expected my mother to love and obey. As it says in the Church's marriage law."

Frustration burned. The limited freedom of her future tightened around her as she met his fiery gaze. "Be that as it may, I am proud of who I am and hope you will be too. However, if you think you will struggle with such a notion and my assertiveness is too much for you to tolerate, why not reconsider Papa's notion of you refusing the marriage?"

"If you're suggesting I walk away—"

"I understand you daren't walk away for fear of breaking your word to your father. You are a good man. A man who stands strong and firm in his family's ambition and values. A man who has made his father very proud. Yet, if you wish to withdraw from the contract and not marry me because you find my conduct intolerable, then I will accept that."

A wry smile twisted his lips. "You must really think me a fool."

"I think no such thing. I am merely reminding you no one is forcing you to marry me. If you do not wish to spend your life with me, then you are free to break our engagement."

The silence stretched even as the carriage came to an abrupt halt outside her house at Royal Crescent. As the clip-clop of passing horse hooves and the calls of children playing in the park resounded, Emily prayed for his surrender.

When he finally spoke, Nicholas's tone was icy cold. "You are more stupid than I thought to mess with me. All you have succeeded in doing is pushing me into finding a way to bring the wedding forward. I will never break the contract. Never!"

Emily's stomach plummeted. "Nicholas, that's impossible. There is no need—"

His smile stretched to a grin. "There is every need and better, it is entirely possible. I am owed favors all over the city. There isn't a priest in Bath who wouldn't help a churchgoing man—and generous donator at that—to cure his heart-wrenching impatience to marry the woman who vowed to be his wife nine years before."

The determination in his eyes left Emily in little doubt of his ability to not just deliver on an earlier date but to make sure everyone in town knew about it, too. She stared, her body devoid of feeling.

"Nothing to say, my dear? How refreshing."

She was trapped like an animal in an invisible cage. There was no escaping her situation or Nicholas if her children were to ever have a future of possibility. The door swung open, and Nicholas's driver stood waiting outside.

"If you are determined to marry me, so be it," she said, finding her voice. "But by doing so, you are accepting Papa's wish to have Mr. Samson escort me before such date as I become your wife whether you like it or not."

Nicholas shook his head. "That is not a condition of the contract, and never will be. This is merely a pathetic attempt at igniting my temper enough that I will sever our agreement. You are determined and wily, Emily. I will give you that." He pushed to his feet and stopped by the open carriage door to face her. "I will respect your father's wishes and condone Mr. Samson's escorting you, my love." He smiled. "After all, the man's time with you is merely a moment in the rest of our lives."

Chapter Twelve

Will came out of his rented room and slammed the door. Thank goodness he'd had the insight to keep paying his rent while staying with the Darsons. If there was one thing he'd learned through his financial struggles growing up, keeping as many options open as possible was always the best way forward.

The night away from Emily gave him the time he needed to refocus on a plan of action. He would avoid another repeat of his total loss of self-control at the milliner's and concentrate on keeping his temper intact. His growing desire to have Emily for his own was making him lose focus on every aspect of his plan to ruin Milne. The thought of her near Milne, let alone marrying him, had become as much of an issue for Will as wringing Milne's scrawny neck with his bare hands.

He knew there was nothing in her heart for Milne. Once upon a time, she'd been secondary to Will, a tool in his agenda. Not anymore. Her smile haunted his nights, her scent his days. Even when he kissed her under the streetlight, it wasn't under false pretenses but with a clear and conscious need to hold her in his arms for a single beautiful moment.

It had done nothing but fuel a seemingly endless hunger.

His intellect told him to stay away after her rebuff at the milliner's, but he could not. He could not leave her with nothing but strong words and missing explanations between them. The only disadvantage to returning to Royal Crescent was he would find it impossible to look into her beautiful brown eyes and walk away again. He wanted her—and the reality was a blow to his gut, his heart, and his once-angry motivation.

A new softness had emerged into his heart, one he didn't know he was capable of feeling and wasn't sure he even liked. Emily had woken a new person in him, a person who cared about someone so much, it consumed him. He hadn't felt like that since his mother died and hadn't thought he'd feel it again. The anger he carried around ate him up from the inside out. Yet, Emily Darson dampened it whenever she was near him. She was the light filtering into his very dark world, and his guilt for deceiving both her and her father stained his soul deeper every day.

Damn Milne and damn that contract.

Blinking, Will refocused on the day's mission. He hoped to dig out some information to break a further thread in Emily and Milne's upcoming union. Having put the last two days since the showdown at the milliner's to good use, Will was confident his research and patience would pay off. Hopefully, if this day was a fruitful one, he would be back in Royal Crescent by nightfall.

Picking up his pace, he made his way along the maze of streets toward the center of town. He passed shops, stalls, buskers, and street jugglers until he came out the other side where the stench of the river grew stronger and the houses more squalid.

Eventually, he stood at the end of the street he'd

followed Milne into a few days before.

Pulling down the brim of his hat, Will lowered his head. He could not risk recognition or to have his presence reported back to Milne. He reached the door of the house Milne had entered and tilted his head from side to side in an effort to loosen the tension in his neck. Exhaling a long breath, he smoothed his hands down the front of his jacket. "Here goes nothing." Will rapped his knuckles three times against the door.

After a few moments, the door swung open. He guessed the woman standing there to be around twenty-five or twenty-six, but she could easily have been younger. Poverty aged a person like nothing else. Her eyes, sadder and bluer than two flints of glass floating on the Dead Sea, struck Will's heart like the claws of a hatchet. Her dress clung to her bony frame like a second skin, and matted dark brown hair showed above the dirty scarf holding it back from her face.

Surely this wasn't the woman Milne visited?

"Are you going to stand there staring at me all day or did you want something?" She crossed her arms.

Will blinked and forced the most nonchalant grin he could muster. "Good morning, miss." He lifted his hat.

"Good morning to you, too. Now, what do you want?"

"A moment of your time."

A flirtatious smile tugged at the corner of her mouth. "I hope you got money, handsome. Moments of time are coins in my hand."

"The time I need won't take me a step inside, but it would be appreciated all the same."

Her smile dissolved and her eyes narrowed. "If you

ain't here for services, what do you want?"

Guessing he was about five seconds away from having the door slammed in his face, Will cleared his throat. It was now or never. This woman would not be bought off with any amount of charm.

"I was given your name by an associate of mine."

Her frown deepened. "My name? Who told you my name."

"An associate of mine. Your reputation precedes you, Laura."

"I'm not Laura."

"You're not?"

She uncrossed her arms and made as if to close the door. "No, now get lost."

Will slapped his hand to the door. "Wait. I need to speak to her. It's important."

"Laura's busy. Now get out of here."

"I'll wait."

The seconds ticked by as the standoff took root.

"Laura ain't at nobody's beck and call." She fisted her hands on her hips. "Not even a handsome bastard like you. What's your name?"

"I'd much rather introduce myself to her."

"She ain't gonna let you get within fifty feet of her without a name or knowing how you learned hers, so if I was you—"

Footsteps sounded behind her, and her mouth snapped shut. She turned, and a man dressed in the attire of a gentleman pushed past her. He briefly met Will's eyes, and Will touched his hat. The man nodded before hurrying on his way.

Will faced her once more. "I assume Laura is alone now?"

She shrugged. "That doesn't mean I'm letting you by."

He reached into his pocket. Extracting a shilling, he held it in front of her. "I want ten minutes with her, that's all."

She smiled. "Ten minutes? You certainly ain't no lover who lasts, are you?"

With the confidence of a man who knew the extreme opposite was true, Will smiled and tilted his head toward the coin. "Why don't you go and ask Laura if she can spare me ten minutes, eh?"

"Fine." She snatched the coin from his hand. "I'll need to know on whose recommendation you're here. She don't see no one who ain't here by word of mouth."

Will pulled back his shoulders. "I'm here on the recommendation of Mr. Nicholas Milne."

Her rosy cheeks paled, and her blue eyes grew wide. "No, you're not." She glanced behind her, before narrowing her eyes. "Who the hell are you?"

Will's gut knotted with adrenaline. What was going on here? "Why couldn't I be here on Milne's recommendation? I know he's a…friend of Laura's."

"He ain't no friend. The man's a piece of…" She pursed her lips together and leaned out of the doorway to look up and down the street. "Just get lost. Now!"

"No. I need to see her. I'm not leaving until I do."

She snapped her gaze to his. "Mr. Milne likes his visits kept quiet, and I can't imagine him telling the likes of you anything."

"Look, whether you believe it or not, I am here with Laura's best interests in mind. I am here to help her, not hurt her."

Her gaze darted over his face, and her hands curled

into fists. "Help her in what way? Is someone threatening her? 'Cause if they are, I'll smash their damn faces in."

The door was opened wide by someone inside. "Bette, that's enough."

The woman who came to the threshold was a little younger than her protector and beautiful. Her burnished brown hair was curled and teased into the latest style but lacked the gleam of moneyed care, and her chemise was clean yet yellowed with age and her red satin wrap had lost its sheen. Will's stomach tightened. So this was the second of Milne's lovers. This beautiful woman might not have been as stunning as Emily, but she damn well deserved to be on the arm of a man who loved her. Not languishing in a backstreet apartment taking in paying visitors like Milne.

Like his mother had before her.

Will removed his hat and swept into a low bow. "It's a pleasure to meet you, miss." He straightened and beamed his widest smile. "Laura, is it?"

She looked him straight in the eye. "Who wants to know?"

"I'm an associate of Mr. Nicholas Milne's. I need to speak to you."

She looked from him to her door guard and back again. "You know Nicholas?"

"Yes."

She pulled back her shoulders. "Then I don't think we have anything to talk about."

His smile dissolved. "Even if what I have to say saves your life?"

She frowned. "What are you talking about?"

"I just need five minutes."

Her door guard stepped forward. "She said no, now sling your hook."

Laura touched her arm, her gaze locked on Will's. "It's all right, Bette. Go on inside and stick the kettle on. I'll soon have this gentleman on his way."

"But—"

"Now, Bette."

The formidable Bette threw Will a look loaded with warning and disappeared inside the tiny two-up, two-down house.

He smiled. It was nice to know Laura had someone looking out for her. He turned and met Laura's gaze.

She crossed her arms. "Well? Let's hear it."

Will locked his gaze on hers, willing her to trust him. "Milne is a dangerous man. A violent man who beat and raped my mother, leaving her for dead on her apartment floor. I don't want you to be his next victim."

The noises from the street at the end of the alleyway filtered toward them, louder than before. Will's blood pulsed as he waited for her response. Two spots of color stained her cheeks, but her eyes gave nothing away.

"You could be lying, for all I know."

"I'm telling the truth. I don't think for one minute he hasn't raised his hand to you. Am I right? The man's a violent woman-beater who enjoys inflicting his power when there is no chance of reciprocation."

She turned and looked along the alleyway. "I take risks every single day with one faceless jock after another, but Nicholas is a different kettle of fish entirely." She faced him. "Nothing is worth upsetting him. If you don't have proof he hurt your mother, don't expect me to put my neck on the line by talking about him."

Will realized his stupidity. Laura had hardened necessity running through her veins instead of blood. She could easily be a mother, a sister…a wife…yet something had brought her to this and she was surviving. Will had more respect for her than she'd ever know.

"She named him. That's enough for me."

She shook her head. "I'm sorry. It's not enough for me."

Will squeezed his eyes shut as frustration scorched his insides. "When she died, I promised I wouldn't go after Milne, but I can't rest until I know he's either dead or locked up." He opened his eyes and met her steady violet gaze. "His poison has seeped into my veins, Laura. Please. You have to believe me. Don't take the risk you'll be his next victim."

She studied him through narrowed eyes. "I suppose your mother was a whore like me, was she, handsome stranger?" Skepticism dripped from her words onto the cracked doorstep beneath her feet. "You must think I'm an idiot. What is it you really want?"

Anger bit at Will's conscience like sharpened teeth. "Milne knew her when she was working, yes."

She smiled. "You don't like to call her a whore." It was a statement rather than a question.

"My mother will never be a whore to me. She was a lady. A mother doing her best to make sure I was clothed and fed."

She stared at him for a moment before her eyes softened, and her shoulders slumped. She blew out a breath. "Look, I'm sorry for your mother, I am, but I'm different from her. I'm not a mother, but I'm doing what I can. I don't need any trouble. I'm sorry."

She moved to shut the door, and Will slapped his palm against it a second time. "I know what Milne is capable of. I want to save it from happening to you or anyone else. You can either work with me or I'll work alone. Either way, Milne will pay. It will just be quicker if I have an ally."

A tear tipped over her lashes as she stared. She swiped her cheek, a soft smile forming. "Who named you our righteous hero?"

Will returned her smile as premature optimism threatened. "I did. That means I have you, his mistress, and his fiancée to look out for. Three women he could kill today or tomorrow. If not physically, then emotionally and spiritually until all three of you resemble living breathing ghosts of who you once were. I will not stand by and let that happen. That man will not hurt another woman while I still have breath in my body."

His heart slammed against his chest as he waited. He daren't breathe nor move and risk interrupting her internal debate. Her eyes flitted over his face and back to his eyes. He needed her. She had the inside information on Milne. She knew him at his most vulnerable. As a man wanting sex—a man out of control. Women like Laura and his mother did not go with men for the hell of it. They were proud and strong. Street savvy and brave.

She put a hand up and let it linger about her throat. "How can I help pay him back for what he did to your mother? I don't know anything."

Quivers of possible victory stirred low in Will's abdomen. He needed something to add to his growing arsenal of information that would ultimately ensure Milne lived the rest of his scrawny life behind bars. He swallowed his hunger for Milne's blood, concentrated on steadying the tone of his voice. The last thing he wanted was for her to sense how close to the edge he really was.

"I need one or two women willing to testify in court that Milne has beaten them, raped them, or—"

"Raped them?" She tipped her head back and laughed. "You seriously think any judge in the country will look at the likes of me or any of the girls I know and give them sympathy? What would they care if Milne or any other bastard took a piece without our consent?" She shook her head. "I appreciate your sentiment, but your head is so far in the clouds, I might as well ask you what heaven looks like."

Frustration rolled like a storm in Will's gut. Doubt edged into his mind on a whisper. Maybe he should just kill Milne. Was that what she was saying? The justice system would fail him? Fail her? Their eyes locked, hers reflecting the hope he'd tell her she was wrong, mixed with the silent triumph of knowing she was right.

Will grappled for something more to say. Something to convince her they could do this. Emily. Adrenaline burst inside of him like a breaking dam.

"I have a friend," he said. "She is as strong and determined as she is beautiful and kind. If he marries her, he will kill her in one way or another eventually."

She smiled. "You love this friend, right?"

Will nodded. "Please, Laura. Take a risk to ensure Milne never hurts another woman again. Whatever is holding you to him, making you risk his murderous temper every day, can be vanquished. You could be in a position to change your life."

"He's a man with money and position. We couldn't win."

He grasped her hand. "How do we know unless we try? Fight with me. Fight for a better life."

She softly smiled. "I guess not many women say no to you, do they?"

****

Will stood outside the milliner's on Milsom Street. Katherine served her next customer, oblivious to him watching through the latticed window. He took the unobserved moment to study her. She, too, deserved a man better than Milne in her life. The boy he met in the back street said Katherine had known Milne since childhood. He understood Emily's tie to him, but what was Katherine's? Did she love him?

He rubbed his hand over his jaw. The man "owned" three women. Three. His gut clenched around his resentment, squeezing it smaller and smaller until it was a manageable heat rather than a blazing inferno. There were questions to be answered. The biggest of which was how Milne managed to get this much control over them. No doubt threats, violence, and a whole lot more played a part.

His mother's face filled his mind's eye. How did Milne come to know her? Was he a regular visitor to their patch of Bristol for business reasons? Social reasons? He started when the shop door opened. Two women walked out, talking and laughing. He touched his hat to them and quickly swept into the shop before the bell above the door announced his entrance.

"Good afternoon, Miss Carter."

Katherine spun around from the hat stand. Her

wide smile dissolved with almost comical rapidity. "Mr…"

Will stepped forward and bowed. "Samson. How are you today?"

She glanced over his shoulder toward the door, as though debating whether to make a dash through it. "I am quite well. How…how are you?"

"Very well."

A flush colored her cheeks, and she turned to the various velvet-lined trays lying on the counter, her fingers trembling as she laid ribbons and feathers back in their allocated spaces. She slid the trays back onto the shelves beneath the glass-topped counter.

Will softened his tone in the hope she'd detect he meant her no harm. "I need your help, Katherine."

She met his eyes, and her gaze deepened with concern. "It's not Emily, is it?"

Will arched an eyebrow. "What makes you ask that?"

Her gaze darted to the door and back again. "Because I know Mr. Darson is insisting you accompany her, and if she isn't with you…have you bad news? Has his condition worsened?"

"No. He is as well as can be expected."

"And Emily? Is she all right? I haven't seen her since you and Nich—Mr. Milne had your argument."

"She is well, I promise. I didn't mean to distress you."

She gripped the counter. "If anyone should hurt her, it would be too much to bear."

Will's heartbeat quickened. "Who would have cause to hurt her?"

"Mr. Milne has been known to have a temper." She

shook her head. "Ignore me. I'm being silly."

Will stared at her bowed head. She knew of Milne's temper yet continued to fornicate with him behind her friend's back. The guilt he had for upsetting her promptly vanished. "I'm confused."

She looked up. "Pardon?"

"If you know about Milne's temper, why would you invite him to share your bed?"

Her mouth dropped open, and her gasp sounded loud in the empty shop. "Shame on you, Mr. Samson. How dare you suggest such a thing."

"Do I not speak the truth? You and Milne are lovers, are you not?"

Closing her eyes, she covered her ears with her hands. "I will not have this conversation with you, Mr. Samson. I would like you to leave."

The seconds passed like heartbeats. He hated having to do this to her, but his motivation lingered far too deep for any other choice. He reached forward and gently lowered her hands from her ears.

He held them as he stared deep into her eyes. "Talk to me, Katherine. Please. I want to help you—and Emily. Tell me about your relationship with Milne. Why on earth would you want to be with someone like that? A violent man. A man engaged to someone else. Your friend. Are you not worthy of more?"

For a long moment, she said nothing and then snatched her hands from his. "Why do you care? What is your interest in Nicholas? Or does your interest really lie in Emily?"

He shook his head and huffed out a breath. "Don't do that."

"Do what?"

184

"Apportion blame to me for your misdeeds. You are having relations with a man who belongs with someone else. Why?"

Her chest rose and fell until she looked away and a tear slipped from beneath her lashes. "You are a horrible man."

Guilt pressed down on Will's chest, and he fought it with all he had. "You know that's not true. I want to help you. Is Emily not a good friend to you?"

She whipped her head around. "Of course she is. I love her."

"Then why would you sleep with her fiancé?"

She closed her eyes. "Nicholas and I have known each other forever. We were friends before I met Emily."

"Friendship is one thing, but your relationship with Milne far surpasses—"

She glowered. "When Nicholas wants something, he takes it."

Nausea struck at Will's gut. "Are you telling me he forces himself on you?"

She stared at him, her eyes wide with fear, as she lifted her trembling hands to her mouth.

"Katherine, please. Think of Aimee."

She lowered her head, her eyes sad. "Don't. Don't bring my baby into this."

"She is the most important person here, isn't she?"

Her trembling became more ardent and Will took one of her hands in his. He held it tight. "Help me to help you."

"He wouldn't hurt Aimee."

Will gripped her fingers tighter. "Can you guarantee that? Forever?"

185

Snatching her hand from his, she crossed her arms. "Why are you doing this? Do you love Emily? Is that it?"

He tightened his jaw, struggled to maintain eye contact. All too soon his feelings surpassed redemption, attraction, and the need to see Milne suffer. He now loved the woman he had only intended to tempt away from his target. He swallowed and met her gaze. "Yes. Yes, I do."

She studied him. Her brown eyes intense and unwavering. After the longest moment, she sighed, and her shoulders slumped. Dropping her arms, she gripped the counter once more. "Nicholas is a man you do not argue with. I learned that a long time ago. The first time was forced. After…afterwards, Nicholas made it clear he would make sure everyone knew I was ruined unless I maintained my relationship with him. So I did. I didn't want to be a social outcast. I was willing to pay the price. That, Mr. Samson, is the sort of woman I am. Why would you want to help me? There is no reason. Now go. Leave me to wallow in my own mistakes."

Will tightened his jaw. "You were fifteen or sixteen?"

"Yes, and now it's too late to do anything about it. You're right. I have Aimee. She is all I have. Nicholas owns every other aspect of my life." She gave a wry smile, a spark of malice showing in her eyes. "Children are of no importance to him, so he leaves Aimee to me. That's the way I want it. Always."

Will balled his hands into fists. "He's an animal."

"Yes, I believe he is."

"What of Emily? What will happen to her?"

Her eyes glazed with tears. "If there was something

I could do or say—"

"You could save her from having to marry him."

"How? Why would you say such a thing? I know about the contract. I know Emily. She will never see her father's money go to Nicholas. Not ever. There is little either of us can do to change our circumstances."

"You're wrong." He turned around and paced a distance away from her lest his growing frustration spill over and drown Katherine in its depths. "Milne not only shares his time between you and Emily but also with a prostitute."

Silence.

He stopped pacing and turned.

Katherine had paled, and her lips turned white.

He returned to the counter. "Katherine?"

She shook her head. "Don't be absurd."

"I'm telling the truth."

"Nicholas would never lower himself to visit a prostitute. To even suggest he does and then comes to my bed is disgusting. You should be ashamed. Now get out of my shop."

Will glared. "I am telling you the truth. If you can't help yourself, then for God's sake, think of your daughter."

She flinched, her eyes brimming with tears. "Get out."

Heat pinched his cheeks, and anger smoldered in his gut. "I have just left the woman Milne pays to spend time with. A woman who has never felt the thrust of his fists but who gave me the names of two other prostitutes who have. I am not lying about this, Katherine. I am telling you the honest truth and intend to tell the same truth to Miss Darson as soon as possible."

Her eyes widened. "You can't. The shame will kill her."

Will shook his head. "Emily can handle whatever is thrown at her. That is the one thing I am absolutely sure of in this entire mess. My revelation will further fuel her desire to be rid of him and the absurd contract she is bound in."

"Even if what you say is true, I have no idea what you expect of me. Nicholas is not a man to cross. I know it, as does Emily, and maybe even these other women you speak of. He is strong and powerful with a reputation that precedes him."

"These women are willing to testify against him in a court of law. They will stand before a judge and tell him what Milne has done to them. But what of you? What are you willing to do to ensure Aimee's safety?"

"This is madness. Whatever you feel for Emily, it cannot be such that you would risk your life, having only known her three or four weeks."

"My life?"

"If Nicholas finds out what you are doing…" She shook her head.

"My motivation originally had nothing to do with Emily. When I came to Bath in search of Milne, I didn't even know of her existence."

"So what has Nicholas done to deserve your vengeance?"

Will tipped his head back, closed his eyes, and told her about his mother.

"I hate him. I hate him with every fiber of my body." He pulled his hat from his head and pushed his hand into his hair. "But I am tired of the hatred digging its claws deeper and deeper into my soul. I want to cut it out of me. The only way to do that is to see Milne locked away and unable to hurt anyone else."

The curtain behind her swished back and little Aimee came running out, holding a wooden doll by its leg. Hastily swiping at her eyes, Katherine lifted the curly-haired little girl into her arms and pulled her close. She pressed a kiss to Aimee's temple.

"I'll help you, Mr. Samson." She met Will's eyes over Aimee's head. "I'll do whatever I can to stop Nicholas from ever coming near my little girl again."

Chapter Thirteen

Emily's heart beat faster as she rested her hand on the drawing room door. Annie had rushed upstairs ten minutes earlier, saying Will had returned and as Mr. Darson was sleeping, could Emily receive him. Could she receive him? She could barely breathe.

Excitement fluttered in her stomach, relief in her heart. He had returned. She should be afraid of the consequences seeing him again could bring, want to banish him out of the house, to leave her in peace to face her destiny. Yet nothing but happiness that he was on the other side of the door reigned supreme.

She inhaled a deep breath and opened the door. "Will."

He turned from the window.

Emily walked farther into the room, not stopping until barely three feet separated them. "You're back." Her voice was barely above a whisper.

He nodded, his jaw tight. "I told you I would not leave you open to Milne's harm. I meant it."

Heat flushed her cheeks and then her entire body as desire lit his eyes. "I don't...know what to say to you, Will. This can't go on."

"What can't?"

Why had she said that? "I mean...I don't know what I mean, but this is wrong. It isn't what is supposed to be happening."

"I won't leave you open to his mistreatment. I can't."

She closed her eyes. "I'm strong. You know that. Whatever Nicholas thinks he can do to me, he can't." She opened her eyes. "I will survive."

"My fear that you won't means I can't stay away. My passion that the man is not fit to lick your boots or even look at you burns right here." He pushed a fist into his stomach. "I can't ignore that."

Emily fought the urge to close the space that lingered like a chasm between them. She tilted her chin against her attraction to him, her need for him. "I will marry him, Will. I have to. My father's legacy means too much to me."

Color stained his cheeks, and he whirled away from her to stare through the window. Her heart ached to go to him, to steal her hands over his back and shoulders. To whisper promises she could not keep. If only things were different. She blinked the tears from her eyes and clamped her hands together in front of her. "I'm sorry."

He huffed out a laugh. "You are the last person who needs to be sorry. It is I who has brought this trouble to your door. If I wasn't here, you would have married him in blissful ignorance. At least for a while until the son of a bitch showed you his true colors."

"Will, look at me."

He turned, and their gazes locked. His eyes shone with fervor, with a passion she longed to have in her life every single day. "This is madness."

She forced a smile. "But it's my madness. You need to move on, forget you ever met me. Whatever it is you think Nicholas capable of—"

"It's not what I think; it's what I know." He blew out a breath through pursed lips and gestured to the settee. "Sit, please. I have something to tell you. Something I think will change your mind and make you see that no one needs to sacrifice their life in the name of loyalty and duty. Especially you."

The sincerity in his gaze alerted Emily's intuition. Whatever Will was about to tell her was about to turn her life upside down. On trembling legs, she moved to the settee and sat.

He sat beside her and took her cold hand in his, then stared deep into her eyes. "I've been busy these past two days. Very busy. And what I have to tell you is not pleasant for me to repeat nor for you to hear."

She drew in a strengthening breath. "Just tell me."

"Milne is Aimee's father."

Emily stared at him and then slumped her shoulders, gave him a wry smile. "I suspected as much. I have for a while." She looked away from his penetrating gaze. "His infidelity doesn't surprise me…but Katherine's betrayal hurts more than you will ever know."

He cupped his hand to her jaw and brushed away her fallen tear with his thumb. "Emily, look at me."

With her heart breaking for the friend she lost a long time ago, she turned.

"Don't blame her. He forced her. She was little more than a child the first time."

Revulsion dropped into her stomach, and she tasted bitter nausea in her throat. His face blurred in her tears. "God, no. Please don't tell me that."

"There's more."

"More?" She stared, a beat aching at her temple.

"What else could there possibly be?"

"There are other women." He took her hand and grasped it. "There are prostitutes."

"Pros…" Emily's gaze locked on his, and the remainder of her words extinguished in the flames of her anger. "You tell me everything you know about him. Everything."

"I have found two other prostitutes so far. I'm sure there are more. He is a womanizer, Emily. A violent and malicious womanizer. I have tracked down a young woman he visits regularly and managed to persuade her to talk to others. I have asked them to testify against him. I want him in court—ultimately prison."

She clutched her free hand to her throat. "He sees this woman regularly? Is she his mistress? I thought Katherine—"

He shook his head. "The man is evil. I have much to tell you that I learned from these women."

Emily's inner tenacity rose up inside her. She tilted her chin. "Then tell me. Tell me everything."

Her loyalty to everything and everyone apart from the man sitting in front of her, closed on her previous intention to banish Will from her life like a slamming door. His voice filtered through her brain and each despicable word he spoke changed who she was forever.

****

The following morning, Emily glanced at her father as he spooned a last morsel of boiled egg into his mouth. Never before had their breakfast taken such a painfully slow time. Having placed her knife and fork side by side on her plate at least twenty minutes before, her nerves were stretched to breaking.

"Emily?"

She started. "Yes?"

"Will you stop tapping your foot up and down beneath the table? Otherwise I will be forced to call for Doctor Marshall and request it be surgically removed."

"Sorry."

"What has you in such a state of impatience?" He touched his napkin to his mouth and reached for his water glass.

"I am not impatient for anything."

He frowned. "I know you better than anyone. What is it?"

She forced a smile. "Fine. You do know me. I am itching to get outside. It's such a beautiful day."

He met her smile. "Well, I think that's a splendid idea, my dear. What did you have in mind?"

"I thought I might ask Will if he would escort me for a visit to Aunt Edith and Cousin Isabelle. I know they get dreadfully lonely being away from town."

"Is that so?"

The knowing glint in his eye brought a searing heat to Emily's cheeks. "Do you not think it a good idea?"

He put his teacup on the table. "Well, indeed. I'm sure they would love a visit from you, my dear...although, I have never known you to take such a task upon yourself without my encouragement before."

She laughed. "I have, too. Didn't I take those muffins to them as a gift in the spring?"

"You did. What was it you said of my sister upon your return?" He glanced to the ceiling before meeting her eyes once more. "Oh, yes. If she deigned to smile, her face would splinter or something to that effect."

Emily widened her eyes in mock innocence. "I said

that but a single time. I was in an unforgivably bad mood after Aunt Edith spent the entirety of my visit suggesting I was obtuse for not getting my wedding to Nicholas over and done with."

"She had a valid point. How has Nicholas been treating you these last few days? I have not heard you utter a single word against him, so I assume things are improving between you two? Is he treating you with the respect you deserve?"

A lump lodged in her throat to see him look without pain for a blessed moment. If she were to share with him what she now knew of Nicholas, it would surely bring his death closer. Her stomach knotted with the pain it brought her to keep things from him, but she would not lay any further burden on his already stooping shoulders.

She forced a smile. "Nicholas has shown moderately more consideration toward me and my feelings over the last few days, I admit. He even apologized for his recent behavior."

Her father gave an inelegant snort. "Apologize? Nicholas? I daren't believe it. Sleep becomes more and more of an impossibility to me as the days to your wedding lessen. Nicholas is becoming worse with age rather than better." He curled his hand into a fist on the table as he inhaled a wheezing breath. "Damn this disease I have growing inside me. I should be here for you, not leaving you in the hands of a man who is as capable of real love as a…a…oh, damnation!"

Emily leaped from her seat as a barrage of racking stole the breath from his weakened lungs. "Oh, Papa."

She rushed toward him and laid her cheek to his head. She closed her eyes as the coughing jerked them time after time together as one. Emily held fast, absorbing the pain from his body. When the coughing abated enough for her to reach for a glass of water from the table, she held it to his lips.

After he'd swallowed a few sips, she set the glass down on the table and dropped to her haunches in front of him, taking his hands in hers.

He looked into her eyes. "I have something I want to say to you. Something I'm sure you will not want to consider, but I think it for the best. For all of us."

"What is it, Papa?"

"I think we should release Nicholas's hold on you and let him have the inheritance in its entirety."

Emily's breath caught. "Papa, no. Everything will be—"

"Everything will not be all right. But you will be free of him. You can go to Aunt Edith's in the country and live there."

"What? No." Dread formed a tight knot in her stomach. She could not think of anything worse—apart from becoming Nicholas's wife, of course. "I do not wish to live in the country any more than you would. We are city people, Bath people. We must not give up hope Nicholas will mellow in time." She swallowed as further shame flooded her heart, but it was paramount for her father to remain ignorant of Nicholas's true nature. "But, if you really feel that strongly against me marrying him, then maybe…" She looked at him from beneath lowered lashes. "The key to unlocking the arrangement is right in front of us."

Her father frowned. "Whatever do you mean?"

She met his gaze and grasped his hand, willing him to trust her to forge her future, her destiny. "Couldn't the key quite possibly be in the form of a stranger who happened to make our acquaintance?"

"Who…" Comprehension emerged in his dark brown gaze and the soft lift of his lips. "You think Mr. Samson can do something about the contract? My dear, whatever would make you think such a thing? He is here for his nephew. With God's good grace, he will soon find the boy, and together they will return to Bristol."

"I know, but there's something about him, Papa. As you've felt, he is to be trusted. I feel safe when he's around, even though I have no idea why." Emily grinned as her growing feelings for Will surfaced.

"How could he possibly help with a marriage contract? An inheritance? It makes no sense to me why you would think such a thing."

She took a shaky breath and exhaled. "He knew Nicholas before he knew us. Of that much I am certain, even though he has yet to admit it. They have a connection from the past, and I will find out what it is if it's the last thing I do."

Their gazes locked, and Emily's heart swelled to see the light in her father's eyes grow brighter. To catch even a glimpse of the man he was before his illness made her want to sing and dance, fight and never surrender.

She took his hand. "Well?"

He lifted her hand to his lips and pressed a firm kiss to her knuckles. "We will talk to Samson, find out what he knows."

Smiling, Emily stood. "That is exactly my intention. If you are happy for me to visit Aunt Edith, Will can accompany me, and I will find a way to raise the subject with him."

Her father smiled. "Excellent. The Darson father and daughter are a formidable team, are they not?"

Emily laughed as the blood binding them together pumped through her veins. She hurried to the fireplace and pulled the bell. Will had told her much of Nicholas's infidelities, of his attitude and lust for violence, but still he had not told her of their connection before he arrived in Bath. Unable to press him when her stomach had convulsed with the knowledge of Nicholas's betrayals, Emily now felt ready to learn what Will knew of Nicholas's past…for she was sure Will carried more knowledge than the insufferable news he had brought back with him yesterday, and she was determined to uncover more about Will, too.

Within seconds, Annie appeared in the doorway.

"Annie, my dear." Emily's father lifted his arm in greeting. "What a wonderful day it is! Could you ask Malcolm to prepare the driving gig for Miss Darson?"

"Of course, sir."

"Have you any idea where Mr. Samson is this morning? Do you know if he has left for the day?"

"I believe not, sir. He was in the kitchen not twenty minutes ago. Would you like me to bring him to you?"

"No, no. Emily will find him. I would like him to accompany her on a little day trip. Just the two of them. Yes, indeed. Alone and unattended."

Emily's face heated. "Father, do not say it like that. Whatever will Annie think of me?"

Annie's gaze lingered questioningly on Emily's before her eyes bulged and her face erupted with a smile of girlish glee. Emily rolled her eyes. If she didn't know better, Annie had more than likely already planned her mistress's wedding to Will. Right down to the place settings and what tins to tie on the carriage as the guests bid them farewell when they set off on their honeymoon.

Emily widened her eyes in warning. If Annie were to give any indication to her father what whirled in her romantic mind, there was a possibility of him changing his decision about the trip. He might not want her to marry Nicholas, but that did not mean he would consent to her being involved intimately with Will.

She pulled back her shoulders. "Off you go, Annie. Speak to Malcolm, and if you see Mr. Samson on your travels, please mention I would like to see him forthwith."

Annie curtsied, her smile wide. "Yes, miss. Of course, miss." She tipped Emily the most atrociously arduous wink before hurrying from the room.

Emily pursed her lips together to stem her laughter at the girl's silly and unsubstantiated enthusiasm.

She turned to her father. "I think maybe Annie sneaked some wine into her breakfast this morning."

He laughed. "I think you may be right. Now, off you go."

She kissed his cheek and hurried from the room intent on heading for the kitchen in the hope of catching Will, when he appeared at the top of the staircase. Attraction struck her very core. Standing big and strong, he met her eyes. His handsome face grew alight with a smile as he closed the distance between them. Could she do this? Could she really lure him away in a bid to interrogate him?

"Miss Darson, how are you today?"

She stepped back from the stairs as he came closer.

"I am very well. In fact, I was looking for you in the hope I could have your company again today."

He arched an eyebrow and stopped so close to her, the dark circles of blue surrounding his jet-black pupils momentarily mesmerized her.

She cleared her throat and fought to keep her gaze on his. "It is such a lovely day and you have been so many hours away from the house over the last few days, I thought we could take a drive into the country to visit with my aunt and cousin."

"It would be a pleasure."

Excitement whirled in her stomach as the thrill of the unknown skittered along the surface of her skin, making her nipples tingle beneath the confines of her stays. She daren't give in to the ardent temptation to inhale the subtle musky scent emanating from him. Her heart beat fast as she recognized the ultimate, age-old challenge in his gaze. His phenomenal eyes languidly traveled over her face before gliding lower to her breasts and back again. He smiled, and a sensation tugged high between her legs.

She took two abrupt steps forward and lifted onto her toes so her lips brushed dangerously close to the side of his neck. His breath hitched, and female satisfaction washed over her, enveloping her in its all-encompassing power. If she reached up and took his jaw in her hand, brushed her lips across his…he would be powerless to resist her.

It felt as thrilling as it did frightening.

"I will meet you outside in twenty minutes, Mr. Samson. Don't keep me waiting."

When she walked away, her legs trembled. She reached the bottom of the staircase and looked back. Will had yet to move an inch.

Chapter Fourteen

Will stared at the horse's forelock, absently patting its sturdy neck, completely lost in thought and somewhat nervous as he waited for Emily to reappear. What just happened? She'd left him frozen to the hallway floor like a love-struck youth. She'd turned away and slowly walked up the stairs with her beautiful behind shifting nonchalantly from side to side. All Will could do was stare after her, feeling as though he'd been slapped across the face with a wet kipper.

He swallowed as his trousers tightened across his groin. He was in far too deep to be comfortable. He couldn't stop thinking about her. A woman who would never be his. He closed his eyes and eased his head against the horse's nose. Its soft velvety texture mixed with the general stench of horsiness and hot breath, which felt strangely soothing to his fraught nerves and confusion.

"How could I have let this happen, my girl?"

"Whatever you're asking her, I can quite assure you Carrington will not provide the answer."

Will abruptly straightened and heard the crick in his neck.

Emily smiled, seemingly ignorant of the pain shooting along his tendon on a wave of heat.

He could handle that. The real cause for concern was the way his heart kicked against his rib cage. "You look wonderful."

Her cheeks flushed, and her gaze dropped to the folds of her dress. "I thought it such a beautiful day it would be perfect to wear my favorite dress. I'm grateful for your compliment."

"It's more than the dress." He stared and warmth spread through his cheeks. "It's you." Feeling like a complete ass, Will stepped away from Carrington, who promptly nudged him hard in the back. He stumbled forward.

She laughed. "Whoops."

He turned to the horse. "Thank you for making me look like a complete moron in front of the pretty lady."

Emily laughed. "Don't blame Carrington. She's only looking after me, aren't you, sweetheart?"

Will turned to face her. Her soft rosy lips were open, showing white teeth and the delicate pink of her tongue. His gaze lingered there, on the mouth he longed to kiss more than anything in the world. The final part of his heart he'd been fighting to keep under lock and key melted. If they had been born in a different time, met under different circumstances, he would have fought to the ends of the earth to make her his, but when he had nothing of substance to offer her, how could he?

She cleared her throat. "Shall we go?"

The embarrassed tone of her voice shook Will from his coma. He blinked. "Of course."

He held out his hand, and her gloved one slid against his palm. Throwing him a final smile, she stepped up into the gig and settled on the front seat.

He inhaled a shaky breath before walking around to the other side and jumping up beside her. "Ready?"

A strange look passed over her gaze. "As I'll ever be."

"What is the mat—" He shook his head. "On second thought, don't tell me. I'm sure I'll find out soon enough."

They exchanged grins. He couldn't remember seeing her look so happy. Foolishly hoping he was the one making her that way, he slapped the reins against Carrington's rump with a thwack, and the gig jerked away, leaving the cobbled street of Royal Crescent behind.

The next half hour passed in silence, punctuated only when either of them commented on the increasing temperature or the ever-changing ladies' fashions on the clothes-conscious streets of the city. The vivid color of the lush summer trees and flowers served as a further distraction. And, finally, as they left Bath, Will's shoulders came down from around his ears. The pressure of sitting next to her and not sliding his hand into hers or brushing the hair from her neck was pitiful. The clip-clop of Carrington's hooves softened as they moved from the streets to the dirt paths leading to the endless countryside surrounding Bath's borders. The changing smell of soot into lavender and stone to bark soothed the tension in his neck and arms.

He glanced at Emily, and his stomach clenched with anticipation. He had a good idea what this trip would entail and relished the beginning of her interrogation. Every now and then, she turned to him as though to speak but then turned away. Time and again, she took a shaky intake of breath and then released it. He would've found it amusing if her obvious discomfort or frustration didn't bother him so much.

He was no stranger to interrogation, but this was entirely different. Gentlemen whose pockets he'd emptied had questioned him; shopkeepers he'd "borrowed" certain items from demanded explanations. He'd been questioned by the good blue-uniformed, silver-buttoned Bristol constabulary, even stood in front of the wigged personage of a fine upstanding English courtroom, and none of them had come close to bringing a drop of sweat to his brow.

Will was not afraid to admit weaknesses, and his biggest right now was silently preparing to question him. Beautiful, intelligent, and witty, Emily would sooner or later turn her soft, dulcet tones and big chestnut-brown eyes on him, expecting answers. There was no doubt in his mind she suspected his reasons for making her acquaintance had nothing to do with a missing nephew and everything to do with Milne.

He grimaced, but he would tell her all, including the real reason why he was in Bath. Lying to her was not an option. The problem was, once he told her, it was likely he'd lose any chance of making Milne pay for what he did to his mother. Emily might dislike the man, but she didn't have the coldblooded hate running through her veins he did. Why would a woman as good as her, as visionary as her, want to hurt a man on hearsay? As Laura had challenged him, what tangible proof could he give other than his word that Milne had hurt his mother?

He had the names of the women Laura had given him—who might or might not testify, should the time come—and Katherine's fragile promise of support. Other than that, it was his word against Milne's, and Will wasn't entirely convinced Emily trusted him enough to accept his explanations, despite her revulsion toward the man she was expected to marry.

He swallowed against the bitter taste of failure. Emily didn't have the image of his mother trying to talk with blood filling her mouth tattooed to her memory. Nor the remembrance of her thin body as she lay in his arms, her skin marked with bruises like black spots painted on with charcoal.

"Will, you're shaking."

He jumped as if she'd struck him. He turned.

Fear filled her gaze, but she didn't move away. Instead, she inched closer and carefully eased the reins from his clenched fists. "Let's stop and rest awhile. We'll find some trees to provide some much-needed shade." A soft smile curved her lips, but concern shone in her coffee-brown stare.

Will forced a smile. "Good idea."

Her hands shook on the reins as she steered Carrington onward.

Guilt burned behind his breastbone, and he swiped his hands over his face. "I didn't mean to alarm you. The last thing I want is for you to be afraid of me."

"Will Samson, stop talking right now."

He arched an eyebrow in amusement. Never before had a woman told him to be quiet. Well, except his mother. He pursed his lips.

"I could never be afraid of you. Ever. If you want to apologize for your unforgivable silence for the last half hour, on the other hand, I completely understand. Don't you know a lady likes to be entertained by a gentleman if he takes her out driving for the day?"

He smiled. "I rather thought etiquette wouldn't be relevant on this trip."

She turned. "Whyever not?"

Will fell headlong into her gaze. She wanted something from him, yet still cared enough to literally take the reins. She handled Carrington with ease, even though something real and tangible gathered momentum between them. Something that would either erupt and destroy or envelop and protect.

Will stared at her mouth and shook his head. "Ignore me. I'm teasing. I want to thank you."

Her gaze dropped to his mouth, and time suspended as they continued along the road, neither of them watching nor caring what was ahead. Seconds ticked by as fate waited for one of them to close those few vital inches between them. She wet her lips and turned away, staring straight ahead. "For what?"

Will followed the direction of her gaze as his heart pounded with the trepidation of taking the next step. "For getting me away from Bath for a while."

"You needed some time away?"

"Something like that…but more, I wanted to spend some time alone with you."

Silence.

He glanced at her. Her cheeks shone pink. He hoped with pleasure. "You're my friend at best, my host at worst." He swallowed. "Unless, you see us as more than that. In which case—"

"You are a"—a smile lifted the corner of her mouth—"a friend, I think. A friend who has come into my life for a reason, and it is that reason I want to uncover. Right here. Right now."

The time had come. She wanted answers. Nerves stole into his belly. He could no longer deny what she meant to him, and if he told her the real reason he'd infiltrated her family home…The thought of disappointment in her eyes should she discover how he deceived her for the last three weeks caught like a spike in his chest. The tenderness in her gaze would be replaced with mistrust, her laughter with contempt.

He forced a laugh. "Do you know you can be quite scary sometimes?"

She grinned, her chestnut eyes wide with feigned innocence as she looked at him. "Me? How could I ever be scary? You, of all people, can handle anything and anyone—"

The carriage hit something hard and unyielding and lurched to the side. Will reached for the reins but was too late.

"Will!" Emily cried. "We're falling!"

Carrington whinnied her protest, and as they began to tumble into a ditch beside them, Will gripped Emily's waist, lifting her into his arms. The gig sharply tipped and her bottom came down on his thighs, and he curled his body around her like a protective cage.

Will's back hit the ground with a harsh thump, almost knocking the wind from him as Emily stared down at him, shock mixed with disbelief and, unbelievably, a hint of laughter. Will's heart raced, but the relief Emily was still in his arms was all that concerned him. Somewhere in the distance of his mind, he was aware that Carrington had got loose of her trappings and paced back and forth, neighing and far from happy.

He touched her face, checking for injury. "Are you all right? Are you hurt?"

"I'm fine. Thanks to you." The tone of her voice slid over his skin like a soothing balm. Soft and husky, full of invitation and raw femininity. Neither made a move to extract themselves from the other's embrace as Will lay on his back, her atop him. With her dark tresses loosened from their pins and her hat askew, she'd never looked so unkempt or beautiful. Will's blood heated as the atmosphere changed from shock to hot needful attraction. Her breasts were pressed enticingly against the thin cotton of his shirt, and her pelvis lay level with his. The first whispers of arousal brushed over his skin and through his blood. Their bodies fit like two pieces of a whole, and Will didn't want to let her go. He drank in the sight of her, knowing this blessed moment of holding her ticked away with each passing second.

"Kiss me, Will."

He looked to her soft pink lips, open and waiting. His penis ached and hardened. His heartbeat pounded. The deepening color of her cheeks told him she felt his need, yet she didn't move away. They were alone. He wanted her. This was a situation more dangerous than him, Milne, and a loaded gun. This was suicide.

"Emily—"

She relaxed her body into his. "Don't talk. Just kiss me before I start to think. Please."

He ran his gaze over her hair, her face, and finally her mouth. Taking his hands from her body, he cupped her jaw and drew her closer. With a final look into her eyes, Will covered her mouth with his and closed his eyes. She sighed into his mouth, and her fingers slid into his hair. Will shivered and increased the pressure of his lips; when her mouth dropped open, his tongue sought hers. She hesitated, and fear struck Will's heart that she would struggle from his arms in disgust, leaving him flailing in the grass, scared of never again feeling the way he did then. Instead, her tongue gently, tentatively touched his, and he groaned knowing she was taking a risk—a risk that meant she trusted him, trusted him not to deceive her, trusted him never to tell they had kissed while lying in the grass alone on the side of a country road. Even though guilt over deceiving her in other ways cruelly seared his heart, she was right to trust him. He held her tighter. Heat and passion were offered and accepted. Will's body awoke with a need to make love to her and worship every inch of her, inside and out.

She broke away.

Her heart beat against his as she stared, her wonderful chestnut eyes wide and her breathing heavy. He wanted to shout out No! and grab her to him once more, but instead, Will forced a smile and reached up to remove a stray length of grass from her hair. "Well, that was…"

An anxious smile twitched her lips. "Nice."

She hastily touched her lips to his once more before rolling to the side and gently falling from his body onto the grass, the broken wheel and panel from the carriage not three feet away from her. Lying side by side, Will turned his cheek into the roughness of the grass, reluctant to stop watching her for a single moment.

"You make me feel different, Will." Her voice was quiet as she turned and met his eyes.

"Different in a good way, I hope."

She smiled. "Yes."

"Then I'm glad."

She turned her gaze back to the sky. "You're

exciting. Strong." Her cheeks darkened. "When I'm with you, you make me think bigger, act bigger. I want to spend every spare moment I have feeling this way."

His heart constricted. "What are you saying?"

She faced him. "I don't know."

His gaze wandered over her face as the words he wanted to say to her lodged like rocks in his throat. Every possible emotion rolled around inside him, and he swallowed hard. How could he confess his feelings without telling her everything? If he did that...she would never again look at him as she was at this moment. "Emily—"

She pressed a finger to his lips. "Don't. Don't say anything. Neither of us needs to say anything. We know what's happening, but it's impossible. It hasn't any future. Let's just enjoy this time. Enjoy it for today."

Their eyes locked, and her smile faltered. "I can't go through with it, Will. I can't marry Nicholas." She pushed up onto her elbow and stared down at him. "I don't know why, but I suspect you're the key to my freedom. Or am I just a fool?"

Relief rushed through him at the same time as desperation ripped at his soul. He would give anything to stop her wedding going ahead—he would ensure it— but like a wounded man who needed healing, he had to know if she felt for him what he did for her. Was she fighting it as much as he was? He'd survived most of his life under a cloak of invisibility, not letting anyone close enough to see inside or hurt him. Known around Bristol as a chameleon, in Bath he'd met a woman who tossed aside his masquerade like it was nothing, leaving him naked and hers for the taking.

He closed his eyes, dropping a curtain over his

thoughts. "No, you're not a fool."

"You know Nicholas, don't you? There is something so rotten between you, I smell it emanating between you whenever you are in the same room. You can close your eyes, but you can't hide from me. I am not going anywhere until I know everything." Her breath hitched. "Please. You have to help me."

Will's eyes snapped open, and his heart lurched violently to see her eyes glistening with tears in the sunlight. "God, don't cry." He pressed a kiss to her forehead. "You cry and I'll come undone."

She swiped at her eyes. "Please. Tell me how you know him."

Milne's face crashed once more into Will's world like a cannonball, destroying and maiming everything in its path. Fire roared in his gut, and he swallowed the heat in his throat. "I promise I will tell you everything, just not yet. The time is not now. You have to trust me."

She rolled onto her back. "Even you won't help me."

"I will. I will do everything in my power to help you." He touched his fingers to her chin and moved her head until their eyes met. "Trust me."

"How can I? Nicholas is two different people most of the time, and I don't know who you are or who you're pretending to be either. I have two men in my life whom I don't truly know or trust."

Will rolled onto his back, clasped her hand that lay between them. The sky was azure blue with only one or two wispy white clouds breaking its perfection. "The less you know right now, the better."

"Why?"

His mother's face appeared above him, and anger once more assaulted Will's senses. "Milne has ruined enough lives. He will not ruin yours. If he suspects you know anything that could be the undoing of him and his fortune, God only knows what he will do to you. I will not risk that happening."

Fear and loathing pumped through his veins. Fear he couldn't resist her; loathing he could never have her. Cupid's arrow had shot across an auction room and struck him straight in the heart the second she winked at him. Should he tell her? Confess he approached her as a playing piece in his plan for Milne's ruin?

Feeling like the biggest fraudster in the world and hating the irony of it, Will kept his gaze steady with hers. "I have feelings for you, Emily. Real feelings."

A blush covered her face and her eyes danced. "You have feelings for me? Truly?"

He smiled, his heart aching. "Yes."

She looked deep into his eyes. "And I you, but no matter what we feel for each other, it is silly to think anything will ever come of it. Even though I want to find a way out of marrying Nicholas, another part of me is bound by loyalty to my father's lifework. We have to find a way to honor him, or else I fear I will never be free."

"Your father does not want this marriage to go ahead any more than you do."

"No, he doesn't, but he is dying, and desperation has him grasping at anything to save me from an unhappy life. If Nicholas were a decent man—"

"He's not." Will tightened his jaw. "He doesn't deserve you."

"So what will we do, Mr. Samson?" She lifted her

eyebrows. "And will we do it before or after you find your elusive nephew?"

He hesitated before hanging his head. "Ah."

She laughed. "Yes, ah."

He blew out a defeated breath. "Fine. That I can tell you. The nephew does not exist."

"I knew it!"

"I needed an excuse."

"An excuse? To move into my home?"

He grimaced. "I wanted to see you again but had no idea how."

"So you invented a nephew and lodged a room?"

He nodded. "Sorry."

She burst into laughter, her eyes shining. "Don't you dare be sorry. It's ingenious…and incurably romantic."

Smiling, he tucked a fallen lock of hair behind her ear. "Then kiss me, Miss Darson. Kiss me until you cannot kiss me anymore."

Chapter Fifteen

Emily could not remember feeling happier. She and Will walked hand in hand along the dirt track toward a secluded farmhouse. Carrington, shaken but unharmed, followed on behind. The boulder they had hit splintered the front wheel entirely, leaving them no choice but to abandon the broken gig in the ditch where it landed.

Emily smiled as Will spoke over his shoulder, reassuring Carrington all would be well.

He was indeed a wonderful and kindhearted man and being with him, like this, made her want to fly free like the birds overhead. But then her father came into her mind, and guilt knotted her heart. If it was not for her beloved papa and the state of worry he was doubtless in, she would not care when they returned home. Or if they did at all. She didn't want to think of anything else but the feel of Will's hand around hers and the memories of their numerous kisses.

"Your dress is ruined."

She looked at the mud-streaked fabric of what had been her favorite foulard day dress and laughed. "Isn't it wonderful?"

He laughed. "Is it?"

"Yes." She grinned. "I have never ruined a dress in my life. And quite frankly, I feel cheated."

"You're mad."

She squeezed his hand tighter and waved her other hand in the air. "It's so freeing. For one blessed afternoon, I feel like me instead of a lady or Oliver Darson's daughter."

"As much as it pleases me to hear you say that, Annie is likely to have a heart attack when she sees it."

She arched an eyebrow. "If I know Annie, she will forget the dress and instead demand I tell her all about what we did today."

He grinned and wiggled his eyebrows. "Will you tell her we were kissing in the grass? Or invent a more acceptable explanation?"

Emily playfully swatted his arm as her stomach shot into a frenzy of illicit excitement. "For your information, William Samson, the kissing will be discussed most definitely. Scandal and romance are what Annie lives for, and I would hate to disappoint her."

He laughed and dropped Carrington's bridle to grip her waist. Feeling so small within the splay of his hands, Emily suddenly longed to know how it would feel to have him hold her that way without stays and petticoats, strings and material barriers separating them. He stared into her eyes, and she gripped the wide breadth of his biceps.

"I don't want to go home. I want to stay out here in the middle of nowhere forever."

His gaze dropped to her lips. "If I could make that happen, I would, but you know it's impossible."

His blue eyes darkened with longing, and Emily's heart swelled. How had this happened between them? So quickly and cruelly. She'd never felt happier or more wanted. She wanted Will to show her…everything. "If we can't have forever," she said, quietly. "We could at least have tonight."

He stiffened beneath her fingers. "Meaning?"

"You make me feel as though I could conquer the world. You make me laugh and feel beautiful. Please. I want you…to show me everything."

"You want to stay out all night?"

The shock in his eyes confused her, shamed her. He must think her a harlot. Tears pricked her eyes, and she looked away from his questioning and unwavering gaze. "Forgive me. I shouldn't be thinking—"

"If you're certain that's what you want, there is nothing that would make me happier. You are all I need."

She turned her gaze to his once more. Her mind battled with reason and rationality versus insanity and danger. "If Nicholas were to discover—"

"He won't." His fingers tightened on her waist, and he pulled her forward, pressing a firm and branding kiss to her mouth. "If you really want to spend the night with me, I will make it happen." He glanced down the road, his eyes narrowed against the late afternoon sun. "We could ask for a bed at that farmhouse. Pose as husband and wife." He faced her and grinned, his eyes burning with passion and fire.

Emily trembled in his grasp as longing filled her soul. She dragged her gaze from him and looked at the farmhouse. "But I have no ring. We will be discovered, and the damage to my reputation will be irreparable." She shook her head. "I shouldn't have suggested…I'm not thinking rationally. We cannot. How will we explain not going home? We have Carrington. Why would we not ride her?"

"Do you really think your father would be happy to have you riding in front or behind me all the way back to Royal Crescent? For all of society to see Miss Emily Darson, a lady no less, riding roughshod with a mere commoner?"

Emily frowned. "Well, yes, as long as I was returned safely—"

"My thoughts exactly. No lady should be seen in such a manner. Not ever. So, I elect to maintain your decorum by sending a message for Malcolm to come and collect us in the family carriage at first light."

Emily smiled. "You are a wicked, wicked man, Will Samson."

He grinned. "Do you think such an excuse will work on your wily father, or will he see straight through it?"

Emily laughed. "Who cares? By the time he receives the message, the night will be over. The question is, how do we get a message to him?"

He pressed a kiss to her forehead. "You leave that to me, my love. The most important thing is if you are the slightest bit unsure, I will take you home right now." He rubbed his thumb over her cheek.

"I want this, Will."

"Then I hope you never look back on this night with regret. You should not be living a life riddled with ifs and maybes. You are a doer, Emily. A woman who wants to make changes for your children. This isn't about what I want but what you want. If there is any doubt in your mind…"

She smiled as excitement churned deep in her belly. "We stay."

His mouth covered hers and Emily closed her eyes.

The sensation of his lips and tongue against hers was exhilarating, strengthening. She'd let him take every part of her without resistance. She no longer had any choice. She was his. The intimate place between her legs pulsed with need, her bosom ached, and her heart soared. She was in love for the very first time, and even though Will promised to help her break her tie to Nicholas, she could not silence the nagging voice in her head telling her there was little either of them could do. At least for the time they were away from Bath, she could be his.

She eased him back. "Shall we go?"

He took her hand and pointed in the direction of the farmhouse. "Forward march, Miss Darson. Forward march."

Laughing, she clutched his hand with both of hers, and he led her into delightful disgrace. They had barely walked more than a few hundred yards when a lone horseman appeared ahead. Will raised his free hand at the same time as he executed an ear-splitting whistle.

"What are you doing?" Panic shot through her. "The fewer people that notice us, the better."

"You want your father to know you are safe, don't you?"

She stopped and turned toward the rider coming closer. "Of course, but—"

"Then I will ask this boy to take a message to him." He let out another whistle.

The rider waved his hand in acknowledgment and, a moment later, drew to a stop beside them. No older than fifteen or sixteen, he frowned. "Can I help you, sir?"

Will patted the lad's horse. "Are you going into

town?"

"Yes, sir. I have a message to deliver at The Circus."

Emily's heart leaped. The Circus was a circle of houses a stone's throw from the Crescent. "Oh, but that's perfect."

The boy turned. "It is?"

"Would you mind taking a message to my father?" Emily smiled. "He lives at number 24 Royal Crescent."

"I'm sorry, but I can't delay, ma'am. I have to deliver my message and get home. It will be getting dark by the time—"

Will coughed, interrupting him. "Wouldn't your parents be pleased if you brought back some additional money for the family pot?"

"You're willing to pay me? Well, that changes everything, sir."

"I thought it might. Here." He reached inside his waistcoat and produced some coins. "This is yours if we can rest secure in the knowledge our message will be delivered to Miss Darson's father."

The boy eagerly eyed the money. "You have my word, sir."

Will dropped the coins into his outstretched hand. "You are to go to number 24, Royal Crescent, and tell them you have a message for Mr. Oliver Darson regarding his daughter. Tell them she is safe and well and with me, Will Samson. Understand?"

He nodded. "Yes, sir."

"Tell them we have had an accident and the gig has lost a wheel, but we have found lodging for the night. They need to send someone to collect us first thing in the morning as we have sought shelter with a kindly farmer and his wife." He turned and pointed to the farmhouse. "All being well, that's where we'll be. Are you able to leave directions to where our saviors can find us?"

"Yes, sir. Absolutely, sir." The boy smiled and glanced to the house. "Old Mrs. Lancaster will see you right for the night, sir. She puts on the face of an angry dog, but she's got the heart of a kitten."

Will gave a curt nod. "Good. Now, all I need is your name."

"My name, sir?"

"Yes."

"Charlie Canton, sir."

"Right, then, Charlie. Look sharp. Now that I have your name, I know that if we are not picked up in the morning, our message hasn't been delivered, and I will be forced to come looking for you. The result will not be pretty."

The boy's cheeks reddened, and his prepubescent Adam's apple shifted. "There will be no need to find me, sir. Your message is as good as delivered."

"Good. Now, off you go then."

Emily shook her head as the boy cantered away. "You almost gave him a heart attack threatening him so. You should be ashamed of yourself."

He leaned close to her ear and she shivered with longing. "You'll soon learn I have no shame. None whatsoever when it comes to negotiating time to spend with beautiful ladies with cocoa-colored eyes and thick black hair."

Emily giggled as his warm breath whispered along her neck. His teasing words and hushed breaths awoke a new and erotic need, and Emily relished it. Her worries melted like snowflakes in the sun, and she came alive like the first blooms of spring. Will had changed her in ways he would never know. She would always remember him as the man who made her realize she could do anything. Be anything. He tugged on her hand, and as they walked farther along the path, Emily studied him from the corner of her eye. He stared straight ahead, his jaw relaxed, his mouth in a half smile. He appeared equally as happy as she was.

Eventually, they came to the end of the dirt track and onto the cracked, sunbaked pathway leading to the door of the farmhouse. Its surroundings were barren but for an overturned barrel and a hunk of rusted machinery leaning up against a sawn tree trunk. Emily did not have the first idea what it would have once been used for, but for the present it was being used as a hitching post for Carrington. Will secured the reins around part of it and gave them a firm tug.

"You stay there, girl. We won't be long."

Taking her hand, they walked to the front door. The smells were of what one would expect on a farm—somewhat pongy and nose-wrinkling yet wholesome and undeniably English. Emily inhaled deeply. The stench would forever equate to liberty and the happiest times in her memory.

Pretty in an understated way, the house bore whitewashed walls and a thatched roof, giving it a picture-book appeal. Before Emily could admire the tiny windows or the decorative yet empty flower boxes beneath them, Will tugged on her hand.

"Change sides with me. Whoever is inside could already be watching us." His concentrated gaze darted over the front of the house. "If I'm holding your left hand, they've no way of seeing a wedding ring."

Smiling, she scooted around to his other side, and he clasped his hand over hers in such a way that her fingers were completely concealed. She loved the unique way he viewed anything new to him—like a predatory fox surveying a henhouse. It was so masculine. His jaw was set and his muscles tense as though ready to pounce on anything that moved.

He looked at her, and his features immediately relaxed. He'd strategized his next move. "Ready?"

She nodded and Will raised his free hand to bang three times on the wooden front door.

A moment passed, and then the distinct sound of shuffling feet, rattling keys, and then the slide and clunk of a key being turned in the lock. The door swung open, and a rather large woman stood on the threshold, her face pulled into such an unwelcoming scowl, Emily moved to take a step back. Will tightened his grip on her hand, keeping her there at the same time as he swept into a low bow.

"Good afternoon, madam. I am so sorry to bother you, but my wife and I have found ourselves in a bit of a pickle and wonder if you could help us."

The woman stared, her hands fisted on ample hips, her eyes so narrowed they were mere slits. "Is that so?"

"Our gig took a tumble that resulted in a broken wheel and its abandonment until morning. If we were to venture back to the city, darkness would be upon us."

Her eyes widened. "You live in the city? What are you doing all the way out here?"

"Oh, but we so love a country drive, don't we, Emilia?"

Emily started when he nudged her none too gently

in the ribs. "Oh, we do. Very much."

"I suppose the tumbling of your gig explains the state of your dress, does it?" The woman ran her gaze up and down Emily.

Emily plucked at her skirt, nerves leaping in her stomach. "Exactly."

Will cleared his throat. "All we ask is for a night in your barn, madam. We will be absolutely no bother to you and be on our way at daybreak. I daren't start the long walk back tonight. God only knows who or what lurks about these lanes at night."

"Hmm." She looked from Will to Emily and back again. "I suppose I can stretch to soap and water, a hot cup of tea, and a bowl of broth. Will that do you?"

With her heart racing, Emily smiled. "That would be most generous. Thank you."

The woman raised her hands in surrender as her face softened and her eyes lost their suspicion. "Come on then, inside, the pair of you. You both look as though a piece of wet flannel wouldn't go amiss either."

Will sighed. "It certainly wouldn't. We feel as though we've been lying on our backs rolling in grass and mud all afternoon."

Emily bit down on her bottom lip to stem the threat of laughter bubbling in her throat. He was impossible. The woman's gaze darted between them once again before she held open the door and gestured them inside.

****

Emily placed her spoon on the table beside her empty bowl and reached for her cup of water. The liquid was welcome against her arid throat. The reality that she would spend the night alone with Will hit her square between the eyes once more, the illicitness of what they were doing shooting into her consciousness with full and alarming clarity.

A night in a barn. Like a pair of animals.

She swallowed as her stomach quivered. As tense as a coiled spring, Emily allowed the goal of hiding her fretfulness to slip and she faltered. She had to put a stop to their hurried arrangement. No matter how strong her pull toward him, to lie with Will was just too much. Mrs. Lancaster, their hostess, locked eyes with her, and Emily slowly returned her cup to the table. Careful to only use her right hand, she knew a slipup was imminent if she didn't keep her nerves under control.

Emily smiled, and Mrs. Lancaster's lips twitched before she returned her attention to the sock she darned. Emily darted a glance to the window for the fourteenth time in the last half an hour. The glaring absence of her "husband" had done nothing to appease her apprehension. Will had seen fit to go outside half an hour ago and was apparently in no obvious hurry to return.

Unable to bear the silence any longer, Emily pulled her shaking hands into her lap. "Goodness knows what is taking my husband so long. He's no doubt wandering aimlessly around as men are so often prone to do."

"He said you were to finish your meal and then follow him out to the barn."

Emily frowned. "He did? He said nothing to me. I had no idea he wasn't coming back inside."

"That's men for you." Mrs. Lancaster didn't look up from her work. "All they think about is themselves."

"Indeed." Even though Emily knew she should get up and move toward the door, her nerves jangled around her body at such a rate that she was struck immobile. She smoothed her hands over the nightgown their hostess had been kind enough to lend her. "Thank you for the nightdress, Mrs. Lancaster. You were very kind to offer to attempt to clean my dress, but please do not bother. My maid is a miracle worker."

Mrs. Lancaster met her eyes and lifted her shoulders. "All I did was hang it out to dry overnight. Hopefully that mud will brush straight off in the morning." She tilted her head in Emily's direction. "I know that nightgown isn't the most flattering thing for a lady with your figure to wear, but I thought it preferable to sleeping in your stays."

Emily smiled. "It is generous of you to let me borrow it. I'm very grateful."

"Are you ready to join him then?"

"Who?"

She laughed. "Mr. Samson, of course. He's out there waiting for you."

"Oh, yes, I see. Yes, I ought, shouldn't I? I am not at all happy he is not here to escort me to the barn though. It's pitch black outside."

"No trouble. I have a lamp you can take with you."

"Well, in that case, I shall be perfectly safe." Emily forced a smile.

Mrs. Lancaster walked to a dresser at the far end of the room. She pulled down a lamp from the upper shelf, took a match to it, and replaced the glass dome over the flame. It flickered and danced as though celebrating the night ahead.

Emily wanted to snuff it out. Why had she thought for one moment it would be exciting, romantic even, to spend a night in the middle of nowhere with Will? Was he not proving himself to be as inconsiderate as any other man? No gentleman would leave his sweetheart alone to find her way across a strange farm to a barn. He was no better than the rest of them.

"Off you go then, Mrs. Samson." Mrs. Lancaster thrust the lamp toward her. "Go and join your husband."

Swallowing, Emily stood. "Thank you. For everything."

She gathered up the huge mounds of excess material from around her ankles with one hand and took the lamp in the other. Mrs. Lancaster swung open the door, leaving Emily no choice but to step out into the darkness.

The temperature was mild and the breeze light. An idyllic evening one might say. Turning, Emily looked again to Mrs. Lancaster in the hope she might want to discuss the weather or the royal family…anything. The door was promptly slammed shut.

"Well, that's just lovely." Emily blinked back hot tears.

She tilted her chin and took her first steps toward the barn. With nerves jumping like beans in her blood, Emily walked all the way around to the back of the house.

"Oh, Will."

Evidence of what Will had been up to for the time he'd been missing was evident before her. At least twenty tiny makeshift fires, held in tin cups and bowls, lit a glowing-edged pathway to the barn. Its doors were slightly ajar as Emily approached, her heart beating fast and her hands clammy. Anxiety and trepidation, mixed with hope and happiness, coursed through her body on an undulating wave. Will was a man who made anything possible. Everything exciting and romantic.

Could she really give him her body? The only thing she could truly call her own?

She stopped outside and clasped the lamp handle tighter. Her conscience shouted NO! Her heart beat Yes! Yes! Yes! Over and over it rejoiced. Rejoiced in her chance to be with him, to steal these next precious hours until daybreak and hold them as hers no matter what the future held. With her mind made up, she pushed open the door and her breath caught. He stood with his back to her, dressed in his shirt and mud-streaked trousers. Her stomach quivered as she silently pushed the door closed, her eyes locked on his physique. He threw one of the two blankets Mrs. Lancaster had given them over a thick, wide layer of hay and straw he'd strewn on the floor.

Emily's body tingled as she shamefully took in the wholly masculine sight of him. His shirt stretched across the breadth of his muscular back, the seams straining across his biceps as he slapped and smoothed the blanket. She flicked her tongue over dry lips. He was perfection. A wide triangular back, narrowing to a taut square backside and thick muscular thighs…

"I know you're there, you know."

She started, and heat seared her face. Gathering her messy senses, Emily walked forward on trembling legs, grateful for the length of Mrs. Lancaster's nightgown.

"It looks wonderful."

He turned and his gaze traveled the length of her body. He grinned, and his teeth showed white in the semidarkness. "I assume that nightgown fits Mrs. Lancaster very well. On you? Not so much."

Emily laughed and forced her nerves into

submission by executing a twirl. "I thank you."

She forced herself to keep her gaze level with his in the hope she appeared confident and flirtatious rather than how she really felt—nervous and almost sick with apprehension.

His smile slipped. "You look beautiful."

The drop in his voice, the thickening of its tone sent bolts of desire through Emily's core. She held his gaze. "So do you."

Her heart beat wildly and her hands shook, but Emily strolled slowly forward until she stood inches from him.

His gaze moved from her eyes to her lips and back again. "Do you like the candles? It's the best I could manage."

Her gaze blurred with unexpected tears. He suddenly sounded so unsure, so vulnerable it melted her heart a little more. She blinked. "It's perfect."

He took the lantern from her trembling hand and placed it on an overturned box beside them. He stared deep into her eyes before lowering his lips to hers. Emily closed her eyes as a swarm of butterflies took flight in her stomach. She must be strong. Must show him she wanted this. If she exhibited even a moment's hesitation, he might not take her—and she now wanted that more than anything.

He pulled away, and Emily opened her eyes.

Gesturing toward the mattress, he smiled. "Shall we sit?"

She nodded, and he took her hand, leading her to the mattress. Emily didn't sit but lay straight back, her inhibitions gone, obliterated by the look of desire in his eyes.

He lay down beside her, and his gaze traveled over her features before he brushed a fallen lock of hair from her face. "Are you certain?"

"Yes. I want this. I want you."

He leaned down to kiss her, and Emily surrendered. She was his. He was all she needed. She refused to allow any residual trepidation to get the better of her. She trusted him. Maybe even loved him. She pulled him closer, her hands moving to his shoulders and up to the nape of his neck.

He groaned into her mouth, and their kiss deepened as his hand slid from her waist and over the bump of her hip. The heat of his touch burned through the thin cotton of her nightdress, melting the last lingering doubts that she could make love to him. Lightning struck her heart when his lips moved from hers to kiss her jaw. She breathed his name into his hair.

His featherlight kisses traveled over her skin toward her ear and the curve of her neck. All those nights alone and ashamed as she touched her body, learning what it desired, had not prepared her for such sensations. His hands were a soothing balm to the open wound of her yearning heart. A wound she'd been waiting for Will Samson to heal.

Tonight she would be the person she wanted to be. The woman who made love to a man who made her feel as though she could change the world in a heartbeat. A man who made her stronger, not weaker. Happier, not lonelier.

Their lips met once more, their tongues entangling and discovering. After a moment, his lips dropped to her collarbone. Her senses heightened as he nipped and gently sucked at her sensitized skin, his hand drawing feverish circles over her thigh and hip. Emily clung to him, her eyes half closed, the tip of her tongue caught between her teeth. A strange ache beat in her breast, and suddenly she yearned for the feel of his hands there.

Blindly, she reached for his fingers and eased them from her hip to her breast. She sensed his hesitation, so she held his hand there until his muscles relaxed and his fingers teased her nipple. It hardened beneath his touch, and when embarrassment threatened, Emily opened her eyes. She needed to see the admiration in his eyes she'd come to adore. He smiled at her, and she smiled back, her self-consciousness slipping away.

His fingers moved to her nightdress, and he loosened the ribbons at her neck. With his eyes locked on hers, his fingers worked until the ribbons came free and cool air brushed her naked breasts.

His gaze dropped lower, and his eyes darkened to midnight-blue as he stared at her bosom. "You're so beautiful."

Emily shivered, desperate for more. He pulled away and took her hands in his. Silently, they lifted onto their knees, and he dropped her hands to pull his shirt from his trousers. Emily watched him as anticipation, curiosity, and a huge dose of excitement swirled inside her. When he tossed the shirt away, she drank in the sight of golden skin stretched taut over a hard chest and thickly muscled torso. A blush struck her face, and Emily dropped her gaze lower. His trousers protruded at the groin, evidence that he desired her as much as she did him.

She shifted on the mattress, drawing the masses of nightdress material from beneath her. With trembling fingers, she gripped the hem and lifted it over her head. The satin of her chemise was tight like a binding around her body, her knickers a restraint. With Will's gaze so intently on hers, Emily lifted the chemise over her head and tossed it atop the nightgown. His gaze wandered over her bared bosom.

She stole backward and lay down. He came down beside her, and their lips met. His kiss was firm and soft, possessive and needful. She scored her hands into his thick dark hair, her fingertips exploring the feel of his scalp, the wondrous shape of his head. He held her upper arms, his thumbs tickling the curve of her breasts. Feeling wonderfully wanton and sensual, she reached for his trousers and popped the button at the waistband.

"Emily."

He breathed her name into her mouth, and she increased the pressure of the kiss, not daring to look at her shaking hands fumbling with the buttons of his trousers. One by one they came free, and the heat of his erection against her naked thigh made her break their kiss. She looked down and swallowed. He was huge. Thick. God help her, he was beautiful.

She looked up.

He smiled and moved away from her. Standing, he lowered his trousers down strong, muscular thighs and stepped out of them. She averted her eyes, not daring to look again in case she lost her nerve. What would it feel like to have such a mammoth thing inside her? Her body shook, but she smiled. It would feel wonderful. To be entirely joined to him.

She opened her eyes and arms. The relief in his beautiful blue gaze sealed their fate, and he returned to her side. With no words spoken, he lowered his head to her breast and took one of her hardened nipples into his mouth. She gasped with pleasure as his tongue rolled over and around it, his hand stealing lower toward her most intimate place. Instead of feeling afraid as she feared, she silently urged him on, wanting to feel him touch where only she had touched. To bring her the pleasure she'd only given herself.

His hand slid over the cover of her underwear, and then his mouth left her bosom. He lowered his body down onto the mattress. With achingly slow progress, he inched her knickers from her body, his lips following their path. Naked and vulnerable, Emily trembled as he moved back up toward her, his mouth capturing hers.

She moved her hands to his shoulders and into his hair, urging him closer, kissing him deeper. He emitted a low growl, and his fingers gently inched into her pubic hair. Emily sighed when they glided over the top and down the sides of her private part. She met his eyes, and he rubbed her. Harder and harder he massaged her, his gaze never leaving hers. Emily clamped her teeth together and lifted her hips. Her breathing labored as the sensations built. His fingers were rough and masculine where hers were soft, his increasing friction intense, yet filled with love and discovery.

He slipped his finger inside her, and Emily gasped.

"Let me do this, Emily. Let me see you surrender."

Her eyes fluttered closed, and she squirmed beneath his skillful hand. She smoothed her hand over his chest, his incredibly hard stomach, and through the dark curls at his groin. Inhaling, she took that final step and curled her fingers around his girth, slowly smoothing her hand back and forth, doing what felt natural and praying he liked it. He moaned his pleasure, and Emily basked in the thrill of female power.

He was large in her palm, smooth like silk, hard and strong. Seemingly by instinct, he matched her rhythm with his fingers as her center pulsed. She fought to stay silent. She would not let her body have its release. Not yet. She wanted more. Wanted to ride this wave, take the prize with Will traveling deep inside her. Her eyes snapped open. Primal lust burned in two blue-hot flames in his eyes.

"Will, please. Make love to me."

He hovered above her, and she raised her hands to his waist, opened her legs. His hand reached between their bodies and with gentle consideration, he slid tentatively inside her. She felt her resistance, his soft nudge, and she broke. At last his body lay flat to hers and they were one.

He moved slowly, gently, until she stole her hands onto the taut firmness of his buttocks and pressed down. He closed his eyes, groaned, and picked up speed. She dug her nails deeper. The sensations roared. Her feelings soared. She lifted her hips, taking him deeper, holding him closer. On and on he urged her, his hips thrusting with joyous precision…

Her release came hard and fast, shuddering through her body with such ardent intensity Emily laughed with the shock of it.

She was a woman. Will's woman. Her joy was unsurpassed.

He made love to her like she would be his for eternity. The words "I love you" spilled from his lips along with his seed, and tears of joy fell from Emily's eyes.

Chapter Sixteen

Will smiled. Emily's eyelids flickered with dreams that appeared to delight her as she slept. He hoped it was him she saw. An hour earlier, the first call of the rooster hailing a new day had woken him. Unable to sleep, Will scoured the barn and happened upon some disused roof slate. Further investigation brought forth some chalkstone, and he fashioned some rudimentary drawing apparatus.

He'd been sketching her since dawn with the hope that, when he was eventually forced to leave Bath, the drawing would bring him some comfort rather than pain each time he looked at it. Will rubbed the side of his finger over the chalky line of Emily's jaw to soften it. God, he loved that jaw. He loved her neck, her collarbones, her breasts…

He shifted as his need to have her rose again. They'd made love twice more during the night and he should leave her be, but even the sight of her naked breasts showing above the wool blanket aroused him. Although she had been a virgin mere hours before, she was so incredibly sensual. She was everything he wanted, but even if he succeeded in getting her away from Milne—correction, *when* he succeeded—he had nothing of substance to offer her.

Frustration burned. He saw no other solution but to let her go. Her loyalty lay with her father and she would never leave him; he could not stay in Bath with neither means nor money. He needed the country where manual work was endless, the fresh air welcome. They were different even if their hearts were so profoundly connected. She deserved a man who could afford to give her everything she desired, and feared her passion to maintain her father's legacy would mean she refused to walk away from Milne. Her conviction to maintain what was rightfully hers and, in time, her children's was palpable.

"Will?"

He started and looked up from the slate. "Good morning, beautiful."

Her eyes shone and her sleepy smile grew wide as she languidly stretched her arms above her head, her nipples showing dark against the creamy white fullness of her breasts. "What are you doing?"

Guilty heat seared Will's cheeks. "Nothing."

Narrowing her eyes, she pulled the blanket around her and stood. "You're drawing. Please, you must let me see."

He smiled and snatched the slate to his chest. "It's not finished."

She made to grab it. "Is it me?"

He held fast. "Yes, but you can only see it once it is done."

She crossed her arms over the blanket and pouted. "That is entirely unfair. Malcolm will be here to pick us up soon. How will you finish it? Please, let me see what you have drawn thus far."

"No."

"Will, please."

He studied her. "Fine…on one condition."

"Which is?"

"You lie back down."

She glanced toward the mattress. "I can't. The day has broken, Mrs. Lancaster—"

"Now that you have risen and covered your beautiful bosom, I have no way of finishing the drawing. However, if you let me see it again, I will sketch faster than a caricaturist befuddled on opium."

"You are incorrigible." Her eyes widened with delight. "I will do no such thing. Your request clearly is in more with wanting to see my breasts than your art."

Laughing, Will placed the slate facedown beside him and lunged forward to grab her. She promptly fell shrieking into his arms, settling her beautiful behind in his lap.

"Kiss me, woman."

Her lips immediately met his, and Will closed his eyes. He breathed in the scent of her skin as it pressed near his nose, sealing it tight in his memory. The night had been short, and these remaining moments with Emily limited. Malcolm would soon arrive to collect them, and then they would be forced to resume their farce of lady and protector.

They parted, and Will stared into her cocoa eyes. "Well, I think that kiss merits you a quick glance at the sketch after all."

She clapped her hands. "Let me see."

He picked up the slate and turned it over. Her gasp warmed his soul. She was his biggest passion, and now he had a permanent memory of her. His gaze wandered over her happy face as she reached out to touch the drawing.

"Oh, Will. I look amazing."

He buried his face in the hair above her ear. "You are amazing."

"But look at the shading, the lines. You are a genius."

"The subject is genius, not I."

She turned, and his heart hitched to see tears glaze her eyes. He brushed them away with his thumb. "Why are you crying?"

Shaking her head, she squeezed her eyes shut. "You have to stay with me."

"Emily—"

She opened her eyes, and she trembled. "Say you'll stay, no matter what happens. This isn't about me, or us, or Nicholas, my marriage. This is about you." She looked back at the slate and lifted it into the air. "Your talent is God-given. If you can do something as beautiful as this from studying me, what could you do with a model? A landscape?"

He smiled and touched his fingers to her chin. Her gaze fell to his lips as his fell to hers. "I fear if I stay I should never draw anything or anyone else but you."

She leaned closer. "Stay anyway."

Will swallowed. He was weakening. His reluctance to leave her tilted on a knife-edge, and when her lips touched his, the cut was deep.

The barn doors suddenly flew open, and Emily leaped from his lap as though she'd been scalded. Will tensed. It didn't matter their feelings; they were not wed and Emily's reputation was in peril. A fact that was incredibly real—but he would never regret their lovemaking. He loved her, and if he'd had the means to offer her a future, he'd ask her to marry him in a heartbeat.

"Good morning, Mr. and Mrs. Samson." Mrs Lancaster smiled but then halted when her gaze fell on Emily's state of undress. "Oh, I do beg your pardon." Two spots of color darkened her cheeks. "I assumed you'd be in your nightgown."

Will stood, hiding Emily behind him. "Good morning to you, Mrs. Lancaster. I assume you slept well?"

Her gaze darted from Emily to him. "I did. It seems your wife was a trifle warm, however."

Ignoring the slight, Will smiled. "We'll be on our way as soon as we can. We don't wish to impinge on your generosity. We appreciate the use of your barn for the night. A true saving grace."

She threw another disapproving glance in Emily's direction. "You're welcome. There are eggs and bacon in the kitchen when you deem it the correct time to eat." She marched toward the door.

Will shook his head and grinned. He turned to Emily. "Quite a character, isn't she—what are you doing?"

Emily yanked the nightgown over her head, her limbs flailing so fast they were little more than a blur. "I'm half dressed! What if Malcolm or Papa or Nicholas had walked through those doors?"

Will stepped toward her and enveloped her in his arms, pressing a gentle kiss to her cheek. "But they didn't."

She threw him a glare. "Only a man would say that."

He held her at arm's length. "What happened here was beautiful. We love each other. We'll have our breakfast, and then we'll leave. No one will be any the

239

wiser."

She grappled from his arms, her cheeks flushed. "Open your eyes. Didn't you see the look on Mrs. Lancaster's face? I have the distinct impression she will enjoy telling anyone willing to listen about the state she found me in. What if she tells Malcolm? He will feel dutybound to tell Papa."

"Then I'll ensure that doesn't happen."

Her eyes stormed with frustration and disbelief. "What is it you suggest we do? Gag her?"

He smiled—but quickly dissolved it when the fire in her eyes inflamed further. "If you prefer, we'll not stay for breakfast. We'll tell Mrs. Lancaster we do not wish to intrude any longer and want to start our walk home."

****

Emily stared into the distance. She and Will walked hand in hand along the same dirt track she'd walked as a virgin the night before, Carrington plodding on behind. She'd given her body to a man she loved. Her stomach swirled with fear and wonder, but not regret. Even knowing their love affair was doomed did nothing to lessen her joy at making the previous hours their own. She'd keep their secret like a hidden jewel forever. Hers to treasure, to hold and remember. The time would never fade. Its prisms would forever surround her soul, filling her with light whenever she needed it most.

She blinked back tears. She wanted to believe they would find a way to sever the contract binding her to Nicholas, yet the wedding date loomed ever closer. She shivered as the chill of impossibility seeped into her blood. Whatever happened next, at least she knew what it was to have a man fill her heart with joy. She'd always have these four weeks with Will to hold as her own.

The sight of an elaborate carriage ahead jolted Emily from her romantic thoughts. The manner in which the driver lifted the reins and lashed them down upon the two horses in front alerted her to impending danger. Piebald horses. Only one person she knew owned piebald horses. She dropped Will's hand as her blood turned cold.

"Nicholas." Her breath hitched, and her heart hammered. "It's Nicholas."

Will stiffened beside her. "It's all right, my love. He will not so much as look at you the wrong way while I'm here."

Emily's heart thundered as she looked at him. His jaw was rigid, his cheeks flushed, and his eyes narrowed to slits. This wasn't the Will who made her laugh with a mere wiggle of his eyebrows, or looked at her with such desire she felt she would melt under the flattering heat of his study. This was a Will capable of murder, and it saddened her he carried such a strong hatred inside so beautiful a vessel.

"Will, look at me."

He turned.

Resisting the urge to grasp his hand, Emily looked deep into his eyes. "We will face him together. Nicholas may be a bully, but he is my fiancé, and it is I who should answer to him."

He scowled. "You should answer to no one but yourself."

The crunch of gravel and the acrid smell of lifted dust turned their heads. With the carriage barely more than a few hundred yards away, there was no time for argument or further discussion. Emily curled her hands into fists at her sides and waited. The carriage came closer, and she recognized Nicholas's driver. He shouted toward the carriage, and seconds later, the horses slowed from their near gallop to a trot. Emily and Will stood together like sentries, standing guard over the precious remaining moments of their liberty.

The horses stopped in front of them, and mustering every ounce of her inner strength, Emily thrust her chin forward and pulled back her shoulders. Staunch dignity seeped into her heart, filling her veins with fortitude and determination. Nicholas would not weaken her resolve to be the woman she wanted to be, nor would he sully her bodily surrender to Will.

The carriage door opened, and Nicholas's ever-present walking cane came first, followed by the man himself. His driver climbed down from his post and bowed slightly. Nicholas passed him without a glance. Despite her silent vows, Emily trembled as his gaze locked on hers with terrifying intensity, but she did not look away.

He stopped directly in front of her. "Disappear, Samson."

Will huffed. "I don't think so."

Foreboding rang in Emily's ears. The tension stilled the birds in the trees and the breath in her lungs. She needed to separate them before something started she'd have no power to stop.

"Nicholas—"

His hand shot into the air silencing her. "I said disappear, Samson, before this turns ugly." His color darkened. "You have spent the night with my fiancée. I should kill you. Maybe I will, but not right now. Go."

Emily risked a glance at Will. His eyes burned with rage, and he dropped Carrington's bridle to cross his arms. "You and I both know you lack the skills needed to kill me, Milne. Is there really any need for the theatrics?"

Emily sucked in a breath, and her stomach tightened.

Nicholas glared. "I could snap your neck like a twig."

Will raised his eyebrows. "Why not do it then? If I stood face to face with the man who'd spent the night with my fiancée, he'd already be dead."

"Why you—"

Emily rushed between them, pressing her hands to their chests. "No, Nicholas. No. Let's talk." A vein pulsed at his temple. "Please. Over here. Come."

He remained frozen, his eye twitching dangerously as he glared at Will.

Will's eyes danced with demonic delight, his smile as wide as the sun.

Disappointment dropped like lead into her stomach. Was he enjoying this? Was last night nothing more than ammunition to further his hate campaign toward Nicholas? She mentally shook her head, refusing to believe it. The feel of his caresses on her skin, her breasts and hair, the words he'd whispered against her ear—none of those things could possibly be veiled in masquerade. His passion beat the same rhythm alongside hers. So why did her heart suddenly feel so heavy?

"Will." She swallowed the lump in her throat. "Stop this, right now."

He didn't look at her. "What do you say, Milne? Are you man enough?"

His blatant snub of her request escalated her simmering anger. "I said stop." Will turned, and their eyes locked. Emily stared into his eyes and silently pleaded with him to back down, to support her. "Your behavior makes me believe everything you did for me last night was not motivated by your regard for my well-being but to further antagonize my fiancé."

His smile faltered and his gaze darkened with concern. "You know how I—"

She raised her hand, cutting him off, even though her heart hitched with relief at his reaction. "Please do as Nicholas asks and leave us to talk."

Nicholas shifted behind her. "You heard her, Samson. Now go and sit over there on that rock like the slimy toad you are. Careful not to croak too loudly."

Breaking his stare from hers, Will tipped his head back and laughed. "Is that an attempt at humor? Good for you. Laughter in the face of adversity is often the only thing a coward possesses."

Emily's heart dropped.

"Adversity?" Nicholas shook his head. "I see no adversity, only an inconvenience. I have been a patient man up until now, but this stops now."

"Is that so?"

Nicholas grasped Emily's wrist, his fingers digging into the tender flesh like sharpened claws. She swallowed back the urge to cry out and give him the satisfaction of knowing he was hurting her. She attempted to tug her arm free.

"Release her. Right now." Will's voice was a low rumble.

Panic bubbled in Emily's stomach, and her mouth drained dry. "Nicholas, drop my arm this instant. If you wish to speak to me alone, Will can make himself scarce for a few minutes." She turned to Will and pinned him with a stare. "Can you not?"

He continued to glare at Nicholas for a few more seconds before slowly turning to face her. His eyes were dark with anger. "I cannot do that." Although addressing her, he shifted his gaze once more to Nicholas. "I fully intend to deliver on your father's expectation that I protect you. If Mr. Milne doesn't release you in the next two seconds, I will break his arm."

Nicholas huffed out a laugh. "I merely wish to be alone with my fiancée. Leave us be. Why don't you be a good boy and run along."

Emily looked from one man to the other as helplessness battled inside her. The air crackled with tension, and the ground shifted beneath her feet. She opened her mouth to demand Will's cooperation when Nicholas flung her to the side and swung his fist toward Will.

As though he possessed a sixth sense, Will ducked. Nicholas roared and threw a second punch. "I'll kill you, Samson."

Will deftly stepped to the side, and Nicholas missed him again. Carrington backed away from their scuffle, seemingly undeterred by their violence. Emily brought her hand to her mouth. Nicholas's fury raged like an inferno as Will bounced from one foot to the other around the dirt track. Nicholas went after him, his punches hitting the air time and again.

It should have been terrifying, yet Nicholas's

humiliation felt entirely just. They moved farther and farther along the track. If she didn't know better, she would have thought Will was purposely leading Nicholas like a blind man to the gallows. A deep ditch at the side of the road lay a few steps behind him. Knowing Will as she did, he would gleefully watch Nicholas tumble into it before strolling back to her, slapping his hands together in the manner of a job well done.

Turning, Emily called out to the driver who watched the brawl with seemingly equal amusement. His grin was wider than his face.

Emily lifted the hem of her mud-stained skirt with one hand and frantically waved the other. "You! Will you not do something to stop this? We cannot stand here and let them fight like dogs in the street."

"That's no fight, m'lady." He laughed. "That's my master chasing his tail."

Emily glared in an attempt at authority. "Now, look here. Mr. Milne will take a stick to you if I tell him how much this display of masculine ridiculousness amused you. Now either you go over there or I'll…I'll…" Emily heaved up beside the driving seat.

"My lady, what are you doing?" The driver scrambled backward.

She grabbed the riding whip lying between the horses and raised it above her head. "I'll whip you myself if you don't climb down and do something to stop them." She wobbled precariously as the horses stamped their impatience.

"Emily, get down from there before you fall." The sound of Will's voice blew toward her on the crest of the faint breeze.

"What on earth do you think you are doing?" Nicholas's shout followed.

She looked at them and blew out a breath. At least she managed to draw the comedy show to a close. They came hurrying toward her, nudging and shoving each other until they stood below her, their hands outstretched, offering assistance so she could alight from the carriage. She looked from one to the other with disdain before replacing the whip and gesturing for both men to move aside.

They stepped back.

Gripping the sides of the carriage, she lowered to the ground unaided and faced them in turn. Her heart slowed to a more normal pace, and her pride bloomed triumphant. Will's gaze burned a brand around her heart. Admiration, love, and more than a little desire burned in their beautiful blue depths—whereas Nicholas looked painfully affronted she'd not needed his help.

Preferring the look in Will's eyes, she faced him with a forced scowl. "You have treated me with respect and consideration since our accident yesterday, yet now you have managed to delete everything you have done by defying both Nicholas's and my wishes."

"Emily, come now, I do not believe—"

With a curt shake of her head, she silenced him before she lost her trail of intention and Nicholas detected her charade. "I am sure my father will be gravely disappointed in your behavior."

Will stared for a moment longer before comprehension shone in his eyes. He dipped his head in submission. "You're right. I apologize."

She turned to Nicholas and when she met his eyes,

her stomach dropped to her mud-spattered shoes. Her confidence wavered, and the hairs on her arms rose.

Violent malice swirled like an angry sea in his emerald-green glare. His smile was terrifying. "Yes, my love?"

She swallowed and straightened her spine. "I would very much like to return home now. Papa must be beside himself with worry."

"That, my darling, is music to my ears. We will leave Mr. Samson here to make his own way back."

"What? We can't possibly—"

"It is as I wish."

Emily glanced at Will and back to Nicholas. "My father would not want that. Even though Mr. Samson has been overly protective of me since you arrived, he was a gentleman to me throughout our entire stay at a kindly lady's farmhouse. I suggest we tie Carrington to the back of the carriage, and Will can sit up front with your driver."

For a long moment, he stared at her and Emily struggled to not step back.

At last he nodded. "As you wish, my dear."

Nicholas offered his elbow and Emily slid her palm against his forearm. They walked in silence to the carriage.

Nicholas addressed his driver. "I want you to drive those horses as hard as you can. The sooner we have Miss Emily looking less like a street urchin and more like the lady she's supposed to be, the better."

From the corner of her eye, Emily saw Will take a step toward him and quickly shook her head. He glared. She silently pleaded. He turned and walked to where Carrington stood balefully watching him. He gripped the horse's bridle and led her toward the back of the carriage.

Satisfied Will was doing as she'd indicated, Emily took Nicholas's offered hand and stepped into the carriage. He came in behind her and slammed the door. Tense seconds ticked by as outside the sounds of Will tying Carrington to the rear ensued. Soon he walked past the window, his chin tilted, before the carriage lurched when he climbed in next to Nicholas's driver.

Nicholas banged his cane against the roof, and the carriage jerked and jolted before it started back along the path. Emily waited with trepidation for the barrage of abuse that was certain to trip from Nicholas's tongue. He sat so close the heat of his arm burned hers.

What was she to say to him? The fact remained that she was an unmarried woman who had spent the night alone with a man. It would be frowned upon if the man had been Nicholas, but another? Emily twisted her hands together in her lap as the silence wore on. The carriage jostled along the path past farmhouses and fields as the soft mumble of Will and the driver's conversation filtered through the open carriage window.

She glanced at Nicholas's leg. It bounced upon the carriage floor—a certain gesture of his suppressed anger. His face looked cast in stone. Unable to bear the increasingly oppressive silence, she sent up a silent prayer for courage and turned.

"How is my father? Is he in a state of panic?"

He remained statuesque, staring straight ahead, a nerve jumping and leaping in his jaw.

Emily's hands turned clammy. "Nicholas? This silence is helping no one—"

His gloved hand clamped like a vise to either side

of her chin, trapping her cry painfully in her throat. His thumb and forefinger shook at her jaw, and his breath blew hot against her face. He pushed her back until she lay half on and half off the velvet seat. He loomed above her. "Damn you. Damn you to hell for doing this."

Emily attempted to speak, but his grip tightened. Her heart raced as his fingers pressed deeper until her teeth cut the inside of her cheek and she tasted blood. She shook her head and clawed at his hand.

"I don't need to ask you what happened, you stupid girl. I will discover that for myself soon enough." Spittle leaped from his mouth onto her face. "Everything you do upsets me. That will not happen once we are married. I know you hate me, but best of all…" His twisted mouth widened to a manic grin, and his eyes flashed with sadistic exhilaration. "I know you love Samson. I have no doubt you let him touch and caress your breasts and cunny last night. You are nothing more than a whore. What you don't know is how I enjoy venting my frustration on your very kind."

Nausea whirled in her stomach, and tears burned hot in Emily's eyes as his weight bore down on her. Panic coursed through her veins, and her heart pounded relentlessly in her ears. She kicked her legs, but it was futile, she could not move him. Her thoughts rushed to Will sitting mere feet away but entirely out of reach.

Cursing, Nicholas released her chin and she opened her mouth to scream, but it was swallowed soundlessly when his mouth covered hers. Violent and possessive, his kiss was filled with hatred. His teeth grazed her lips; his tongue sought hers like a venomous snake. Saliva smeared her lips, his breath hot in her mouth. After a harried few seconds, he pulled away but his lips were immediately replaced with his hand, sealing her screams like a slamming lid.

Humiliation burned in Emily's heart and dripped like poison into her soul as he grappled hungrily at her breast over the top of her dress. Terror hitched in her stomach, threatening to rise higher and higher. Sweat broke out on her forehead. His eyes bulged with feverish delight. He'd lost his mind. He began to pant, his tongue stuck to his bottom lip in concentration as his hand left her breast to snatch and pull at her skirts. Fear and revulsion turned her blood cold. No! She would not allow this. Not here, not now with Will so close yet so far away.

She struggled and kicked and clawed at his hair and face, but he bucked and yanked out of reach time and again. It soon became clear this was not the first time Nicholas had overpowered a woman in such a way. The knowledge sunk into Emily's heart, filling it with anger and murder. He would have to kill her before he touched her. His icy-cold fingers touched her bared thigh, and she strained with all her might against the suffocating weight of his hand. Finally managing to open her mouth, Emily bit down.

"You fucking whore!" he yelled.

The carriage ground to a halt.

Chapter Seventeen

With the word "whore" ringing in his ears, Will leaped from the carriage, anger burning in his veins. He ripped the carriage door back on its hinges.

Milne's hand was raised above Emily, poised to strike.

Blind rage tore through Will. First his mother, then the other women he knew of, now Emily. It was over. Milne would never lay a finger on another woman. Jumping inside, Will hurled his entire body weight at Milne, knocking him off his feet. Grabbing him by the throat before he fell, Will manhandled him to the opposite seat from where Emily half lay, half sat, her skirts rumpled at her thighs.

His heart pumped with revulsion. "I'll kill you. I'll rip your head off and stick it on a spike, you son of a bitch."

"Will, stop." Emily's cry bounced from the walls. "He can't breathe."

Her pleas were muffled beneath the words in his head. *Do it. Kill him. Kill him right now. Think of Emily. Think of your mother.* Years of resentment, rage, and hate whirled inside him, burning down Will's arms and peaking in the wide span of his hands. He could throttle him, watch him turn blue...He tightened his grip, squeezing harder and harder until Milne's eyes grew wide with fear and the bastard's pulse beat beneath Will's fingertips.

"I should've killed you years ago." Will clenched his teeth.

Milne clamped his hands to Will's wrists, yanking and pulling, but Will held fast. He shook with rage, his mind blank but for the need to end this, to kill the scum with his bare hands and toss him onto the side of the road, forgotten and abandoned. Prison was too good for him; he should be killed and buried six feet under. His mother's beaten and bloody body filled his mind's eye. She was curled in the fetal position, the bedsheets strewn and tangled around her shaking body. Her lip split, her cheek swollen, bite marks upon her breast...

"Will, stop."

Aware of Emily's hand tugging at his bicep, he felt her, heard her, but his wrath was too great.

His knuckles turned white as Emily yelled at the driver. "Driver, help me! He will kill your master right now if you don't do something. Help me!"

Knowing there was no room for the man to enter the carriage even if he had the courage or lack of sense to try, Will continued to stare down at Milne, his stomach sore with bitter resentment. When Emily pulled on his arm again, he blinked and tried to focus on what she said.

"Will, please. This will solve nothing."

"Get out of the carriage, Emily. Now!"

"No. I won't let you do this. You will not go to prison for the rest of your life over him. Think of your painting. Lord in heaven, think of me." Her voice cracked.

Her words sliced through his hypnosis like a knife through flesh. Emily. His beautiful, amazing Emily.

Hadn't his mother said the exact same thing? If he killed Milne, would his life really change for the better?

In prison, Will would lose his liberty. He'd never touch Emily again. He would have no future opportunity to help the women Milne hurt. He opened his hands, and Milne slid to the carriage floor in a crumpled heap, his six-foot frame an awkward mess in the narrow foot well.

Milne coughed and sputtered, his hand at his throat as he glared at Will. "You will pay for this. I will have the authorities track you down and arrest you without so much as a blink of an eye."

Will bit his teeth together, no longer trusting his words or his fists to behave. The only two women who truly cared about him had both begged him to spare Milne. Was it fate? Or was it cruelty? He had no idea, but he could no sooner ignore Emily's protests than he could have his mother's.

He turned and cupped Emily's face in his hands. He kissed her cheek. "It's all right. Everything's all right."

"Get your hands off her, you filthy moron," Milne spluttered behind him.

Shaking his head, Will kicked out his heel, and it connected with something hard enough to make Milne curse and fall backward.

He looked into Emily's tear-glazed eyes. "We need to talk." He gestured toward the door. "Outside. I refuse to say a word in front of him."

"I mean it, Samson. Get your hands off my whore."

Will dropped his hands from Emily's face and curled them into fists. He trembled as he looked at Emily. She was his anchor, his miracle.

"Outside. Go."

Her face paled as she threw a final glance at Milne before turning and stepping from the carriage. Will spun around and leaned his hands on the seats on either side of the carriage. His vision was red with rage as he lowered his face until it was inches from Milne's. Satisfaction churned in his gut when the coward shrank back. "From now on, you will spend every day looking over your shoulder because I promise, very soon, you're going to find a sharp and rusted hatchet in your back or the firm hand of the law on your shoulder. Either way, you're a dead man walking."

Milne's lips curved into a slow smile. "I don't think so."

Will pushed to his feet, took a breath, and planted an almighty kick to Milne's testicles. The scum's feminine shriek echoed around the interior before Will thumped the bastard square in the face. Knocked out cold, Milne was now exactly as Will wanted him. He needed time alone with Emily, free from interruption or distraction. Turning, he jumped from the carriage and slammed the door.

"What did you do to him?" Emily's face was drawn, her gaze darting from him to the carriage and back again.

"I haven't killed him."

She shook her head. "You have to tell me what he has done to you. What history is there between the two of you? Do you dare to deny you knew him before you knew about Katherine? The others? I am not stupid. This comes from something far, far deeper."

He ran his fingers gently over her face. "Are you all right?"

She nodded, a lone tear escaping and running over her cheek. She pressed a kiss into his palm. "Tell me."

Will swallowed. She had every right to know, and he couldn't keep it from her any longer. It wasn't fair and it wasn't right. He dipped his head and placed a gentle kiss to her lips before cupping her elbow and leading her away from the carriage. Walking to its rear, they stopped beside Carrington. Will looked deep into her eyes, praying she understood what he was about to tell her and didn't turn away.

"My mother was a prostitute."

She flinched. "Your mother?"

He nodded. "A prostitute Milne mercilessly beat and left for dead. I came to Bath to find and ruin him, if not kill him."

"Nicholas beat your mother? My God. No wonder—"

"He beat her so badly when I found her, she had blood in her mouth and bruises on her body. The man is an animal, and I cannot let him have you. I've felt that way from the moment I laid eyes on you at the auction rooms."

She glanced toward the carriage. "Does he know who you are?"

Will drew in a breath through flared nostrils, took her hand in his, and exhaled. "No. I doubt he could even differentiate my mother from the others."

Tears filled her eyes, and he brushed his thumbs under her eyes. "He's not worth your tears."

She shook her head. "I'm crying for your mother, the other women he's hurt…oh, God, Katherine and Aimee. With Nicholas in jail, what will they do?"

Loving her deep kind soul more than ever, Will

pulled her into his arms. She settled her head beneath his chin. "That is not your concern."

The carriage creaked, and they turned. The door opened and Milne wobbled on its threshold. His face was twisted in an ugly grimace, his color red and teeth bared. "I will see you dead, Samson."

"The hell you will." Dropping Emily's hands, Will yanked on the buckle of Carrington's harness.

Milne awkwardly climbed from the carriage. "What the hell do you think you're doing?"

Will continued working the buckle with lightning speed until the horse was freed, barebacked and with only its bridle. He was taking a risk Emily would even say yes to his request, but it was one he had to take.

He glanced toward Milne who was being coaxed by his driver to stay back. Intelligent man.

Gripping the horse by its bridle, he stepped close to Emily, his eyes searching hers. She stared back at him in wide-eyed wonder, and he took her hand.

"Come with me. We'll go back to the city, and I will return you to your father where you will be safe. I will tell him everything I know, and we will work from there. I have to do this. I have to release you, Katherine, and every other woman I have met from Milne's violence." He tightened his fingers on hers. "If we do this together, the rewards will be more than retribution. They will give us hope for the future. We can be together. Do you believe the same?"

She glanced over his shoulder where Milne scuffled with his driver, and Will stared at her turned cheek, praying she came with him. They were seconds away from escaping. Seconds away from the possibility that Will might have to knock Milne out cold again.

They were leaving. The question was whether Milne would be conscious when they did.

Emily's intelligent brown gaze bore into his. "I'll come with you."

Will's relief rushed through his blood, and he released her hand. The scuffle behind them grew in volume, and Will turned to see Milne shove his driver backward onto the dusty ground.

Will gripped the horse's mane. "Once you are safe with your father, I will have to leave for a while, but I will be back. Quickly, take my hand."

She stared at him for a moment before her gaze cooled. "You're leaving?"

"Yes, but I'll be back."

"I see."

Even though her tone had turned decidedly colder, Will had no time to question her. Milne marched toward them, his arms swinging like pistons, visible steam blowing from his expanded nostrils.

"Quick. We must go."

With a final glance in Milne's direction, Emily placed her hand in his and Will hauled her up so she sat sidesaddle in front of him. He grinned and saluted Milne before kicking his heels into the horse's girth, leaving the bastard coughing against a cloud of dust.

****

Emily shook her head. "I am a fool, Annie. Worse, a fool in love."

"It's only been two days. Mr. Samson will be back."

"He won't. I need to accept my fate." Emily pulled back her shoulders as Annie pushed another pin into the hem of her dress. "He was the first man to turn my head, but now I must grow up and understand love affairs for what they really are."

"Miss?"

"A means to an end, Annie. A step along the path to reassurance for the next generation. I should never have thought my marriage to Nicholas could be delayed, altered, or canceled. Love does not exist."

"You do not mean that." Annie shook her head. "You love Mr. Samson, and you should be with him. Even Mr. Darson thinks so."

Emily looked at the crown of her maid's head and pursed her lips. "Father thinks a lot of things, but his hands are equally as tied as mine. He's dying. He is weakened by his illness and deep down knows Nicholas is in far too good a position for us to fight him and not lose every penny." She looked to the open window. "I know Mr. Samson promised Papa he'd be back with a plan to make everything right, but I can't afford to believe a word of it."

"Why? I think Mr. Samson is capable of anything."

Emily met her gaze. The girl's eyes were dreamy as she stared ahead at absolutely nothing. Emily frowned. "He might have told me the truth about his history with Nicholas in the end but still…"

"You cannot blame him for keeping something like that to himself." Annie stared, her eyes wide. "How was he supposed to tell you his mother was a prostitute? Or that he intended to bash Mr. Milne into next week? Which I think he fully deserves, by the way."

"Oh, I am not berating him for it. Nicholas deserves it. All of it. I am merely facing the reality that Will can look anyone in the face and convince them white is black." She sighed. "Even though I have feelings for him, it would be stupid of me to act like a blind woman. If I fail to carry out my promise to marry Nicholas, not only will I lose all Papa's money, I'll have nothing of my own."

"But what he did…tried to do." Annie shook her head. "You can't marry him, miss."

Humiliation whispered through Emily as she thought how close Nicholas had come to assaulting her in the worse way possible. "I just don't know what else to do to make everything right for Papa."

Annie sat back on her haunches. "It's not fair. None of it."

"We're not alone." Emily's mind wandered to each of her female friends who were tied in abusive marriages. "I do not know how I'd survive or where I'd go without a penny to my name. Father's illness has used all we had. I allowed myself to revel in the fantasy of true love. That was foolish." She laughed, the sound sharp and devoid of emotion. "What a dimwitted little girl I am."

"Dimwitted is the last thing you are." Annie frowned. "What else has happened to make you doubt Mr. Samson's return so fervently? He is a good man, a handsome man…a man most women would give their eyeteeth to see swim naked in the river." She gave a saucy wink.

Emily's cheeks heated with knowing and a little longing, but she kept her face somber. "I have no idea why you find any of this amusing. If I lose Father's legacy to Nicholas, what do you imagine will happen to you? I will never be able to afford to keep a maid in employment."

Annie shrugged. "What of it? I will find work

elsewhere. It's your happiness that matters right now. I wish you wouldn't doubt Mr. Samson."

"Nicholas will see this marriage through to the end."

"Mr. Milne is a thug and a bully. He raised his hand to you. You cannot marry him. What about everything you stand for? You will find a way to get your money and your man, just you wait."

When tears threatened, Emily lifted her skirts and stepped down from the overturned box, annoyance prickling her agitated nerves. "Will used me to get to Nicholas. Men are a race unto themselves." Her emotions lodged in her throat, threatening to choke her. "A race that, for now, we are bound to rely on. Our job is to ensure that is not true for our daughters too."

Annie pushed to her feet and planted her fisted hands on her hips. "Mr. Samson will be back. I know it and so do you. You're afraid, that's all. There's nothing wrong with fear if you channel it to make you stronger. Mr. Samson loves you."

She couldn't bear holding on another day to the hope Annie's declaration was true. Her belief in Will had grown weak. He had left, and his absence rocked her to her very core. She needed him, had thought they were destined to be together. That separated they were strong, but together they were invincible. She swallowed as tears burned her eyes. With him gone, there was no use in contemplating the dreams they could've achieved.

"Oh, Annie." Emily thrust her hands to her face as the tears she fought so hard to contain burst forth. "If he doesn't return, my heart will be broken forever."

"Oh, miss. Don't cry."

Emily let Annie take her in the soft circle of her embrace. Closing her eyes, she rested her head against her maid's shoulder, and tears slid warm and soft over her cheeks. "I love him, but my need for him is hardly his fault."

"You and Mr. Samson are meant to be together, and you will be." Annie's fingers were comforting over the surface of her hair. "He's more of a man than any I've ever met. He loves you. Whatever comes after that, the two of you will face united."

Emily shook her head and eased back from Annie's arms. "He told me he needed to go back to Bristol to collect some more money and then return to find a solicitor willing to help his quest for Nicholas's incarceration."

Annie grinned. "He has money? Well, that's even better."

"He is comfortable, but you are missing the point. He came to Bath looking for revenge, nothing less, nothing more. He lied to us all, and I fear my feelings for him have blurred the truth."

Annie's smile dissolved. "What truth?"

"He has no missing nephew and managed to infiltrate his way into our home to get closer to Nicholas. Why would I think just because I gave myself to him—"

"You laid with him?" Annie's eyes protruded from their sockets like two eggs from a hen's behind.

Heat seared Emily's cheeks even as undeniable excitement pulsed at her most illicit place. Memories of their night together flooded her senses and warmed her heart. She tried and failed to stem her lips curving into a smile. "Yes."

Annie squealed and gripped her hand like the friend she really was, pulling Emily to the bed. They sat side by side, their hands joined. "I don't believe it. That is...astounding."

Emily laughed. "Despite the ache in my heart, I'll never regret what I've done. Ever."

Annie grinned. "Mr. Samson will be back to claim you as his own. Mark my words."

Hopelessness twisted at Emily's heart. "Real life rarely turns out the way we wish it."

A sharp rap at the bedroom door had Annie leaping to her feet.

With a quick nod to each other, Emily cleared her throat. "Come in."

Malcolm walked in carrying a letter. With a curt bow, he held it out to her. "This arrived with the afternoon post, Miss Darson. Your father told me to bring it straight to you." He grimaced. "It appears to be from Mr. Milne."

Dread turned Emily's blood cold. "How is Father?" She rose from the bed and took the envelope. "Has his fever reduced since Doctor Morgan left?"

Malcolm shook his head, his forehead creasing. "No, miss. The badness inside him has strengthened its grip. I really don't know what else I can do. I try to think of new ways to help him but..."

Emily patted his arm. Malcolm had worked for her father for close on twenty years. "I know. More importantly, he knows. My father is strong. He wants to see me married. He won't be going anywhere soon." She smiled, forcing optimism into her voice.

The weight of losing Will bore down on Emily's chest. She cupped Malcolm's elbow and turned him toward the door, lest he see her distress. "Now off you go and try not to worry. All will be well."

With a bow, he left the room.

The moment the door closed behind him, Emily hurried to her bureau and took out her letter opener. She sliced the seal and extracted the letter, hating that her hands shook so vigorously. She quickly scanned the words until sickness settled like a hardened lump of gruel in her stomach. "Nicholas wishes to take me out driving at eleven tomorrow morning."

Annie stood beside her and touched her hand to Emily's shoulder. "Does he say where he is taking you?"

"It's not that which concerns me." She looked into Annie's eyes. "His presence will upset Papa immeasurably. It is too soon after Will's revelations about Nicholas's past...and present. He can't come to the house. I must prevent Nicholas from coming here until I'm sure Father won't risk a heart attack by launching at Nicholas upon sight."

"How will you get a message to Mr. Milne before tomorrow morning?"

Emily snatched her writing box from a drawer in the bureau. "I will send Malcolm right away. He can deliver a note asking Nicholas to meet me at the Pump Rooms for tea instead." She met Annie's eyes. "That way I am in the safety of public company, if nothing else."

Annie pulled back her shoulders. "I'll come with you."

Emily smiled and touched her palm to her cheek. "There's no need. I will be quite safe."

"Please, miss. Let me. Mr. Darson does not wish

you to go out alone, so there is no use in trying to dissuade me. Mr. Milne would not dare attempt to strike you again if I am there. A coward like him would never risk your father's or Mr. Samson's wrath."

Emily frowned and slipped her hand from her maid's cheek. "Mr. Samson is not coming back. We must move on."

Annie's expression brooked no debate.

Taking out a sheet of writing parchment, Emily turned from Annie's unwavering gaze. "Fine. You can come, but please, no more talk about Mr. Samson's return. My heart cannot take it."

She could not let Annie sway her acceptance of Will's rebuff. She was a woman of fortitude, and she would take whatever Nicholas threw at her alone and without Will. Nicholas did not scare her. His attack in the carriage had shocked and frightened her, but he would never get close enough to her to be able to do something like that again. Even if they married. Nicholas would never sleep with her or even eat with her. They would tell the world she was barren. Emily's eyes smarted with tears. Did that mean without a child her fight for her father's legacy was wasted? No, she was still here, and her father meant the money he'd earned to pass to her as much as he did his grandchildren.

While Annie busied herself with other duties, Emily wrote a clear and decisive letter to her fiancé. The last time she'd seen Nicholas, he'd been enveloped in a cloud of dust. The next time she saw him, he would be cleaned up and undoubtedly angry enough to beat her as he had Will's mother. The only difference was, Emily was forewarned, and if he so much as laid a finger on her, she would give him as good a fight as any man.

Chapter Eighteen

Will wished Emily were with him. The choice to leave her for a few days had been as necessary as it was difficult. She needed to be home with her father, not dealing with the likes of police, prostitutes, and the horror stories of what Milne had done throughout the years she'd been tied to him. He'd taken a couple of nights in a rented room in the heart of Bath and prayed to God she didn't come across him.

In case anything happened to him during his investigation—God only knew whom Milne would pay to have Will's head in a box—he preferred she thought him a cad than dead.

The lie he was returning home for money stuck like a jagged rock in his throat. When he told her the truth about Milne, he'd hoped the end of the lies came with it. It just hurt too much to see the hope in her eyes. The hope they would one day be together, come what may. He prayed it would happen but until he was certain...

With each hour that passed, Will's need to return to her grew.

Today he would.

Pride swelled behind his ribcage as Laura and the other ladies spoke to Sergeant Middleton in front of him. One by one they told him their truth, and he wrote their statements on his notepad. Will's heart beat like a drum, admiration and respect for each of the prostitutes running through his blood and filling him with the promise of vengeance for his mother.

The world was in for a change bigger than Will ever imagined. Women were shining supreme. He was honored to be in the presence of such courage. Despite Emily's confidence that things would be different for the next generation, his belief in that possibility had often wavered. How could the dreams of the women surviving in poverty come to fruition, when he saw time and again how they struggled with daily abuse? Their confidence was shaken and their optimism crushed with each blow of their lovers' fists.

Yet here. Now. This was how things changed. He smiled. Fire pulsed in his belly to see how stupid he was to doubt the combined power of women on a mission. Something bigger than he could have ever hoped for when he arrived in Bath was unfolding right in front of his eyes. All he'd wanted was Milne dead or begging for mercy at his feet. What happened now was a million times better.

Katherine Carter stood shoulder to shoulder with Laura and two other women Milne had paid money to in exchange for sex. Katherine, in her tailored clothes and beribboned hat, wore the same expression as Laura and the poorer, if not more elaborately dressed, women of the street. Disgust twisted their lips, anger flashed in their eyes, and determination turned their cheeks rosy. Nothing separated them. Wealth, class, and creed vanished when you suffered a man's fist at your temple. Having found a man of the law willing to listen, the rest was up to them. Middleton was a respected and upstanding copper who believed in a woman's voice being heard as much as Will and Emily did. This was all the vengeance Will needed. The very women Milne used would be the ones to slam the bolt on his prison door. A perfect circle ending.

"Each of you is willing to testify against Mr. Milne in court?" Sergeant Middleton looked at each woman in turn. His steel-gray eyes invited no leeway or doubt. "If I am going after a man of Milne's stature for physical assault, rape, and attempted murder, I need to be sure I have your backing. Anything less and I risk my professional position…and pride."

"I want him dead, but if this is the only way…" One of the prostitutes shrugged. "He tried to strangle me, sir. If my son hadn't been in the other room—"

"He stamped on my hand and broke four fingers." Another woman raised her hand. The bones were healed but horribly misshapen.

Will's gut twisted with anger. They could not fail.

"He deserves everything coming to him." Laura fisted her hands on slender hips. "This has gone on for too long. I don't want to hear about a girl being killed by him when I could have done something to prevent it."

"And you?" The sergeant looked at Katherine. "You don't seem as vocal about this as the rest of these ladies."

Putting his hands behind his back, Will clenched them together. As unjust as it was, he needed Katherine more than the others. She was the golden ticket to sealing Milne's future in prison. A lady who owned a business, who kept herself and her child well-dressed and respectable, was their only real chance of a judge making the decision to retain Milne indefinitely. If she balked, Will doubted Laura's and the others' testimony

269

would be enough to ensure Milne served time behind bars.

Katherine's gaze darted from each woman to Will and back to the sergeant.

Will's stretched nerves got the better of him, and he stepped forward. "Katherine?" He gently touched her arm.

She started. "Yes?"

"The sergeant asked if you are willing to testify in court against Nicholas. Are you?"

She stared at him, her eyes as sad as any he'd ever seen. "Does Emily know?"

"About you and him?"

She nodded.

Will swallowed. "Yes. And that he is little Aimee's father."

She squeezed her eyes shut. "God, how I wish that wasn't true."

"Emily doesn't blame you. She knows what Nicholas is capable of now."

"And yet she has to marry him."

"If you don't testify, yes." It was a low shot. Even without her testimony he would find another way. There wasn't a hell's chance of Emily marrying Milne, but allowing Katherine to believe as much might be the only way to harness her strength.

Tilting her chin, Katherine faced the sergeant. "Yes, sir. I am willing to testify and tell the world everything he made me do, say, and put up with over the last ten years. Nicholas Milne may be the father of my child, but he is also the reason I've little of my own and the reason my best friend risks spending the rest of her life in misery."

The sergeant's lips tilted upward in a near smile. "Then, in that case, I will take this to my superior, and unless I am completely inept at my job, I believe we have reason enough to get this piece of...this man put under arrest."

All four women turned to Will, their faces and eyes alight with triumph.

Will grinned. "Well, thank you, Sergeant. We look forward to hearing news of that over the next few days."

"Indeed, Mr. Samson. Indeed." With a click of his heels, the sergeant walked away.

Will faced his new best friends. "Right then, ladies. Who's coming with me to tell our good news to Miss Darson before she goes ahead with the stupidity of marrying a man not fit to clean her shoes?"

****

Emily glanced at Nicholas from beneath lowered lashes. A business associate intercepted their departure from the Pump Rooms, and now they spoke in earnest. The late afternoon sun was still high in the sky, and the Abbey cast its shadow across the flagstones at their feet. Enduring tea with Nicholas had been arduous and the increasingly fraught atmosphere had bored down on Emily's chest, making it hard for her to breathe. The conversation was forced at best, veiled in accusation at worst. Annie sat beside her, silent and straight-backed, her face drawn into a permanent scowl.

Neither Emily nor Nicholas made mention of her night away with Will or the ensuing tussle between them. The signed marriage contract hung between him and her like a death warrant, and any chance of Nicholas having a modicum of genuine feelings for her were well and truly quashed. The weight of obligation threatened to crush her. Now deeply in love with another man, Emily understood wounds to the heart were apt to bleed for a long while—possibly forever.

Blinking back the sting of tears, she glanced again at Nicholas's profile. She'd seen no hint of lust or possession in his eyes as she had before, only contempt and disdain. He suspected she'd given Will her maidenhead and thus meant no more to him than a streetwalker. Nerves and apprehension tumbled like falling rocks in her abdomen.

He finished his conversation and returned to her side, offering his elbow. "Shall we?"

Emily slid her hand into its crook and lifted her chin. The ax would fall; it was just a question of when. They strolled from the Pump Rooms to the courtyard at the side of the Abbey. Thankful for Annie's presence a few feet behind, Emily forced the rapid beat of her heart to slow. As long as they remained in public view, Nicholas would not harm her. He would not risk losing face in society. His status was his only power—he had nothing else to give.

He stared ahead, his jaw tight. "We'll take a walk along Pulteney Bridge, I think."

Emily forced a smile into her voice. "That would be lovely."

He huffed out a laugh. "And her charade goes on."

Emily turned. His smile was tight as he slowly moved his head from side to side. Impending danger screamed along her nerve endings. The battle had commenced.

She inhaled a long breath. "If you have something to say to me, please say it."

"You act as though I have forgotten what happened."

He tightened his fingers around her hand as it lay on his arm, and Emily sucked in a breath at the wretched and purposeful pain.

She glanced around her. "Let go of me."

"Let go of you? It's taking all my strength not to throw you to the floor."

Her stomach lurched. "Release me, Nicholas. Now."

"You are mine, Emily. Mine. From now on you will do as I say, or so help me God, you will end up dead."

Terror clutched her heart in a fist, and Emily halted, yanking her hand with all her might from his arm. Adrenaline thundered through her body. He might as well strike her dead right then if he thought she would submit to his every demand.

His eyes flashed with venom and violent hatred. She would not be his next victim.

"You cannot threaten me like that. What you say is not law."

Emily's heart picked up speed. She was so thankful Annie stood not a foot away from them. She trusted her maid's loyalty, and Nicholas would undoubtedly know, together the two of them would be a force to reckon with.

He clenched his teeth. "You will do exactly as I tell you."

"No. My father is dying, and I am fighting my love for another man. You do not control me, nor do I care what you say or do anymore. We are bound under a business arrangement, nothing more."

Nicholas slowly smiled. "Is that so?"

Emily tilted her chin, confidence building like a smoldering volcano inside her. "When I think of you sitting alone counting my father's money, I cannot walk away from you. I cannot let you have everything he worked for."

His smile widened. "Oh, dear. Well, you're stuck with me then, aren't you? Once we are married, as your husband, it is my right to expect you to perform every wifely duty."

The insinuation was rife, and nausea burned hot and sour in Emily's throat. She stared into the eyes of the devil. With full and sudden clarity, she saw how to permanently sever his sexual pursuit of her.

"I will never be yours mentally, emotionally, or physically." Pride swelled in her chest. "Will Samson took it all."

He stared for a long moment, revulsion contorting his face until his mouth curved into a slow grin. His eyes gleamed. "Oh, Emily. I am not a fool. I know you are a slut, and I know Mr. Samson has had you."

She shook her head, bitterness twisting inside her. "You are an animal."

"Me? Samson is the one who took what he wanted and disappeared. He used and tossed you away like yesterday's rubbish, my dear. Do not think for one minute he felt anything for you. Look at you. I don't want you and neither does he."

Her belief that his words were true slashed at her heart, but she tilted her chin. "What if you are wrong? What if he comes back?"

He laughed, the sound icy cold. "You are a blind fool."

Pain and anger tripped along her nerve endings, making her shake. "I am not as big a fool as you seem to think. I know enough about you to hate you for the rest of my life. You will be as miserable as I in this marriage. I will ensure it."

He waved his hand dismissively. "Blah, blah, blah. You know nothing about me. Nothing at all. You are an ignorant, silly little girl who—"

"I know you beat Will's mother and left her for dead. I know you keep Katherine as your mistress and Aimee is your child."

His eyes grew wide and his glare more dangerous. Emily stood her ground, even as Annie's hand slipped into hers.

Something had snapped inside her. She could not marry him. A new truth—a new legacy—swept through Emily's heart. Her father wouldn't be here to see the challenges she would face and feel endless guilt upon his shoulders, and if a life of struggle meant a life without Nicholas's evil residing over it, that was a life she wanted.

"What of it?" Nicholas shrugged. "You will marry me knowing everything, and you will be grateful."

Emily glared. "Grateful? Grateful knowing you are capable of such violence and betrayal?"

"At least I do not hide my past from you...as your precious Samson is."

"I know everything I need to know about Will. I love him and will for the rest of my life."

He laughed. "The man has told you nothing. He is a liar and a fraud. A confidence trickster with a past on the street. The son of a whore and a criminal since childhood. He came into your life by design, nothing more."

Will was a confidence trickster? A criminal?

No words formed on her tongue as perspiration burst cold at her upper lip. What else hadn't he told her? Instinct told her Nicholas spoke the truth. Will's anger, his ability to deal with every situation, no matter how unexpected. Surely it could only come from a life of true experience?

She swallowed and met Nicholas straight in the eye. He would not see her pain, her confusion, her heartbreak. "Even if what you say is true, it does not make me love him less. One day Will and I will meet again, and I will ask him the truth."

He sneered. "Samson targeted you like a pawn in his game. He doesn't love you. He doesn't desire you. He just wanted to take you from me. He thinks I actually care about you. None of that matters now. He failed. You're mine."

His words struck at her soul like a knife, but she would not falter until she heard the truth from Will. He would explain and soothe the pain ripping through her blood on an unrelenting wave. She drew in a long breath and exhaled.

"I will never regret lying with him." She gazed around the Abbey courtyard as though bored with their conversation. "Will is a real man. A man who made love to me over and over again—"

The vicious sting of his open palm sliced her cheek. She fell, and the side of her face hit the flagstones with a crack. A blinding pain ricocheted through Emily's head, blurring her vision.

Annie dropped to her knees beside her. "My God, Emily."

"Get up now." Nicholas's voice boomed above her. "How dare you address your mistress by her Christian name."

"She's bleeding. How could you do this?"

Emily stared upward, her vision clearing just as Nicholas raised his hand again. Emily sat up. "Don't you dare hit my maid."

"I will do whatever the hell I like."

Despite feeling nauseous and lightheaded, Emily struggled to her feet with Annie's trembling grip at her elbow. Holding her hand to her throbbing face, Emily glared. "Look around you, Nicholas. See what you have become, what others now witness."

Men and women stared. Gentlemen shook their heads in disapproval, and women clung to the arms of the good men they were lucky enough to marry. Other men stood smiling, their eyes glistening with admiration as their spouses looked to the ground in shame or fear. The world was nothing but a game of chance. Women were fortunate if they found a partner who understood them, loved, and respected them, but more often than not, they were matched for money or ambition, their lives spent in misery.

Emily dropped her hand from her face and straightened her spine. She would find a way to live and make money. Forgoing her father's fortune was the key to her liberty. Maybe even her life.

She met Nicholas's stare. "I will never marry you."

With an arrogant smile, he focused on the admiring men who watched. "Yes, you will."

Emily stared at his turned cheek as fear whispered inside her. The truth was Will had taken her virginity and disappeared. Yet, the look in his eyes when he'd made love to her was too honest to be misjudged. The way he so gently caressed her could not have been tainted with the intention to seduce and abandon. No one—not even a confidence trickster—could be that convincing.

"And at last she cries."

Nicholas's taunt cut through her reverie, and Emily swiped at the tears she did not know had fallen. "I cry, not out of fear but loathing."

He smiled. "You are a brave soul in so many ways, my love, but even you are not brave enough to walk away from a fortune and live a life without luxury."

"I am and I will." She covered Annie's hand with hers. "Let us go home, Annie."

Nicholas moved to stop her and then pointed his finger instead. "If you walk away from me, I will make sure you never see a penny of your father's money. Not ever."

Turning, Emily headed for Royal Crescent and the family home she adored but that would soon belong to Nicholas.

Chapter Nineteen

Exhausted, Emily and Annie stood outside the front door of Emily's house.

"Now remember, Annie," she said. "I want none of your hysterics. Papa's condition has worsened considerably over the last two weeks, and I fear the next few days will be his last."

Annie's eyes were sad and afraid. "You must tell him what happened with Mr. Milne. He cannot get away with treating you that way."

"I will find the words once I am in front of him."

Annie's gaze lingered at Emily's cheek. "What of your face? Mr. Darson will—"

Emily closed her eyes. "I know. I know. It will be all right. I will tell him marrying Nicholas is no longer an option."

Annie's eyes glazed with unshed tears. "What will you do? What if Mr. Samson does not return?"

Emily smiled, the prospect of adventure sweeping through her stomach in a loop the loop. "Then I will seek him out. If I do not find him, at least I will have tried. I will do just as well alone."

"You can't mean that. There is no one else on this earth as perfect for you as Mr. Samson."

Emily unlocked the front door. "Come. Enough of this romantic fantasy. Let's face what has to be done and tell my father I am to break the contract, regardless of certain struggle."

Emily stepped into the hallway and stopped. Something was significantly different. Malcolm did not greet her, and there were far too many voices coming from the drawing room that was normally so quiet. Frowning, she hastened forward and strode into the drawing room.

"Papa? Is everything…" Her question died on her lips.

Will stood on the edge of a circle of women, his handsome face split into a smile the breadth of the River Avon. He met her eyes over their heads. He stood in her home as though he'd never been away. Emily's heart turned over in her chest, and her skin tingled. She longed to run into his arms, but her feet would not move. Her brain whirled with a million apprehensions of why he was there and who the women were with him.

Emily took a step toward the circle. "What's happening?"

Katherine immediately emerged from behind Will and came toward her, a huge smile brightening her pretty face. "Emily, you're home." She held out her hands as if to clasp Emily's when Katherine's gaze fell on her cheek and her smile dissolved. "Your face. What happened? My goodness, is that blood?"

Emily lifted her fingers to her wound as both cheeks turned hot beneath the sudden silence. "It's nothing. I—"

Will came forward and stood in front of her. His gaze targeted her cheek, and his blue eyes darkened to almost black. "Who did this?"

Fear shot through her. If he knew Nicholas struck

her...She ignored his question and looked over his shoulder. "Who are all these people?"

"Friends of mine." He lifted his hand to her wounded cheek and then curled it into a fist. "Was it Milne?"

Emily snatched her gaze to his. "Will, please. It does not matter."

"Emily? Emily? Is that you, child?" The sound of her father's rasping, struggling voice broke through the tension between them.

She brushed past Will and hurried to her father's side. Three gaudily dressed women stepped back to let her pass and Emily dropped to her knees beside her father. He lay awkwardly on the heavily cushioned settee, his condition clearly deteriorating with each passing hour. His breaths wheezed from his chest, his skin white as he battled his pain.

"Papa." She dropped her forehead to his and closed her eyes. "I'm here. It's all right."

"Look at me, child."

Emily squeezed her eyes tighter. He had no doubt heard what Will and Katherine said. She opened her eyes.

His gaze wandered over her cut cheek. "I want you to answer Will's question."

Heat seared Emily's face, and she met his shrewd gaze. How could she tell him in front of a roomful of people that Nicholas had hit her? Some of whom were complete strangers. Humiliation washed through her, heating her face.

"Papa, this is not the time." She smiled. "Later. When we are alone I will tell you everything."

His jaw clenched. "I am dying. My days are

numbered, and I have heard more about Nicholas in the last two hours than I care to think about. If he has struck you, I want to know this instant."

Emily stared at his ashen face, tears burning the backs of her eyes. How could she defy him? Although weak and riddled with disease, her father was her father. As long as he had breath, he would want to protect her.

She nodded. "Yes, he hit me, but—"

"I damn well knew it." He raised his arm. "That's it. Then it is done."

Emily flinched. "What is done?"

"You will never marry that man. Do you understand? Never. I will find a way to finish this contract. Make it null and void with every penny going to you. Every damn penny, or so help me God, I will come back and haunt Milne into an early grave."

His body trembled under Emily's hand, and she quickly got to her feet to support him as a barrage of coughing rendered him speechless. "I cannot bear seeing you this way. Will, help me lift him from the settee."

Silence.

Dread tripped up her spine with silent fingers. She turned. "Will?" The place where he had stood was now empty.

She closed her eyes. Like a panther hunting its prey, he would scour the streets for Nicholas. If he found him and killed him, Will would hang. Torn between her father and the man she loved, Emily's heart ached with helplessness. She had to do something.

She looked to Annie. "Has he gone after Nicholas?"

She came forward as Emily continued to rub her father's back and offer sips of water from a glass beside him.

Annie nodded. "He took off the moment you said Nicholas hurt you. He was like a rock from a catapult, I couldn't have stopped him…even if I wanted to."

Emily looked at her father. "Papa? I have already told Nicholas I will not marry him. I am happy for him to have the money. Look at you. Look at me. What good does money do anyone toward finding happiness? You were happy with Mother when you struggled from week to week. I am happy when I am with…"

Her father managed a smile. "I think it's about time someone introduced you to these ladies. They are here about Milne."

Emily looked at the women, and realization dawned. Their painted faces and brightly colored clothes told their story. Emily smiled as camaraderie settled like a blanket around her shoulders. What did it matter if a woman was a streetwalker or lady of the manor? If a man hit you, class did not alter the humiliation.

"How do you do? I am Emily Darson."

The three women executed brief curtseys, their eyes showing their embarrassment. Standing in her drawing room was as uncomfortable for them as sitting astride a stool in a tavern would be for Emily. Her father gently cupped his hand to her elbow.

"These ladies have been on the receiving end of Nicholas's fists as you have, Will's mother has, Miss Carter has, and goodness knows how many others." He shook his head. "If Will does not kill Nicholas with his bare hands when he catches up with him, you have my promise I will do everything to make sure my money is yours. Nicholas will spend time in prison for what he has done."

Rendered speechless, Emily met Katherine's gaze as she stepped forward and took Emily's hands. They embraced.

"I am so sorry." Katherine sniffed. "So very, very sorry."

Emily squeezed her eyes shut. "You have nothing to be sorry for. If Nicholas wanted you as his mistress, you would have had little choice in the matter. You were barely more than a child."

Katherine pulled back and tears streaked her face. "He threatened to hurt me so many times. He made me feel I was nothing without him. I didn't know what to do."

Brushing the tears from her friend's face, Emily smiled. "You've found the strength now. That's all that matters. Nicholas gave you Aimee. She's precious, Katherine. Precious and deserves a better father. Find her one."

Emily turned and faced the three women. "Thank you so much." She touched each of their arms in turn. "I am not sure a thank-you is enough, considering everything you are prepared to do. Please, tell me your names. Did Will bring you here?"

Smiling, their eyes glassy with tears, the women nodded. A beautiful woman of no more than two and twenty stepped forward.

"I'm Laura. Your Mr. Samson tracked me down like a bloodhound, determined that I'd testify against Nicholas and find others willing to do the same. This is Thelma and Meg."

She smiled a hello to each of them, before laughing and brushing at her tears. "He's not my Mr. Samson. In fact, the more I know Will, the more I realize he's a free spirit and tied to no one."

Laura shook her head. "Maybe once upon a time. But not so much anymore, not now he's found you."

Emily looked around the room at the smiling faces, hope and trepidation written there in equal measure. Who knew what the future held? Neither she nor Will could predict what would happen in the days to come. Could they have a future together? He had come back after all.

She spun around to face her father. "We must alert the authorities. We must tell them Will has gone after Nicholas and what Nicholas has done."

His face was stern. "You must not go after him alone." He turned to the woman named Laura. "Did you say you have spoken to a policeman? A policeman who believes everything you have told him?"

"Yes, sir. A constable named Middleton."

"Right. Then you must find him. He will track down Will."

Emily's heart picked up speed. "What if we're too late? What if Will finds Nicholas and kills him? What then? He'll be hanged."

"Then there is no time to waste. God only knows I wish I could do something to help but I cannot. You must go. All of you. You split up, and you each go a different way until you find this Middleton. Then and only then do you find Will. Do you understand me?"

Emily stared. She could not trawl the city looking for one policeman when there was one man who meant so much more to her than any justice system. She nodded. "I understand."

"Good. Then go."

Emily hurried from the room with Annie, Katherine, Laura, and the others close behind. Once they were out on the street, she whirled around to face them. "We will split up, but half of us look for Will, the other half the policeman."

They all nodded their agreement, their faces flushed with enthusiasm, their eyes wide with determination.

Their unity flowed through Emily's blood, making her feel anything was possible. "Good. Laura, you take the girls and find Middleton. Annie, Katherine, and I will track down Will. It's the only way."

Laura clutched her arm. "Godspeed, Miss Emily. Godspeed." Her eyes widened. "Wait. Did you say Nicholas hit you after you told him you knew about him visiting me?"

Emily frowned. "Yes, why?"

"Oh, my God." Laura's hand slipped from hers, and she teetered back on her heels. "He's gone to the house. He'll hurt Bette." Her face turned pale. "I have to go. I have to protect her."

Fear and loathing rose up in Emily's chest. "Then we'll all go."

"I admire you, Miss Emily, I really do, but where I live is no place for a lady."

Emily pulled back her shoulders. "We all go. Come on, we are wasting time."

****

Will's heart beat faster and faster, burning like a ball of fire behind his ribcage. Milne ducked into the alley like the caped criminal he was. His coat was inappropriate and heavy for the summer's day, and instinct rocketed through Will's blood, knowing he concealed a weapon. A weapon meant for Laura.

Over Will's dead body would Milne use it on anyone unfortunate enough to be in her house.

He drew in a long breath. "Milne. Stop."

Milne halted and spun around. For a long moment, he said nothing and then his face broke with a manic smile. "Well, well, well. Mr. Samson is here to save the day."

"You're a dead man, Milne." Will stepped closer, his hands curled into fists at his sides, his mind clear.

Will drew in a long breath, accepting Milne's death meant his own, too, but it did not matter. Emily would be free. The money would be hers, and Milne would be six feet under.

"I don't think so, Samson." Milne opened his coat to reveal a claw hammer.

Will's vision tinged red. He meant to kill Laura with a hammer.

The man was an animal.

With a roar, Will ran at Milne and ducked his head, wrapping his arms firmly around Milne's waist. Keeping his head down, Will pushed him to the ground as the whoosh from the hammer's swing brushed his ear. With Milne on the ground, Will pulled back his arm and punched Milne full force in the face, the sound of cracking bone filling the squalid alley.

The hammer left Milne's fingers, and Will pulled back and punched him again. His mother's voice filled his ears and tried to break through his mania but nothing would stop him. Not now. Not ever.

"You're scum, Milne." He gripped his slack chin in

his fingers and savored the bloody mess of his face. "Scum."

Just as he closed his hands around Milne's neck, he heard a scream. A feminine scream followed by another and another. Straddled over Milne's unconscious body, he turned.

His eyes met Emily's. He was vaguely aware of others, but it was only her he saw.

"Emily." Her name whispered from his lips.

She rushed forward, tears running in silver streaks down her face, her eyes wide as she shook her head over and over, her gaze not leaving his.

Slowly, Will pushed to his feet and stumbled toward her, his arms outstretched. She slumped into his embrace, her body shaking with her sobs.

"Is he dead? Am I too late?"

Will held her tighter. "No, no. He's alive."

She pulled back and looked into his eyes. "If he is found guilty, the inheritance will be mine. Let him live, Will. Let him know what he has lost. Please."

Knowing there was nothing he would deny her, he dropped his mouth to hers and they kissed as Laura and her girls stood guard over Milne's unconscious body and waited for the police.

Chapter Twenty

Emily pushed her arm through Will's, and their eyes locked. The chilly November breeze fluttered the feathers in her hair and blew the leaves across the steps at her feet. They stood at the front of the courthouse while Annie, Laura, and Katherine stood huddled in a circle to the side. Emily looked into the dark blue of Will's eyes, and her heart swelled with love.

"Nicholas is gone."

He brushed a lock of hair from her cheek. "For the next five years or so anyway."

"Will it be enough?"

He covered her hand with his and led her away from the doors and slowly down the steps. "It is enough for us to be married and to move away from here."

She stopped. "Move away? But where? Father is buried here. I can't leave him."

"We have to if we are to be together. I have tried and failed to find work in Bath. Now that my past has come out because of the trial, it is doubtful anyone will employ me. I want to marry you more than I want anything in the world, but we cannot stay here without income."

"Our future together is the most important thing, not how we pay the bills."

"They are equally as important. We should have known Milne would want everything about me exposed. It was his last chance of kicking me where it hurts. He succeeded."

"No, Will, he failed. You will find work, and we will be happy in Bath."

Emily looked out at the bustling street. People rushed back and forth, calling and shouting and talking. People came to Bath to make their fortunes; it was almost second to London in its popularity and possibility.

He touched his finger to her chin. "I promised your father I would look after you for the rest of my life, and that's exactly what I will do. I love you."

Her stomach tightened. Fear and sadness shone in his eyes. They would do what they had to. She just wasn't capable of saying goodbye to her father, not yet, not until they had exhausted every possibility of staying close to him.

"Miss Darson?"

"Yes?" Emily turned.

A man in his early fifties stood to her side, his face etched with concern. "How are you?"

"I am better than I have been for a long while." She smiled. "I'm sorry, I do not know…"

He held out his hand. "Mr. Granger. Your father's solicitor. Executor to his and Mr. Milne's estate."

Realization shot into her stomach, and she raised a hand to her mouth. "Oh. Oh, with everything…" She looked into Will's eyes and her face blurred with tears. "It's mine."

He frowned. "What is?"

"The money. The tobacco company." She snapped her head to Mr. Granger. "That is why you're here, isn't it?"

His mouth curved into a grin, and his eyes sparkled. He held out an envelope. "I had to wait until Mr. Milne was sentenced before I could give you this."

Emily's hand shook as she took the envelope; her gaze darted to Will's and back to the envelope. She slid her finger under the seal. She looked down at the papers and urgently scanned the text. Her fingers curled around the papers until they crumpled. She looked into Mr. Granger's eyes.

"Is this possible?"

He smiled. "Yes. It's there in black and white...if you and Mr. Samson want it this way, of course."

"But how?"

"The moment Mr. Milne was incarcerated, he became ineligible to carry on the business. Even when your father was on his deathbed, he saw the love between you." He beamed at Will. "So, if Mr. Samson wants to accept the position, it's his."

Will stepped forward and stole his hand around Emily's waist. "What is this?"

Emily's love for Will swelled as she thrust the papers at him. "Read it. It's ours. All of it."

His smile slipped along with his hand from her waist. "But..."

He frowned as he read, and a shot of fear swept through Emily's blood. Will was his own man. A man used to sole survival, to living and working on the streets. What if he saw this as charity? Or control...worse, failure to provide for her himself? What if he was determined to move from Bath? Her father? His legacy?

"This is our future." He turned and gripped her waist. He drew her close. "We can be together, Emily.

Together."

She met his eyes, her body trembling with hope and anticipation. "You mean…"

"As long as we are together, we can make this happen. I will not let you or your father down. I promise. I'll work harder and straighter than any man ever has before."

Emily laughed. "That's good to hear."

He grinned. "Well, there's nothing else for it. If I am to learn the business and become a tobacco merchant, we need to join forces."

She laughed. "We are already joined."

"Not properly."

He released her and dropped to one knee, taking her hand in his. "Emily Darson, will you do me the honor of becoming my wife?"

Happiness soared through Emily, warming her heart and bringing her father's face to her mind's eye. She nodded, tears threatening to spill.

"Yes, Mr. Samson. Yes, yes, yes."

Everyone burst into cheers when Will stood and lifted Emily off her feet, swinging her around until they kissed again, sealing the start of their new beginning…

A word about the author...

Rachel Brimble lives in the UK with her husband, two daughters and beloved Labrador. She is a member of the Romantic Novelists Association and the Female Entrepeneur Association. When she's not writing, she is reading, walking or watching dramas on TV while nursing a chilled glass of white wine!

www.rachelbrimble.com

Thank you for purchasing
this publication of The Wild Rose Press, Inc.

For questions or more information
contact us at
info@thewildrosepress.com.

The Wild Rose Press, Inc.
www.thewildrosepress.com